SENTIENT

SENTIENT

MICHAEL LEON

Published in Australia by Australian Inspiration 2020
www.australianinspiration.com.au

Cover, design and typesetting by Luke Harris
www.workingtype.com.au

ISBN:
Print: 978-0-9944731-7-2
Ebook: 978-0-9944731-8-9

CONTENTS

EARTH 2120 AD

The world of the 22nd century has undergone rapid transformation as international government grapples with the key issues of that era: global warming and rapid technological change. The population has peaked at ten billion, consisting mostly of 'post-humans' (commonly referred to as castes), humans who have opted to have substantial technological implants. Minority groups consist of 'humans' without implants, and 'biots', human looking robots who are manufactured to loyally serve either the humans or post-humans they are commissioned to assist.

Human population quickly declined as more and more chose to become post-humans, enabling them to couple their consciousness to technology, thus using its power to enhance intellectual capability, but also to protect against rampant global pandemic diseases afflicting the young.

World governance had been handed to AI two decades earlier to avoid an ecological disaster, leading to the re-optimization of resources into 'super cities' around the globe, where mega corporations increasingly wield power at the expense of the State.

Humans with less influence in the new technological structure are mostly left with the task of halting the degradation to the world's natural environment or the terraforming of new off-world environments. The largest human-based organization is Gaea — its vision, to enable Earth's environment to return to pre-industrial levels, as well as the terraforming of Mars.

Post-human-based groups oversee the acceleration of technological change, where unnatural selection advances the next evolutionary leap to technological man. The largest post-human-based group is Apollo Corporation — its vision, to accelerate the advancement of inter-solar and inter-galactic exploration and emigration.

Prologue

The Center for Environmental Infectious Disease, nick-named the Ice Cube, was busier than normal. That usually meant there would be a day of 'transfers'. Castes filled the foyer, supporting my hunch. A large party from the neighboring Center had assembled, waiting for their interview facility to be made available. I searched for Hali in the crowd, hoping she'd located Chryse's ward. The Ice Cube stretched out like a tray of ice cubes, all neatly squared buildings set among manicured greenery. With some dozen or so purpose built opaque glass-walled buildings, each interconnected, the Ice Cube was the best facility in California offering pulmonary care for children.

"Tell me you know where Chryse is located," I shouted, in the noise of the crowd.

Hali squeezed a nurse's arm appreciatively, before join-ing me. "She's in the D1 Block, so we're close."

Simply nodding, I signaled her to lead the way. Hali strode through the glass maze of corridors as if she were one of the many hundred biot nurses who inhabited its walls, before opening the door into Ward B. "To your left, Dane."

Just inside the doorway, my daughter greeted us. "Daddy! Hali!" Chryse exclaimed. She'd have jumped into my arms long before I made it to her bed, if she hadn't been connected to an oxygen mask.

I walked toward her, holding her gift in front of me, drawing an excited reaction. "Thank you, Daddy. What is it?"

I shook my head before placing the gift on her lap. "I can't spoil your birthday surprise. Can I?"

She eagerly eyed the large gift wrapped in red paper and gold ribbon, before Hali offered her gift, a smaller parcel wrapped in gold paper and red ribbon. "They're both in my favorite colors! They look so beautiful together," she said, extending both hands, inviting Hali and I to sit on either side of her as she opened her gifts.

Her room was sterile white, bar the vase of red carnations on her bedside table. "Are these Mummy's?"

Chryse didn't look up, more interested in opening her presents. "Yes. Mummy came earlier while I slept."

Paper and ribbon fell in all directions as she peeled away the wrapping. "Daddy. You didn't forget!"

She held the lifelike baby in her arms, overjoyed with her gift. Chryse looked so like her mother at that moment.

Full of life. I savored every moment of her happiness, knowing her days were not always so kind. Hali diverted her eyes from Chryse across to me, expressing a knowing glance and I nodded in appreciation. Hali may have been a biot but she could respond in a human manner, learned from our many years of working together.

"What name will you give her, Chryse?" Hali asked.

"Cyane. Is that a good name?"

"I like that name. She'll have a Martian name like you," Hali replied, looking at her gift. "I think Cyane will want this, too."

Chryse eyed the golden wrapper before undoing the ribbon. "A life ring for Cyane. Thank you, Hali!"

Hali gently stroked Chryse's rosy cheek. "Now you'll be able to talk to her."

Chryse slipped the life ring on her doll's finger. It pulsed a number of times before the biot doll's silver pink eyes flashed into life. She immediately snuggled into Chryse's arms then looked up to Chryse. "Are you my big sister?"

Chryse checked Hali for confirmation. "Yes. I have already programmed her ring. You are Cyane's big sister."

I sat back in the chair and watched my daughter for a time as she became acquainted with Cyane. The toy biot was lifelike but carried only a limited range of emotions and responses. Environmental laws had long ago outlawed pets, so baby biots were used to fill the void for the young. Chryse held her baby sister close, showing an over protectiveness, no doubt born from her own insecurities. I was leaving her at a vulnerable moment in her life for a lengthy period, and the decision troubled me. Was I asking too much of my own family? Unfortunately, the decision was based on a broader need. Chryse, like most of her generation, were susceptible to global environmental degradation and answers had to be found.

Chryse was in deep conversation with her new sister, until her gaze was suddenly diverted. Lia walked into the ward, beaming a smile that matched the bright white medical coat she wore. She hugged Chryse and Hali before sitting beside me and leaning close into me, showing her exhaustion.

I rubbed her back and shoulders. "Long shift?"

"Yes, another all-nighter. We're transferring a lot of children today."

"I saw the crowd. How many?"

"Around two hundred. They're briefing them, now. So, I couldn't come until all the transfers were settled.

"Two hundred! That's a record."

Lia responded with a sharp glare before deflecting my faux pas.

"Do you like your gifts, darling?" Lia asked.

"It's the best gift I've ever had, Mummy!"

"You know I have one more for you."

"A dress?"

"Yes. They're delivering it this morning, so you can wear it to your party tonight."

The thought excited Chryse. "Can you and Hali come tonight, Daddy?"

"I'm sorry, but you know Hali and I must go to the base, shortly. Promise me you'll send highlights of the party."

"I promise. I'll write every week."

"So will I, darling. Who's coming to your party tonight?"

"All my friends. Except Zoe," she replied, trying to hide her disappointment.

"Zoe's your best friend. Is she sick?" I asked, but she didn't reply.

Lia squeezed Chryse's arm before responding for her. "Zoe's one of today's transfers, so we won't see her again."

"Zoe? I spoke to Bill only last week. He never mentioned anything."

"They never do," Lia responded, before turning to Chryse. "You know Zoe would see you if she could, darling, but she will live somewhere else now."

Chryse hugged her baby sister close. "Why can't I go

with Zoe? She said they are going to make her just like Hali. What's wrong with that?"

Chryse diverted her gaze from her mother to Hali, waiting for a response. My daughter was of an age where peer pressure mattered. She'd watched many of her friends move to the neighboring hospital — the Center for Post-human Rehabilitation.

"If you went with Zoe, you wouldn't be allowed to stay with your mummy and daddy," Hali replied.

"Zoe said she won't be sick anymore."

I wanted to reassure Chryse, but she was right. Technological implants offered the best solution to the chronic illness sweeping the Earth's young, albeit a high emotional price.

"That's why your mother is working so hard on a cure and why Hali and I are going to Mars. When we find the cure, you and your mother will join me on Mars."

Chryse lay back on her pillow and held her baby sister tight. "I won't have any more operations on Mars?"

"No more. We promise," Lia said, before running her com over Chryse. "It's time you had some sleep so that you're strong enough for your birthday. Hug Daddy and Hali. They have a space ship to catch."

Hali hugged Chryse. "Take care of your new sister."

"I'll love her with all my heart. Will she love me, Hali?"

Hali smiled. "She can't love, but if you love her enough, she'll be a loyal sister to you, always."

I held my daughter, knowing it would be a long time before I could be close to her again. "I'll com you every week, until you join me on Mars. You look after Cyane and Mummy for me."

I took Lia's hand and the three of us walked out of the hospital to the autonomous vehicle waiting to take us to the space station.

Lia hugged Hali before doing the same with me. "Thanks for seeing her this morning. I know the schedule's tight."

The significance of the moment made me struggle for words. I held her tenderly, knowing it may be our last embrace. "Remember what we said."

"A week at a time," Lia replied.

"Yes, a week at a time until we reunite on Mars. We owe it to Chryse's…to everyone. That's worth a few years, isn't it?"

"Is it? Go, before I change my mind," Lia said, fighting tears away.

PART ONE

DELIVERY

Chapter One

BREACH

An ambulance roared past, its red lights pulsing, signaling the scale of the emergency. I remembered calling out to my sister, Zi, before I woke from the dream. A similar intermittent red light streamed through my pod signaling a real emergency, a 'Code Red' and potential hull breach. I straightened my uniform, annoyed I'd fallen asleep while working, again. I slipped two pairs of socks on before standing. Months of space travel had made the soles of my feet soft and more sensitive to the aluminium composite floor. It also made me lose track of time, so I checked in with Hali.

"Did I sleep long?"

"A few hours. You were talking in your sleep again."

I nodded. "Yeah. Can you run a com scan for implants?"

The dream was uneventful, except that I'd had the same dream over a dozen times now.

Hali stood in front of me and flashed her metallic chrysochlorous eyes directly into mine. Her unflinching technological gaze could detect a myriad of abnormalities from potential blindness to cancer. My request was simple, the detection of digital implants. In the post-human world, there was one thing humans valued — naturalness, but even humans carried a small number of tech implants to better function in a fast-paced society. The cost, susceptibility to being hacked.

Hali finished her scan. "All clear. No abnormalities."

"Thanks. How long has the alert been flashing?"

"Since the second it woke you," she replied,

I nodded. The alert could be significant but there was nothing Hali or I could do. We were paying customers and had to wait for instructions to come from Quinn, the ship's captain.

"I dreamed again that I was home."

"That would be logical, given we have nearly arrived at Mars base."

"There was the same explosion. Then an ambulance drove past, heading for the mines. I called out to Zi."

"Yes, I heard you. It's to be expected, don't you think?"

Hali's chrome eyes softened, reflecting an empathic

response. It was my favorite shade. It made her look almost human. In those moments, her beauty radiated out always catching me unprepared, as if she were human. Biots had come a long way in the last two decades. They didn't possess real feelings, but they had mastered the art of appearing to. Appearances aside, Hali was right. I was returning to the home of my youth after a ten-year absence. The closer we came, the more I thought about events I'd spent the last decade trying to forget.

"You're right. I guess I've shut out those memories for so long."

I left Hali to her work and returned to my quarters. A personal message had arrived while I slept, so I took the chance to check it. It was the weekly com from Lia and Chryse. Com capability on a cargo ship was sparse with navigation using up most of the load capacity, meaning personal communication didn't figure highly, but short as it was, the one-minute com meant the world to me.

I lay back on my bed and opened the video message. Lia sat with Chryse at her hospital bed. Chryse must have just had treatment as she wore an oxygen feed. She was perky despite it, as she played with her biot doll. Both waved into the com.

"Hello, Daddy! Do you think Cyane has grown? She's six months old today," she announced proudly.

Lia prompted her. "Tell Daddy what you're doing today."

"I'm taking Cyane to the playgroup, and we're going to play in the doll house. I think she'll like it there because I'm going to bake her a cake and invite all my friends to join us."

Lia chipped into the conversation. "You should see the new VR doll house, Dane. It's the best in the country. Chryse has invited her best friends." Lia turned to Chryse. "Who's helping you to bake the birthday cake, darling?"

"Mummy is!"

I paused the message and studied my daughter's pale face. Her eyes lit up when she was happy, making me wish I could be with her. I was about to continue the message, but the breach signal stopped, allowing Quinn to make an announcement.

"Attention: navigation sensors have picked up a hull breach in the cargo hold. All crew follow emergency procedures, immediately. This is not a drill. I repeat, this is not a drill."

The six-month transit from Earth to Mars had been uneventful until now. I had started to believe our return flight to Mars would be incident free. Then just as we approached the final difficult deceleration into Mars orbit, a potential breach. My first reaction was to reach out and touch the pod wall, feeling for the pulse of the nuclear fusion engines. They steadily pulsed, which reassured, even though a breach of the cargo hold would not immediately affect them.

"Should I investigate?" Hali called out.

Emergency procedures required one of us inspect the cargo hull. I returned to where Hali was working. "No. I'll check it. You complete the project briefing for the Mars team. How's the progress?"

"The briefing is complete. I just need to run all possible analytics to support our position on…"

I cut Hali short, squeezing her shoulder in appreciation. Research grade biots were programmed to err on the side of over-providing information. I'd learned a long time ago to circumvent her programming, using human signals. Hali recognized my gesture and smiled back in a knowing way, one of many human-like responses she'd learned over our five years working together.

"I'll check the breach, then report to the captain. Anything you want to share with Quinn?"

"No. His mind will be fully occupied with the breach."

I nodded in agreement. Quinn's one and only priority was to offload our cargo on time. The breach would only further build his irritation towards having 'non-essential passengers' like Hali and me on board. He was good at shipping cargo, not so good with people. That mostly suited me, for the cargo belonged to the organization I worked for, Gaea. The less Apollo personnel knew about our work, the better.

My com showed that three of Quinn's crew were already in the cargo hold, Ander, Cluste, and Shell. I quickly secured my space mask and focused on reaching the bridge to the cargo hold. This was a tricky procedure as the stern hub of the Deliverance, the crew's quarters, operated in G1 conditions, whereas the cargo hold, the largest area of the ship, was a gravity-free container hold.

Entry through to the hull was controlled by strict procedures that I followed. "Close stern pod hatch." I waited the allotted time for all the safety procedures to be checked and the airlock hatch to be automatically secured.

"Bridge secured. Open hatch to cargo hold." The titanium enforced hatch slid open and I entered, wondering what awaited me. How severe was the breach? Importantly, where had it occurred? Quinn had sent three crew members, so that couldn't be good.

"Connecting port safely traversed. I have entered the cargo hold." The airlock hatch closed behind me, releasing my body into zero gravity motion.

The cavernous cargo hull was as quiet as an empty cathedral. I gazed down to the containers assembled in grid-like uniformity. No sign of a major breach. I pushed up from the rail and floated up toward the hull's dome for a better view, gripping support rails and traversing the dome, monkey bar style. Floating freely always brought back happy childhood memories, roaming the low gravity valley of Chryse Planitia and the elevated grounds near the base of Ascraeus Mons. A decade back on Earth hadn't changed me. Despite its challenges, Mars was and always would be my home.

I saw Ander first. He stood on a central container, directing his obedient crew like a conductor as they scurried to his every order. Their inspection centered around Container 64, revealing one important fact to me. This breach had been initiated by Gaea, meaning my superiors held fears that my mission had been infiltrated. *Is Ander the infiltrator?* I was eager to find out, but pointed my com light upwards instead, checking for any physical signs of a micrometeoroid breach in the ship's hull, while slowly maneuvering in his general direction.

Even from a distance, Ander's giant frame was commanding. All military grade biots were built larger than your average human. All were clothed in armor and an array of armaments that only a military biot had the strength to carry. He looked none too pleased as he signaled me to join him. I responded, purposely timing a faultless landing, before reaching to the security rails for stability. Ander didn't acknowledge me, seemingly engrossed in the com readings he scanned. *Has he identified the breach?*

"Nothing on my com. How have you fared?" I asked via com audio transmission.

Ander offered a brief, terse glance, before continuing his survey. Whatever he knew, I'd be made to wait until he was ready.

Ander was a typical biot, possessing advanced cognitive skills and a limited capability to act out human emotions, tailored to suit his operational requirements. Despite those limitations, he would be more than capable of running the ship. It worried me that Ander, a defence grade biot, was working on the *Deliverance*. Such skills were usually reserved for military operations. Unusually, there were two others as well. One of them approached us.

"Shell. Run a 3D scan of the container group I just scanned," Ander ordered.

Shell, a female biot and Ander's highest-ranking crew member, hovered over the containers from the aft side of the ship. As with all biots, she was created to loyally serve the human or caste she was assigned to, in her case through Ander, who in turn loyally served the ship's caste captain, Quinn.

Shell was similar in stature to Ander, but she was

a deadly Medusa, carrying bee-like miniature drones, every bit as deadly as the mythical goddess's vipers. On landing, she released a dozen drones from inside her tech-enhanced sleeves, half the formation veering left, the other right, as she guided them from her com. The buzz of drones echoed across the cargo chamber for some time before Ander finally acknowledged me.

"Have you identified any anomalies?" he asked, holding his stolid gaze.

My confidence plummeted from Ander's intimidating presence. This giant of a soldier looked down at me, seemingly enjoying my nervous silence. He asked me a question that required I lie. He played with his high-tech sleeve while waiting for my reply, further highlighting his physical presence, a mixture of muscle and technological armor, making him the perfect interrogator. *Was he toying with me?* I wondered, his piercing metallic eyes turning from his armor to me.

"None at this point. You?"

Ander looked toward the maze-like sea of containers. "Com models suggest a noise lasting no more than a micro-second emanated from this location. What's in this grouping of containers?"

"They carry our newly developed terraforming equipment."

"Unusually expensive and heavy cargo for such a long journey. Couldn't they be manufactured on Mars?"

"No. They could only be built on Earth in our best laboratories."

"Extreme security. Don't you think?" Ander asked.

Ander was fishing again, trying to unnerve me. "Gaea insisted on securing this section, given their value."

"Perhaps the machines were disrupted and activated?" Ander continued, falling just short of accusations. Did he know much more than he should? That would account for his unwelcoming demeanor since I boarded the ship.

"That's impossible. One activated machine would disrupt the whole cargo. Billions of credits would be lost, not to mention five years of research. We won't activate them until they are safely delivered to the surface of Mars."

An uneasy silence remained until the formation of reconnaissance bees glided seamlessly into Shell's outstretched arms, disappearing into widened sleeves and docking.

"Report," Ander commanded.

"There is no evidence of any micrometeoroid breach, but I detected a minor disturbance within a fifty-meter radius of this area."

"That represents eight containers. Continue with your reconnaissance of the other containers and pinpoint the disturbance. I need to report back to Quinn within the hour."

"That's twenty minutes. I request Cluste assists. His superior radar will provide pinpoint accuracy."

"He's already in the cargo hold. I'll have him join you shortly."

Shell nodded, then turned to me before re-commencing her inspection. "If you need help with your review, com me," she said smiling. Shell was the more communicative of the biots, fitted with facial response features such as empathy, emotional enactments deemed important for a surveillance specialist.

"We may have to search the contents of these containers. Do you have access?" Ander asked.

"I think that decision can only be made by your captain, with the support of the appropriate Gaea officials."

"Unless the breach is a threat to the ship."

"Only Quinn can make that call."

Ander held a silent gaze, seemingly enjoying my unease, a human reaction he could never have, but one he had learned to copy well through years of interrogation experience. I looked away and watched Shell fly to the surrounding containers. Cluste joined her, then both split off to commence a more detailed reconnaissance. Time was running out for me to act.

"I won't waste another minute arguing about protocol. I'm going to check the east side of the containers. The sooner we find the breach the better."

I didn't wait for Ander's response, leaping from the container and continuing my own search. The sound of Ander's commands to his crew steadily grew faint. To my relief, he didn't follow me.

I descended into the pitch black, my com lighting a small radius where my hands maneuvered along the container wall. On reaching the bottom, I switched the light off, the darkness now my friend as I enacted a well-drilled security procedure should the mission be infiltrated.

I activated an undetectable encrypted area of my com. A more detailed map of the cargo hold appeared, pinpointing the exact locations of the crew and their secured communication channels, allowing me to hear conversations not intended for my ears. Their investigations had been narrowed to the set of containers 62 to 66. It wouldn't take long for them to identify container 64 and the secret cargo.

I knew what to do next, yet I hesitated. This would be the first time I'd actually engaged in counter intelligence operations, stepping from imagining to doing. There'd be no turning back. My time to act was short, yet doubts lingered. *What would my sister Zi do?* She may have already paid the highest price, for all I knew. "This is for you, Zi," I whispered, before determinedly studying the com screen for the array of hidden explosives at my disposal.

A coded message from Quinn to Ander drew my attention.

"Where's Dane at present?"

"Carrying out his own inspection of the cargo hold."

"Bring him to Navigation. We need to extend this investigation to inside the containers."

The net was closing. I had to act, so I selected container 63, knowing two biots were in the vicinity. 'Sufficient damage to ensure deflection is effective' were my orders if Gaea activated the breach signal. My heartbeat raced, knowing that the quiet that was the vacuum of space would soon be disrupted by explosives, turning my crew into foes for committing a crime against Apollo Incorporated.

My mind raced. *Were there any other alternatives?* The secret cargo would be difficult to locate and it would take much negotiation with Apollo and Gaea to access the codes. Given they were close to docking, would Quinn undertake such a politically charged action? If not for his crew, Quinn would smooth over the incident, but his biots were military grade. Perhaps they worked to another agenda?

"Bring all personnel to navigation except Shell. Let her finish the reconnaissance, alone. Create no suspicion with Dane or his biot."

Quinn's order shook me from my indecisiveness. Ander was coming for me. Memories flooded through my mind: the incident; the loss; and the enduring pain from the explosion. Now, ten years on, fate revolved around another explosion. The vivid memories finally brought me the resolve I needed.

I pressed the detonator and braced.

Two distinct blasts shook me. First, the noise of the blasted container shell. Second the force of container 63 as it reverberated against the container beside it. Container 62 slammed into my right shoulder with the force of a truck's side swipe. Zero gravity magnified my predicament as I rammed into container 61. Stunned and disoriented, I looked up to the flickering lights of my com spinning ever higher. As the light faded, my pain adversely grew. Had the explosion been stronger than expected and damaged the cargo hull? If that were the case, we would all perish. In the dark silence, I expected the force of a hull breach, but instead another light emerged from above. It was Ander.

"Can you move?"

"I can, but there's pain."

Ander scanned my body, before wrapping his left arm around my waist. As he returned me to my quarters, I wanted to know more about the explosion, but dared not ask anything specific, for fear of being exposed.

"What happened out there?" I asked, but Ander ignored my question. Were they aware of my involvement or were they still analyzing the event?

Ander placed me on my bed, before he turned to Hali.

"He sustained heavy bruising and some minor internal bleeding, but nothing more. Take care of him for now, and Quinn will contact you as soon as we have rectified the emergency," Ander ordered, leaving immediately, not answering any questions.

Hali looked to me, just as confused as I, but for different reasons.

"What happened out there?"

"I was inspecting a container, then a blast from one of the other containers knocked me sideways. Is the ship okay?"

"I haven't heard anything. We are in code red until further notice," said Hali, before injecting a pain killer into my ribs. "This will help you rest," Hali said, also returning my com to me. "Ander recovered this."

"Thanks. I'll be fine now. I just need to sleep."

I rolled over in my bunk, looking away from her, feigning sleep, but unable to rest. I'd carried out my first counter intelligence operation. *Had I succeeded?* I turned my com on and accessed the encrypted code. I would soon learn what actions Quinn and his crew would take and where their suspicions lay. If I'd failed, the project was in grave danger of being exposed. Either way, I faced a grueling interrogation. I couldn't sleep, but the injection did take away the pain as I lay in the silence knowing I would soon have to face them.

I lay on my back and finished the com message from Lia. She had walked away from Chryse. "I miss you, but the work you're doing is so important to everyone. It's getting crazier in the Center. We're transferring record numbers of children from our wards. I fear our patient numbers will get so low, we'll lose funding for the Center. The pressure from post-human groups isn't helping," she said, before walking back to Chryse. "Let's wave to Daddy." They both waved and blew kisses until the message froze at the one-minute limit.

I studied the frame for a time, wishing I could be in the hospital room with them, but knowing the chances of reuniting were diminishing. I'd started a deadly process that would not go away any time soon. Military biots had not been included on this voyage without reason. Some or all of them may be my enemy and I would soon find out exactly who. *If there's a way through, I'll find it,* I whispered to the frozen image of Lia and Chryse, holding my gaze toward the com, hoping I'd see my loved ones again.

The cargo hold had been secured and the inevitable review quickly followed. With Hali's assistance I struggled to Navigation. The bruising had steadily swelled and the soreness lingered, despite the painkillers, but pain was the least of my worries as I took my place alongside the crew, supported by Hali who stood watchfully beside me.

A 3D com hologram lit the center of the makeshift area, showing a smaller scale representation of the cargo hold for review. The crew of six plus Hali and I formed a close semi-circle, except Draven, another military grade biot, who stood directly behind me. Of the three military biots, I knew the least about him. His presence always unnerved me. Could he have been in the cargo hold at the time? I politely nodded Draven's way, receiving only a steely, accusing gaze. Had he seen something? If he had, this review was about to become my inquisition.

Quinn commenced proceedings in a no-nonsense manner. He had the looks of a craggy mariner who valued only the journey across the seas, in his case, space. He stroked his cropped grey beard as if it were his badge of honor. "People, I draw your attention to the two monitors above you. They will be streaming this meeting to Apollo and Gaea representatives. There is a half hour delay, so they will not be contributing to this review, but they will report back to me with their recommendations. I don't need to tell you the sensitive nature of this incident, so stay on subject."

Quinn dimmed the surrounding lights, giving sharp clarity to the hologram, then he switched the two monitors on, commencing the formal review.

"The simulation we are watching is the four-minute lead up to the explosion, which damaged our navigation officer, Cluste. Fortunately, he remains operational. Importantly, no hull damage was sustained and the threat was quickly contained by our team. Within a minute, force fields were activated to ensure any further explosions from the suspect area could not impact on more containers. However, the cargo hull floor remains vulnerable."

"Just the one explosion?"

"I'm sure you felt like there were more, Dane. You experienced the aftershock as surrounding containers were destabilized from the explosion. We are monitoring all containers in the force field perimeter, and there have been no other disturbances."

I gripped Hali's arm, repositioning my stance to lessen the pain, drawing Quinn's attention.

"What's your commander's condition, Hali?"

"He sustained minor internal bleeding and bruising to the left and right ribs. Recovery should be quick, given time for rest, recuperation, and supporting medicine."

"We may need your support for an inspection. Are you up to it?" Quinn asked.

Hali's report was accurate. I was sore and struggling to move. Rest would be the best antidote, but that wasn't what Quinn wanted to hear. "I'm as anxious as everyone to investigate the containers. Should Gaea support it."

"Duly noted," Quinn replied, casting a slightly annoyed glance toward a monitor.

His response sparked discussion, starting with Shell. Her wide eyes darted around the room with the speed of her drone arsenal, before speaking. "Given the risk of another explosion, I recommend we don't wait for clearance from Gaea."

"Your report suggests otherwise, Shell. What are your concerns?" Quinn asked.

"I'd have no concerns, if Cluste hadn't been damaged in the blast. He was completing his own reconnaissance just before the explosion, robbing us of a second verifiable report. Together, we would be certain of the condition of the cargo, something my drone reconnaissance can't guarantee."

"Margin for error?" I asked.

"Small. But we're talking about a potential fatal explosion. I vote we go inside the containers to be sure," Shell replied.

Quinn interjected. "We can make that assessment soon enough. Let's focus on the initial breach signal. What caused it, Ander?"

"We carried out a full inspection of the cargo hold and detected no micrometeoroid breach."

"Conclusion?" Quinn asked, through pursed lips.

"The only possible reasons for the breach were a systems malfunction or some movement within the group of co-joined containers."

"Or sabotage," Draven interjected.

Quinn nodded slightly, seemingly not choosing to support Draven's accusations, instead deflecting. "What is the cargo, Dane?"

"All the containers in that area hold our new terraforming equipment."

"The length of time of this breach, Ander?"

"A microsecond."

Quinn looked around the group. "Would anyone care to offer an opinion as to what we should do next?"

This was my best chance to sway Quinn. He seemingly had no suspicions of foul play and appeared more concerned about rectifying their situation as quickly as possible.

"In my mind, the breach warning and explosion emanated from the same place, meaning it is almost certain that a faulty terraforming machine had ignited. While we wait for Gaea orders, I could undertake a more detailed external scan of the area, using my biot assistant. She is programmed with seamless technology, linked to all the terraforming machines, so I'm confident she would pick up..."

"Why not do an internal inspection?" Draven interrupted, moving to the front of the group.

"The less disturbances made around this equipment the better. I assure you, Hali's sensors will deliver you a detailed evaluation."

All eyes turned to Quinn, who stroked his beard, seemingly considering his options.

"I can't see how your biot's programs would be any better than Shell's. But a second opinion can't hurt. Carry it out if you think it'll help, but what we really need is an internal inspection of all the containers."

"I agree, but you know as well as I that there will be a time delay to gain approvals. Gaea holds the codes to these containers, given the sensitive nature of this project."

"How long?" Quinn asked, openly showing his annoyance.

Knowing negotiations between Gaea and Apollo officials would delay the answer Quinn sought, I merely shrugged.

Quinn shook his head in frustration. "Rendezvous time with the space-tug, Ander?"

"Thirty hours and twenty minutes."

Quinn studied his operational crew for a time, "Any other suggestions?"

Draven took his cue. "Why do you need Gaea support? You're the captain of this vessel."

"Did you not just hear that Gaea has the codes to the containers?"

"I could break these codes," replied Draven, with authority.

I learned a little more about Draven then and there. No normal crew member would speak with such brazenness, particularly given the meeting was being streamed to Earth. He was either very foolish or in a position to challenge authority.

"Your thoughts are duly noted, Draven, but I shall wait until I am briefed by more senior representatives. Is that understood?"

Draven shrugged. "You're in charge." He turned his gaze on me, not hiding his suspicions before he walked out of Navigation. No one challenged him, which again was strange. He supposedly reported to Ander, yet the powerful biot did nothing in retaliation. He and Quinn exchanged knowing glances, but if they were annoyed, they did not share it.

Instead, Quinn turned to me. "I'll follow your advice for now. I want you and your biot to undertake a sweep, immediately. I expect the report on my com in three hours, so I can brief Apollo and Gaea. Is that understood?"

"Yes. Hali already has the relevant program. We can start immediately."

"Good. I want a comprehensive and accurate report in three hours." Then Quinn turned the monitors off.

"We have the eyes of the most senior officials on this delivery, so brief me about any concern, no matter how minor. Is that understood?" Quinn ordered, a steely expectation in his expression.

"This report will be one hundred percent accurate. If there is any problem, you will know when I report."

"Very well, Dane. If you have any doubts before then, I expect you to report it to me immediately. I do not suffer fools. Even worse, I will not tolerate mistakes. If you are hiding a fault with these machines, I'll have your arse hauled to the brig, followed by a lengthy court case. Am I clear?"

"Perfectly." I stood up and walked from the meeting with Hali's assistance. It was clear from the meeting that Draven was not who he seemed. I had to act swiftly, while the opportunity remained. I had to brief my Gaea contact, for he was the one who initiated the security breach. Only he knew what I should do next.

Chapter Two

COVER UP

Hali and I hovered above the central containers, analyzing the impacted area. The external damage to container 63 was minimal, but the internal explosion must have set off other explosions to the surrounding terraforming equipment, given the unanticipated damage. I filmed the area in preparation for my report to Gaea, before we moved toward the security force field.

"Request perimeter entry."

"Force field disengaged," Ander replied, allowing us through and re-engaging it behind us.

"Commence by sweeping the stern side of the containers, Hali. I'll inspect the aft."

"Standard sweep?"

"Negative. We have no room for error. Perform a

detailed scan. I'll undertake an internal inspection of the aft side."

"Internal? You have access?"

"No. It's just the periphery. I want to manually inspect the internal skin around the explosion area. Contact me when you've finished, and I'll join you on the stern side."

"Very well. I expect to complete it in fifty minutes," said Hali, confident in her estimate.

"Get this right," I said, exaggerating its importance. Unbeknown to Hali, her assignment was an unnecessary one. I had a fifty-minute window to contact Gaea.

I floated thirty meters down a narrow vertical aisle to the base of container 64 to a small entry in the container's protective skin and unlocked it. Scanning my com confirmed Hali and I were alone in the cargo hold, so I entered securing the panel behind me. The narrow cavernous space was pitch black, but it felt reassuringly familiar, given the endless training drills I'd undergone on Earth. Using just touch, I moved twenty meters forward to a second camouflaged entry. Scanning a security code at an innocuous area of the internal skin opened a secret passageway containing the secret cargo destined for Mars base.

The flash of my com lit an area filled by a three-meter charcoal, rectangular shaped monolith, linked to seven other monoliths in an octagonal shape, looking more akin to Stonehenge than Gaea's finest technological achievement. The Multiverse Quantum computer, nicknamed 'Trojan' was contentious from its inception and the flash point between Gaea and Apollo.

The specially designed fortified container walls ensured no noise or signals could pass through it, except one. I triggered the encrypted transmission code, supposedly detectable only to my Gaea contact, then waited for the delayed response from Mars. *Could Ander detect it?* He was a military class biot. If he could, my work and the sacrifice of many, not least my family, would be put at risk.

A reply flashed back from Earth, lighting the enclosure. I switched on the encrypted, 'stealth com', preparing to report. A small light beamed from above, forming a large 3D image of my Gaea contact, Latatious. He stood tall in the middle of the surrounding monoliths, the beamed image flattering his small, stodgy frame. He was adjusting the large framed glasses he always wore, emphasizing his intense, suspicious eyes.

"Your position is secured?" Latatious said, ignoring pleasantries.

I re-checked my surroundings. "Yes. All entries secured. I'm alone."

"Scan the enclosure again," Latatious ordered, a hint of concern in his voice.

I scanned a second time to reassure him. "Scan all clear."

"Sorry to draw attention around the perimeter so close to docking, but we had to contact you. How has Quinn reacted?"

"As expected. He is suspicious of anything that impacts his mission. His second in command, Ander, didn't help."

"He will follow defense protocol," said Latatious, with a familiarity born from his extensive military experience.

"Yes. He wanted to undertake an internal inspection of the containers, but Quinn accepted I carry out a machine assisted inspection."

"Good. How long until you report?"

"Two hours."

"My team will send you your report."

"What will you identify as the problem?"

"A malfunction in a terraforming machine sent a radiation burst, tripping the breach signal. Quinn will accept it."

"That's a start. What about the rest of the crew?"

"That's where it gets tricky. There has been an Apollo infiltration."

Latatious confirmed what the breach had already signaled, but it didn't lessen my foreboding. The whole project was at risk. "Serious?"

"We don't know. But we received a com report from one

of our undercover operatives. It seems Apollo is aware of the advanced nature of the Trojan project."

"How aware?" I replied, alarmed at the development. If they located the machine, the cargo would be held in a secured area of the Apollo zone on Mars, halting progress on the project years, perhaps decades and most certainly ending my career.

"Aware enough to involve Apollo operatives to investigate."

"Shit! How soon?"

"Unknown. But you can bet they'll make the delivery of the cargo slow and difficult, if we let them," replied Latatious.

"Time's against them, unless…"

"They order your ship to remain docked until operatives arrive," said Latatious.

"Then the game will be up."

"It could be, but we will create a little chaos before then. The commissioning of this cargo was approved by both Apollo and Gaea."

"Political pressure?"

"That will be one of the fronts. We'll also create some incidents on your ship."

"What do you want me to do?" I asked, keen to make a difference to the deteriorating situation.

"In the first instance, I want you to witness it."

"Eyes and ears?"

"Precisely. We will need both points of view to what will unfold. Is your biot aware of the secret cargo?"

"Negative. The risk would be too great if our cargo was discovered."

"Fine for now. Hali could be a good ploy, if needed."

"Understood. What chaos are you planning?"

"Some will be planned, but others will be in reaction to what Apollo operatives initiate. For now, I want you as confused as all the other crew members."

Latatious wanted me left in the dark, for no good reason. I had put my future on the line for this project. Why would he withhold information? Had the infiltration moved beyond containment? I voiced my concerns.

"You're going to leave me exposed without more information?"

Latatious chose not to immediately respond, preferring to read his notes. "I need to know about your crew and their habits and idiosyncrasies. Let's start with Quinn."

"I'll brief you as you've briefed me!" I smarted, saying no more.

"We have precious little time, Dane. I suggest you spend it wisely."

I'd made my point, so I reluctantly answered. "I've seen

less of Quinn than any of the other crew. He's obsessive about procedures, so much so that he never leaves navigation."

"Never?" Latatious said, surprised.

"Never. He works long hours, sleeps and eats in an adjoining pod no bigger than a cupboard and delegates all duties outside of navigation to his second in command or one of the four biots."

"He never inspects the crew's quarters?"

"Not once. He always requests Hali or I meet with him in navigation."

"Handy to know. What about his 2IC?"

"Ander. I wondered why a military biot was on a cargo ship. Now I know. He's a typical 'defense-grade'. Massive unit, inscrutable face, but a hostile demeanor. His eyes alone are intimidating, and he's quick to flash his weaponry to unsettle."

"Is he loyal to Quinn?" Latatious asked.

"Totally. He's a 'one-off' assignment for this project, which raises my suspicion."

"Possible, but this is an expensive cargo. They would want security. What about the other four biots?"

"An impressive quartet. Two of them are military grade, so Ander has surrounded himself with some heavy-duty fire power."

"You think they are Ander's lieutenants?"

"I thought the two defense grades were, but they acted like independent units in our de-briefing. The other two are commercial grade biots and report mainly to Quinn. Are they operatives?"

Again, Latatious ignored my question. "Let's go through the biots one by one. The two that report to Ander."

I was resigned to remaining in the dark. Latatious knew a lot more about the crew then he cared to reveal. At least one of the crew had to be Apollo's agents, but for now he didn't intend to let me know who.

"Shell, the female, is Ander's deputy and more than capable of taking charge."

"Drones?"

"I've seen her surveillance drones. My guess is she's fitted with a full arsenal of assault drones, too. If so, she could take on a star ship and win."

"And Ander's second sentinel?"

"Draven? A mystery. Keeps to himself. Dark hair, dresses in black, seemingly to blend into the background, where he likes to be. A biot of few words. Born to be a spy. He left our de-brief without permission and unconcerned, as if he reported to a higher chain of command than anyone on this ship."

"Capabilities?"

"I've no idea. Maybe his skills are finding and keeping secrets? I asked Ander once, and he told me he was a structural engineer. He spends a lot of time examining the ship, inside and out."

Latatious studied his notes. "We have very little intelligence on him. Like Ander, he's been assigned to the ship for this one project."

"I've never seen him in the cargo hull, but maybe he makes sure I don't?"

"Put Hali on extra watch, just in case. What of the other two biots?

"They are Quinn's support team for navigation and tech and highly skilled in ship handling."

"That checks out. You said earlier you think the four biots appear more loyal to Ander than Quinn. Explain?"

"I'm not sure why. Just a feeling, I guess. Maybe it's because Ander has such a presence. I wouldn't blame anyone for not disobeying him."

"Does that count for every biot on the ship?" Latatious asked.

"Are you talking about Hali?"

"Yes. Has her behaviour changed in any way since you boarded the ship?"

"I haven't detected any change. She's entirely focused on the Trojan program."

"She does not suspect the early completion?"

I had worked with Hali for all of the five years on the project and never found reason to doubt her commitment. She was the lead scientist. If she was the infiltrator, our project was way more than infiltrated. The thought disconcerted me more than I expected, for I'd developed a friendship of sorts, as had my wife and daughter. Could my feelings cloud my judgement? Normally, I'd voice my concerns, but Latatious was sharing precious little information with me.

"No. I'm certain she suspects nothing."

Latatious was about to speak, before he was interrupted by a staff member who handed him files. He glanced over it before handing them back. "We are sending your report. This should satisfy your captain."

"Then what?"

"Act as if nothing has happened. We will do the same, unless unseen events begin to occur on your ship."

"And if they do?"

"A lot of this will be out of your hands. As I said, remain the eyes and ears for Gaea. You have two priorities. One is to protect the cargo and continue to deny any knowledge of such cargo existing."

"And the other priority?"

"Protect yourself!"

I wanted to ask more, but the holograph terminated, leaving me alone to consider the ramifications. My com flashed, signalling Latatious's report had been delivered. Hali had also sent a message. She was heading toward my coordinates and had noticed a biot in the cargo hold. It was Draven.

I exited making sure all entries were secured, before floating to the top of the containers, where Hali and Draven were waiting. I was surprised that Draven had for the first time appeared in the cargo hold. *Was Latatious's prediction of 'chaos' beginning?* Draven stood a half meter taller than Hali, his tight charcoal uniform accentuating his lithe body, whereas his long, dark hair and beard hid his youthful face. He looked like a man who enjoyed living in the shadows. The unusual texture of his uniform made me wonder if he had technological enhancements that could camouflage him from unwitting crew members. Hali's niveous complexion was accentuated by his presence, as Draven questioned her.

I interrupted their conversation as I approached. "Did your surveillance pick up any anomalies, Hali?"

She immediately turned to me. "All clear. Shall I scan the stern side?"

"Yes. Continue your surveillance. I need the report within the hour," exaggerating the urgency for Draven's benefit. "Have you been instructed to check the breach, too?"

"I've heard you are finalizing your report for Quinn. I'm making sure there are no mistakes," Draven replied.

"We have it under control."

"So, you should. Two hours to carry out an inspection? Anyone would think you are buying time, Dane."

"Your captain emphasized he never tolerates mistakes."

Draven smiled from behind his beard, seemingly happy he'd got a reaction. "So, what did your internal scan reveal?"

"You'll hear that from your captain, once I have Hali confirm my readings."

"I read the cargo files. It says this cargo is high security and cannot be opened, without official clearance? And yet you have come from that very place?"

"Your research is correct. I undertook the scan inside the protective skin of the containers. There is no access to the machinery until it's delivered to Mars."

"This is the first mention of an internal skin. I'd like to investigate it." Draven asked.

Draven's request sounded more an order. A curious action from a biot. "I'm happy to give you access, if Quinn supports it."

Draven smirked, seemingly enjoying my discomfort.

His military biot skills were on full show, as he unsettled and interrogated in equal measure. "I'll keep that in mind," he replied, before hovering down to where Hali was carrying out her inspection and overseeing her every move.

I remained on the container rooftop and studied the report Latatious had sent. I didn't need Hali's report. She would find nothing new. But I remained there anyway, keeping an eye on Draven, who was showing an increasing interest in the cargo hold. Was he the Apollo operative assigned to stop my mission? If he was, my first reprieve lay with Quinn, so I contacted him. "I have nearly completed the report."

"Report to me immediately on completion," he replied, his tone tense, no doubt from the pressure his superiors would be applying.

"Draven is harassing my biot. Is that because of your orders?" I asked, hoping Quinn wouldn't tolerate his actions."

"Negative. Bring your biot to navigation, too," he replied.

When Hali finished her investigation, I quickly ordered her to accompany me to navigation, nullifying Draven's intimidations. Our situation was fast descending into a political battle between secret operatives. Unpredictability had been unleashed on the Deliverance, and my future mission was increasingly shrouded by uncertainty.

Chapter Three

BAYLEY

The spiritual chant 'Om Mani Padme Hu'M' repeatedly echoed throughout the Chenrezig valley casting a lyrical serenity over the small Buddhist institute nestled deep in Chenrezig's mountain forests. It was as if all things living were calmed by its steady rhythm. Buddhist disciples filled the meditation room chanting the familiar prayer before the 'weekenders' would join them after they had dined.

Bayley Cheltham studied the human procession from his small verandah, drinking generously from a jug of distilled water, as if every glass would further perfect his youthful skin and lean body. His thirst quenched, Bayley leaned back on his chair, hands clasped behind his head, satisfied he had connected with his humanness.

"You look content," said Louise, joining him on the veranda. She sat down, continuing to towel her damp hair.

"Enjoy the shower?"

Louise rolled her eyes. "No hot water is the one thing I won't miss about this place."

"The price you pay to connect with nature," said Bayley, holding his gaze toward the monastery. All the nuns had assembled inside and a meditative quiet had taken over. "Peaceful, isn't it?"

"Chilly, more like it," Louise replied, furiously toweling to dry her damp hair.

Bayley ignored her complaint, trying to hold his mood. He wasn't one to have weekend romances as he always felt uncomfortable about it, but passion had become the mainstay of this weekend's retreat. One opportunity lost, another gained. He wanted to leave Louise on the verandah and eat, but he owed her some appreciation. Both knew this would not be repeated. They were merely passing time, undertaking taboo-like activities. Sex was 'off limits' in this place, according to the carefully typed House Rules placed in each of the dozen cottages rented to the public, but Bayley played by his own rules.

He saw another opportunity to test his humanness, ignoring his desire to leave. "I love your long hair, especially when it smells of fresh lavender."

Louise stopped toweling her hair, instead flicking it back over her shoulders. She sat forward on her seat, revealing bare breasts under her loose white robe. "There's still some time left before I leave."

Bayley immediately regretted his decision. "It's a pity my meditation starts so soon," he said, feigning regret.

Louise looked at her watch. "You'd skip dinner if it meant that much to you," she challenged.

"Sure. Why not."

"That lacked a certain amount of conviction, my darling lover. Let's not bother," said Louise, as she finished drying her hair.

Bayley stood, straightened his tailored jacket and ambled down the veranda stairs, somewhat relieved, before Louise goaded him.

"You wouldn't feel anything anyway," she taunted, abruptly stopping him.

"What do you mean?"

"I've never known a biot to enjoy sex."

"Sorry to disappoint you, but I'm human."

"I may not be an intelligent scientist like you, dear, but I've had many lovers, human, caste and biot, and you're a biot.

"Care to show me how you make such accurate observations?" Bayley asked, returning to take her hand and lead her back into the cottage.

Louise dropped her robe on the floor, before reclining on the bed, naked.

Bayley gazed at her body for a time, before speaking. "So, what makes you so sure?"

"It's harder to pick you, given your eyes are blue not metallic. I thought that was against the law? Do you have connections?"

"Eye recognition is impossible to evade unless you happen to be at the very highest levels of biotic research," said Bayley, reaching into his coat pocket and taking out a small metallic disc.

"What's that? A listening device?"

"No. Quite the opposite."

Bayley lay beside Louise and kissed her neck passionately, before pressing the disc firmly against her neck.

"What are you doing?" she exclaimed as she tried to remove it.

"I wouldn't do that if I were you," he warned, holding her arms firmly. "The disc will naturally disengage from your skin in around ten minutes. It will leave no marks as long as you make no attempts to remove it."

"If I do?"

"You will be left with some rather unfortunate scars. Trust me, in ten minutes it will fall off, and you will have no residual effects from the nanotech drug."

"Drug! What have you done to me?" she cried, before growing drowsy.

Bayley lay closer, releasing both arms, before comforting her with warm kisses. "Don't worry. You'll just sleep for a short time." He cradled her in his ams "You'll forget this weekend. More importantly, you'll forget me," he whispered soothingly to reassure her.

Louise would sleep until the next morning as the drug systematically erased her experiences with him. As she fell into a deep slumber, Bayley covered her with the bed linen, then he headed for the Chenrezig café, enjoying the freshness of the cool evening air, thoughts about Louise already erased from his memory. He had erased many human's memories, even killed when required. His near humanness was a sacrosanct action believed impossible according to biot laws, but Bayley was special, one of just a handful of biots granted clemency.

He approached the special prayer wheel situated halfway down the hill. *"Buddha guide me to my glorious achievement,"* he said to himself as he quietly walked around the spinning prayer wheel the required three times. There were over one hundred million prayers on microfiche contained in this special wheel. He imagined Buddha paid close attention to his prayer.

The sun was setting behind the steep hillside when

he arrived at the popular Big Love café for his evening meal. It was aptly named given its open and welcoming architecture. The majority of the nuns ate dinner at four o'clock, their final meal for the day. Unlike normal biots, Bayley was a class of biot containing a human digestive system, an expensive and important addition to aid his cover. He was ravenous and thanked Buddha that he did not have a similar curfew. An assortment of vegetarian meals was made available for the weekend guests every night between six and seven o'clock.

Bayley walked past the tables toward the cafeteria line. There was a hive of activity scurrying around the many occupied tables and a line of students waiting to be served. He stood patiently in line as the team of nuns diligently served the hungry guests. It was his last evening at Chenrezig, before leaving in the morning to return to work. By the time Bayley got served, hunger had made him forget the wisdom of the 'Eight-Fold' path taught in the morning session. Maybe this was the last test for guests? To learn patience.

"I'll have everything," he said, hunger in his tone but backed by an amicable smile. *At least the serving was generous.* He whisked his full tray to a quiet corner and hoped for no interruptions. He quickly gorged the food, finishing the main course before another of the students, an older woman, joined him.

"I'm Clare," she said, extending her hand to greet him.

Clare would have been in her sixties, but her thin, fit frame belied her age. She had a small serving of food compared to Bayley and appeared in no hurry to start her meal. He remembered her from the morning's class, as she was one of the more outspoken and probably more learned students. He soon found out that Clare had been attending Chenrezig Institute for many years.

"Did you enjoy this morning's lecture?" she asked.

"Yes, I came especially for this morning's session. The whole area of Karma fascinates me."

"I think 'cause and effect' makes more sense than a life that is bound only by fate."

"I agree. Our lives are so much a result of our own actions. We're the architects of our own fate. But whether we have past lives which impact on our current life is purely speculative, don't you think?"

Clare smiled. "What do you do for a living?"

"I'm a research scientist for Apollo Corporation."

"Ah, I thought so. Your rational mind will only accept what it sees, correct?"

"I have an open mind, but yes my training is Socratic in nature. We can be too easily fooled by our feelings. Once we believed we lived on a flat earth, did we not?" Bayley replied, enjoying the challenge of the conversation.

"Yes, that is the question. Do we as humans possess a mind with innate abilities that stretch beyond what science can account for? Do we possess the capacity for telepathy, clairvoyance, premonitions, or retro-cognition? Have you had any of these experiences in your life?"

Bayley searched the data base of his neural network for his dead host's experiences, selecting the most appropriate to share. Before dying, the human Bayley was a well- regarded scientist, committing much of his life to the pursuit of nature's universal truths with patience and rigor. He headed a team of renowned scientists who were investigating the speculative end of scientific research – biological quantum transference. It was considered the 'holy grail' of technology and robotic biological engineering. In short, he was searching for the soul. Could biots ultimately function as humans in every sense of the word? Could they possess a soul? His decision to pursue such research was decided by a single dream he had in his youth, a dream so vivid he never forgot it. Twenty years later, the predictions of his dream came true.

"Yes. I saw my future in a single dream that changed my life. I've been determined to find those answers ever since."

"Maybe it was more that you were born with the determination to achieve your dreams."

Bayley nodded in agreement. "I have many weaknesses, but lack of determination is not one of them."

Bayley's com flashed an incoming text from Apollo. He glanced briefly at his message. *Project Blue is live. Report to HQ 0800 hours, tomorrow*, it said, an order from his commander, Zhang.

Bayley stood. "Sorry about that. I've been waiting on an urgent message. If you'll excuse me, I have to leave, now."

"Of course. Good luck!"

He waved his hand in appreciation, not for her well wishes, but her belief that she was encouraging a fellow human. His slow conversion to that which he had been programmed was nearing its completion. Project Blue was live. Finally, he was in a position to change the course of human evolution, a cause he was programmed to kill for if necessary.

Bayley called Zhang to confirm his commander's message. "I'll be there at 0800."

Bayley said no more, intent on returning to the cabin to remove all traces of his stay with Louise.

Project Blue was finally live.

The hidden war was soon to begin.

Chapter Four

ANDER

Ander methodically inspected the ship's sectors, increasingly reassured the Deliverance was running smoothly. The incident in the cargo hold appeared to have been an accident, confirmed by Dane's report. That didn't stop him from undertaking an exhaustive security sweep in a challenging hour that included real examinations laced with digital scenarios to test his response time to security threats.

Ander ran a final diagnostic on his 'sleeve', a purpose-built bay fitted to all defense grade biots. Similar to his female assistant's drone filled sleeve, Ander held a deadly armory of defensive and offensive weaponry. His was the most expensive, befitting a superior military biot. Ander wasn't assigned to make up the numbers; he could fight off a hostile fleet if need be.

Satisfied with his security sweep, Ander contacted the captain. "Security and maintenance completed. No abnormalities."

"Have my biots reported?" Quinn asked.

"Cluste and Fragg are running maintenance checks in the docking area, in preparation for the Mars tug-ship docking."

"Neither have reported to me. Check the situation. I will need them back on the Navigation pod to oversee docking."

"Following through, now." Ander replied. "Cluste – confirm status?"

"I'm checking a minor fault in the Docking Bay pod. I will be delayed fifteen minutes."

"What's the fault?"

"It's just a minor electrical."

"And Fragg?"

"He's undertaking a security sweep of our reconnaissance ship in preparation for the arrival of the Mars tug."

"I want you both back in Navigation in ten minutes, maximum. Is that clear?"

"Clear."

Ander headed for navigation himself, satisfied with Cluste's response. "Contacted Cluste. He and Fragg will be in Navigation in ten minutes."

"Reason?"

"Cluste is repairing a minor electrical fault. Fragg is running a security check of our reconnaissance ship in preparation for the tug docking."

"Monitors have picked up that the reconnaissance craft has been activated. That's not part of security procedures. Investigate now and return them to Navigation, immediately!"

"I'm on my way." Ander replied, without argument. The biots were committing a serious breach of protocol.

"Report to me immediately. Fragg, you're committing a security breach. Cease immediately!"

Neither biot replied. Instead, preparation of the reconnaissance craft launch continued unabated. Ander's com confirmed the external docking bay doors were being opened. He had only minutes to stop them, otherwise the ship would be lost, leading to more investigations. It was clear the actions were premeditated, as the internal docking bay entries were in full lockdown.

"Give me immediate entry, Cluste. That's an order!"

His request was ignored, so Ander positioned his right palm against the security door and with the gentlest of shoves, knocked the six-inch Teflon and aluminium door aside, as if pushing a toy to the ground. He moved forward and unhinged the second security door before walking into a hostile response.

"Stand clear or I'll fire," said Cluste, standing beside the operational helm, weapon in hand and a preparedness to do battle.

Ander engaged his defensive force field, before contacting Quinn.

"He has a twenty-first century ballistic weapon. Shall I disengage him?" Old fashioned weaponry had been banned in space vehicles, given a misfire could breach the hull of a ship.

"Disarm or decommission. It's your call," Quinn replied.

"You'll stay perfectly still, or I put a round of bullets through this hull," Cluste threatened.

Ander activated a pulse that formed a shield around Cluste's weapon, eliminating his threat. Then he engaged the biot in combat, easily defending Cluste's attack before laying a decisive blow to his head – half power – designed to paralyze movement capability only, but importantly saving his neural network for interrogation. Cluste fell to his knees, powerless against his superior officer.

"Who gave you these treasonous orders?"

Cluste refused to answer, before tilting his head toward the sound of the reconnaissance vehicle's thrusters being ignited.

Ander was too late. Cluste had somehow overridden navigation security protocols, giving clearance for the vessel to exit the mother ship. He turned from Cluste to the navigation panel.

"I cannot override Cluste's command. Request permission to disable the reconnaissance craft's defense shield."

"Affirmative. Do anything to halt that vehicle!"

The vehicle had already launched, but Fragg remained within range for a strike. Ander set his holographic to hand weapons and selected a Smithen Pulse Gun. Once selected, it turned from a 3D image into a real weapon capable of deactivating the escaping vehicle. Ander fired the first pulse to its left side, predicting correctly it would turn in that direction to attempt evasion. The first pulse slammed into the side of the vehicle, destroying its defense shield. The craft was vulnerable and could be destroyed with another direct hit.

"Craft vulnerable. Shall I disable?"

Several valuable seconds passed as Quinn deliberated. Whatever happened now, there would be an investigation.

"Disable the satellite navigation only. No damage to the ship's hull. We need to recover Fragg and interrogate both biots. He cannot escape."

Ander's next shot was more difficult, given the growing distance between the ships. Ander took further valuable seconds changing his weapon from the Pulse Gun to a Laser Gun, capable of firing a single, more accurate shot at the craft. He aimed for the exterior satellite navigation antenna, a small target at this distance. Again, Ander predicted the craft would move further left to continue its evasive path, so he fired one degree left, but the craft straightened to its original course. The shot destroyed the communication satellite, but only grazed the navigation antenna, not disabling it. Ander watched helplessly as the craft flew out of range, making a second shot impossible.

"Fragg has escaped, but I've immobilized Cluste. Your instructions?"

"Secure Cluste into a holding pod. I shall interrogate him myself. We have more pressing concerns now. I'll notify the authorities of these events and try to calm the shit storm that will follow. When you have secured Cluste, have all the remaining crew report to the Navigation pod."

Ander returned to Cluste, effortlessly lifting and carrying him to the entry of the holding pod. There, Ander turned off his com and Cluste's.

"What next?" Cluste asked.

"Quinn will interrogate you."

Ander lowered his incapacitated body on the floor, before scanning a programming device into his left eye.

"Is my project memory being erased?"

"Yes," Ander replied, applying the specially encrypted program. "Program erase, commence."

In a few seconds, all records of Cluste's clandestine commands were deleted. Cluste now looked on in bafflement.

"What's happening?"

Ander ran a review across Cluste's eyes verifying the program had been erased, before running a second scan. "Erase his memory of me running these scans."

Ander hibernated his neural network before carrying Cluste to the holding pod, confident Quinn's interrogations would face an empty shell. Chaos on board the Deliverance had commenced.

Chapter Five

ASSIGNMENT

Bayley entered the foyer of Apollo Corporation, his appropriate passes in hand. He was well known to the security staff, but that never stopped them from running long, tedious checks. This level of scrutiny was reserved for humans, no matter how long they worked for Apollo.

"Look into the scanner, Mr. Cheltham," the guard requested, before directing him to a nearby seat, to await official clearance.

Bayley sat and watched the procession of castes who walked through security and into one of the many elevators servicing the city's largest building. Castes had inbuilt identification systems installed in their adolescence, affording them freedoms humans would never be given. Many minutes passed before Bayley was allowed through. The small number of humans that worked for Apollo tolerated the treatment, but not Bayley. He would be concerned if he were not treated in that way. Every time a caste displayed their mistrust or indignation was more proof that he had achieved his goal. To them he was just another annoyance, part of the dwindling number of humans who rejected becoming post-humans.

"You can go now," the guard said.

Bayley nodded, ignoring the caste guard's superior tone before taking the first available elevator. He pushed the top floor button, drawing curious looks from the hand-ful of castes. Bayley enjoyed watching their reaction. Of the fifty thousand employees who worked or lived in this 'super-scraper', only a token number were humans, making up the required international employment quota. Humans, for the most part, worked in the human indus-tries, devoted to the maintenance of natural biosphere systems, of which Gaea was the largest multinational company on Earth.

Bayley joined his operational manager, Zhang, who sat at the head of a long meeting table, its backdrop an expansive view of the city. Another operative sat to Zhang's left, scanning notes on his com.

"Welcome, Bayley. This is Hogan who will be briefing us about the Trojan project."

Bayley merely nodded, before taking a seat to the right of Zhang and opposite Hogan.

Hogan's cropped greying hair looked out of sync with his youthful, lithe, military trained physique. He wore a standard military uniform, tapered on the body but bulked on the shoulder and arms to carry his technological armor. He proudly displayed military pins on his uniform and on the cap, he had placed on the table, displaying his elite commando pedigree. Hogan studied Bayley for a time. Digital silver pupils flashed intermittently, revealing his caste credentials. Any details he didn't know about Bayley would be clarified through inbuilt augmented reality vision.

"Thank you, Commander. Before I commence, may I ask what Bayley's role will be in my proposed mission?"

"He is a research scientist, with some secret operative credentials."

Logan's metallic fingernails moved across his com as he checked Bayley's data. "Commander, may I speak frankly?"

"Granted," Zhang replied, with a hint of resignation in his voice.

"We are discussing a military mission. This is hardly of relevance to a research scientist assigned to a peripheral project."

Hogan's slight had little to do with Bayley's capabilities.

Though he didn't say it outright, Hogan believed him to be a human. Like any caste, his covert judgement was that a human would be at the least a hindrance, at worst untrustworthy.

"Thank you for your opinion, Hogan, but I shall be the judge of Bayley's relevance. Please continue," he replied.

"Very well," Hogan replied frostily. "I won't bore you with the background of the Trojan program, as I understand you're well briefed about the details?" Bayley nodded his head. "The issue at hand is that operatives in my team have discovered that the Trojan program is far more advanced than Gaea representatives would have us believe."

"They claimed the program was two years from completion at the last international forum," Zhang added.

"That's correct, but we have uncovered the truth. The Trojan computer was recently completed and they have plans to ship it to Mars base, where they will bring it to full operation, under the protection of inter-solar law."

"Do you have time lines for this planned shipment?" Bayley asked.

"Our sources believed it was imminent, but recent events have made us consider that it may already be in transit." Hogan replied, turning to Zhang. "A recent incident occurred on one of our Apollo freighters that has raised concerns."

"I read the brief. Two biots went rogue soon after an explosion occurred in their ship's cargo hull. The ship's captain filed a report on the explosion. The cause sounded clear cut. I have his report if you'd like to see it," Zhang replied.

"No. I read it. It didn't look suspicious, until we were made aware that a Gaea employee wrote the report."

"Yes, a human research scientist with the help of his biot assistant," Zhang said.

"Both are intimately involved with the Trojan project, Commander."

"True, but the findings were accepted by our best field experts."

"Even if we accept the findings, two biots going rogue would appear an interesting coincidence." Hogan replied.

"True. Quinn's report claimed that both were close to the explosion. One was temporarily decommissioned. Is it possible that the explosions led to the malfunctions?"

Hogan shook his head. "Possible, but again the odds of this occurring are improbable. I recommend we send a team to the ship to carry out our own investigations."

"There are two rogue biots. One is still on the ship under guard. The other is piloting a transit ship to Mars orbiting station. It may be more in your interest to carry out an inspection on Mars station and Mars base. You have operatives in both sectors. Why not engage them?" Zhang asked.

"None of our operatives have the security clearance to undertake this investigation. As you know, it is highly classified."

"I don't need to remind you, Hogan, that the program is not gifted with unlimited funds. When do you want to enact this investigation?"

"I understand that the ship is in orbit awaiting clearance to transfer their cargo to the orbiting station, before shipment to Mars base. We have a one-week window. Maximum."

"One week? That means a starship!"

"And an appropriate crew."

"An ambitious request! That would mean hundreds of millions of credits. Many times your budget entitlement," Zhang replied.

"And if the Trojan computer was on that ship? What would that be worth, Commander?"

Zhang sat back in his chair contemplating. "If I was to entertain your project, and that's a very big if, tell me what crew you would need and why?"

Hogan withdrew pre-prepared files and passed it to Zhang. "I took the liberty to develop a program brief that includes all the funding requirements."

Zhang perused the file. "I'm not familiar with the crew. Brief me?"

"Locke would be my second in command. He's a specialist biot, trained in space warfare. Step is a Starfighter pilot. He would command the navigation as well as the AI fleet of four fully automated Starfighters as support. We would also require another biot, mainly for navigation assistance."

"Are you expecting an incident?" Zhang asked.

"This close to Mars base? It's almost certain, if they actually carried the contraband."

"Your team could hold any retaliation?"

"My crew is small, but they are among the best of our Apollo biots."

Zhang turned to Bayley and transferred Hogan's file to his com, immediately getting a reaction from Hogan.

"This information is classified, Commander!"

Zhang ignored him. "Take your time reading it, Bayley".

Bayley slowly read the brief, despite Hogan's remonstrations. Then he passed judgement. "Hogan has good reason to be confident. His team has the capacity to handle any external attack. But the brief assumes we have a matching capability inside the ship. I'm not convinced we do."

"With all due respect, I've been briefed on the crew of

the Deliverance. If there is hidden cargo there, it will not leave the ship," Hogan retaliated.

"Yet, two biots disobeyed orders, one abandoning the ship. Explain that?" Bayley replied.

"The rogue biot will be picked up at the space station. He poses no problem for us."

"That is hardly reassuring. Explain why you think your team can handle who is on the Deliverance?" Bayley asserted.

"There are only two Gaea employees. The human, Dane, and his assistant. The biot is not military grade. Neither pose a problem."

Bayley intervened again. "Your knowledge of the Gaea presence on that ship is limited. I request to join the mission."

"This is preposterous..." Hogan replied defensively, turning to Zhang for support.

"Hogan. You and your team are the best for this mission, but there are certain facts you are clearly unaware of," Zhang replied, angering Hogan further.

"I know nothing of this agent, Zhang. He could compromise my team. I..."

Zhang cut him off. "Enough, Hogan. I want Bayley to join you and your team and report to you at 0800 hours, tomorrow. You will be in command of this mission, but

Bayley will partner you in all interrogations on board the Deliverance. Is that clear?"

Hogan stood up in defiance, "Surely you see there is a potential for compromise of our mission by including a human?"

"I have another team waiting in the wings, should you step down. But I'd prefer your team. Is your Starfighter ready for takeoff?"

"Yes. Everything is set for departure."

"I can't make you accept this mission, Hogan, but it goes without saying, Apollo command would not consider your refusal in a good light, given the urgency of the situation."

Hogan sat down, resigned to Zhang's verdict. "There was no need to brief you on my project. Your mind was made up well before this meeting. How about you tell me what's really going on?"

Zhang sat forward in his chair. "I can't reveal everything. I can tell you that I need an operative who will support my decisions. If you can't accept that, I suggest you stand down from the mission. Give me your decision now, captain.

Hogan looked to Bayley than back to Zhang, who sat stony faced. "Fine, have it your way," he replied, raising his arms in a surrender position.

"Excellent." Zhang replied with satisfaction, before

standing. "I'll leave you two to sort out any differences before tomorrow. I'll have to leave you both now. Another pressing meeting, I'm afraid."

After he left, Bayley studied Hogan's com files in silence for a few tense minutes. "Are you going to tell me as little as Zhang just did?" Hogan pressed.

Bayley looked up from his com. "The flight specs show you and your team will report to launch pad twelve at 0800 hours tomorrow. Your fighter pilot, Step, and 2IC, Locke, will perform pre-flight checks of our Starship and the four accompanying AI ships in preparation for an 1800 launch. Correct?"

"Yes. And what will be your role?"

Bayley closed the file. "While in flight to Mars orbit, I'll follow your command. But when we start the interrogations on the Deliverance, we work as a team."

Hogan smirked. "Sure, but if we encounter danger of any sort, I expect you to follow my orders. I won't endanger my men."

"I'd expect no less. You must protect your ship while docked, but you must also protect me as I carry out the investigation of its crew. Is that clear enough for you?"

"Any military crew could do this. Why waste my time?" Hogan replied, indignantly.

"Zhang requested the best for this operation, because

we can't make mistakes. If the Intel is right and that cargo ship is carrying the Trojan computer, then Gaea will have a presence of agents with one aim — get Trojan to Mars at all costs. Zhang selected you to counter that threat. He selected me for reasons that are highly confidential. It's imperative that you support me. You were seen as highly reliable, but perhaps Zhang made a mistake."

Hogan looked Bayley in the eye. "I can do that. But can you tell me one thing?"

"Shoot."

"You studied my specs. I'm not a biot."

"You have over forty percent implants. You're a caste. That makes you more than qualified for this mission."

"You're the first commander to accept a post-human so willingly. Most request biots."

"That's why you have mostly worked alone. I know. It's all in your specs."

"It doesn't worry you?"

"Your team is the best. Two military grade biots. They appear to have the utmost confidence in you. Loyalty from biots doesn't come easy."

"Exactly. Loyalty from biots will never come easily. And yet..."

Bayley smiled. "And yet? What is it you want to know?"

"Who am I working for? Biot or ..."

Bayley stood up. "Or human? I've learnt that both biot and human require loyalty in our line of business and given the high stakes, loyalty is inevitably hard earned. I will report to you at 0800 hours, Commander. Let's begin the process of earning each other's loyalty." As he left the meeting room, Bayley half smiled. Hogan, an experienced operative, was not sure if he was human or biot.

Chapter Six

DEBRIEF

I struggled to Navigation, with Hali's help. All the crew attended bar the two errant biots. Quinn studied everyone as if we were all guilty. His normal gruff brand of certainty was replaced by cautious observation. Disloyalty was not a behavior Quinn had faced from his crew before, and it clearly rattled him. Had his investigations uncovered anything? It was unlikely, as the chaos Latatious predicted unfolded around him. This career captain had skills to handle freight hauling, not the nest of vipers that currently inhabited his ship. Quinn maintained his silence for an unusually long period as he seemingly willed his crew to confess their guilt, but none was offered.

Quinn looked directly at me. "Either this is the

worst luck I've ever had in a thirty-year career or there's a pattern of disruption occurring on my ship that is coordinated."

All followed Quinn's accusing gaze, prompting me to take the offensive. "You think I'm not worried, too? You're carrying the most expensive cargo ever sent to Mars by Gaea, and I'm responsible for it."

Quinn raised an eyebrow before turning to the other crew. "We have had our first Category Five emergency. Today at 0500 hours, Fragg took possession of one of our reconnaissance vehicles. He's currently on a course to Mars satellite base. Reasons unknown."

"Is Mars orbiting base aware?" I asked.

"Already contacted."

"Is it too late to retrieve him?"

"Yes, Dane. The ship is outside Ander's weapons capacity. Fragg escaped with the help of Cluste. Fortunately, Ander immobilized him and we hold him in security. For now we will follow emergency protocols. I briefed Apollo, and they're sending a Starship and interrogation team to our ship. They are expected to arrive in 30 hours."

Apollo was closing in and with it my window of opportunity to deliver the secret cargo. "And the tug ship?" I asked.

"It has already launched and will be docking with our

ship in 24 hours. Apollo wanted the docking cancelled, but we were too late to stop it."

"Have you questioned Cluste?" Draven asked.

"I have, but I can't give you the details of my interrogation."

Draven didn't hide his annoyance. "Can you tell us anything useful?"

"I can say that I have encouraged our prisoner to provide important details about the objective of their treasonous actions and the reasons behind them."

I supported Draven's discontent, even if for different reasons. "We work alongside these biots. One disobeyed orders and another abandoned ship. For the safety of the crew and this ship, you should tell us more."

"I'll tell you everything I've learned, once command gives me clearance to do so. What I can share is our new project directives. We'll remain in orbit around Mars, until further notice."

"Instructions for the tug ship?" Ander asked.

"It will be allowed to dock, but that's all."

"No unloading?" Ander pushed.

"Absolutely not."

My window was all but closed. I had to try and influence Quinn. "We're going to float in space for an unknown period, while you carry the most expensive payload ever sent to Mars? I remind you that this Gaea funded project is high priority. I hope that Gaea has been included in your decision making?"

"The value of this cargo hasn't been ignored, but it appears your program is shrouded in highly sensitive protocols that are not meant for my ears. For now, our priority is to hold the Deliverance in orbit until further notice."

"There's still a possibility that all your biots are equally compromised." I warned, looking to Ander, Draven, and Shell.

Ander nodded in the affirmative before speaking. "I will personally maintain a high security watch over the remaining crew. There will be no more protocol breaks," he responded, in a determined manner.

Quinn backed him. "Your concerns are duly noted, Dane. For that reason, I will maintain a red alert over the ship until further notice."

"I request access to the cargo during this period. It's too valuable to be left to Ander."

"Request denied. For now, you and Hali are confined to your quarters until further notice. The same goes for all other biots, with the exception of my 2IC," Quinn ordered.

"Preposterous! You have no jurisdiction over me. I demand counsel with Apollo." Draven exclaimed.

"Request denied. All biots except Hali will be confined to their quarters and follow my orders only, until the investigation team dock. Is that clear?"

Draven moved to the front and stood beside Shell. She appeared to react, lifting her sleeve. *Was she working with Draven?* The potential threat was soon dissipated, as Ander moved his sleeve, ready to answer any challenge. A silent stand-off ensured, before Quinn finally spoke.

"All crew except Ander are confined to the assigned quarters until further notice. Is that clear?" He barked, staring down the two biots and receiving no more argument.

I wasn't about to argue and make things worse. Better Quinn maintained control of the ship than Draven. For now, I only had one ally I could trust. Hali stood loyally alongside me, her objectives unchanged, even after the chaotic events. She would continue to work on the Trojan file review until otherwise commanded. Had the time come for me to bring her closer to the real events that were unfolding? She no doubt held opinions about the unfolding chaos, but she would not veer from her orders unless ordered. I resisted that option for now, for unknown to Hali, she had the capability to change the game should Latatious consider it required. The clock was ticking and a decision had to be made before the investigation team arrived. Somehow, I had to break protocol and get to Latatious.

Chapter Seven

DOCKING

The starship thrusters fired in full reverse, slowing from sub-light speed to a relative crawl. Step masterfully steered the small ship into the docking procedure under his commander's watchful eyes. Hogan delighted in showcasing his team's abilities in front of Bayley, every command highlighting the superior technical skills castes and biots possessed. This drive to showcase the evolutionary inevitability washed over all human, post-human relations. Bayley watched on, secretly enjoying the precision but knowing Hogan would not be so amenable to him after docking.

"Request external docking clamps be opened," said Step, as he slowly maneuvered the starship to the docking bay.

"Docking clamps released, ready for dock. Proceed." Quinn replied.

Within a few minutes, textbook docking was accomplished. Hogan tapped Step's shoulder in appreciation, before signaling Quinn.

"Docking process complete. Request three of our crew board your ship, Captain?"

"Affirmative. Procedures to open adjoining hatch in process. Expected boarding time is 03.20 hours."

Hogan thanked his crew for a flawless flight and dock, before turning to Bayley, seemingly as an afterthought. "How did Zhang want us to proceed with the interrogations?"

"Hogan, you'll directly assist me with the individual interrogations of the crew, while Locke carries out a search of the ship for any suspicious contraband."

Hogan predictably questioned the decision. "Shouldn't I assist Locke?"

"Negative. You'll attend every interrogation. Locke is more than capable of carrying out the surveillance."

"And if I should face resistance, Commander?" Locke asked.

"You're on a war footing the minute we board their ship. Remain at that level until I say otherwise." Hogan ordered.

"Is there a need to show such force? It may give rise to an unnecessary incident," Bayley questioned.

"There are three military grade biots aboard that ship with the capability to retaliate. Locke would be outnumbered. I protect my men. Would you?"

"Duly noted," Bayley replied.

Hogan continued with his orders. "Step, put the starship and the four automated Starfighters into war footing, too. If there is any sign of resistance, act."

"Shall I remain docked?"

"No. Once we board, I want you to leave the docking station and hold your position in tandem with your autonomous fleet."

Hogan then addressed all the crew. "Gentlemen, we board the Deliverance in less than an hour. I suggest you use this time preparing to carry out your assigned duties. Clear?"

"Where should I focus my investigation?" Locke asked.

"Study the cargo hold formation and the contents of those containers. I want a thorough inspection. Stay focused on that, unless I order otherwise."

Nothing else needed to be said. The interrogation was set at the highest of security levels. A deadly game of poker was about to unfold.

Chapter Eight

INTERROGATION

The ship had been in lockdown for thirty-five tense hours. Three of the starship's crew boarded our ship, immediately commencing interrogations. I expected to be the first called, but five hours in I remained confined to quarters. Hali had been called to their interrogation room an hour earlier and still hadn't returned. Leaving the guilty to last. As the only human on the ship, I was certain to be the chief suspect. They'd gather little information from Hali, except for the official review of the Trojan program. That would reveal nothing they didn't already know, that being the Trojan computer was years from fruition.

Hali finally returned, accompanied by Ander.

The wait was beginning to frustrate me. "Is it my turn?"

"Not yet, Dane. The investigators are reviewing their findings. They'll call for you when ready."

"What's happening, Ander?" I asked, hoping for any snippet of information.

"There are two undertaking the interviews and a third inspecting the cargo hold."

"Have they reported anything?"

"I don't think they intend to reveal anything. We know as much as you." Ander stopped to listen to a communication. "I have to go. I will return when they are ready to interview you."

Ander turned and left, seemingly ordered to minimize communication with me, yet Hali was left behind. It was likely they were scanning our communication, so I spoke cautiously.

"How did it go?"

"They were initially interested in the explosion, but they realized I knew little about it.

"Did they ask you to recount anything I said about the incident?"

"Not the explosion. They appeared more interested in our follow-up inspection of the cargo hull."

That worried me. My report of the events offered a perfect explanation, perhaps too perfect. Were they closing in on me? "You said they?"

"Yes. Bayley, a research scientist, and Hogan, a military man."

"How did they react to the report?"

"Bayley showed no reaction one way or the other, whereas Hogan was suspicious, bordering on hostile. That was interesting to me."

"Why?"

"I can't be certain, but I believe Bayley's a human, where Hogan's a caste."

A human on the investigation team was interesting. I expected specialist biots to be the interrogators, or high-grade castes. Why would Apollo risk a human to head the inspections?

"You said Hogan was suspicious. Did he press you on any events?"

"His line of questioning tested my knowledge of events, both current and past."

"In relation to the Trojan project?"

"Mostly."

"What else?"

"He was aggressive at times, challenging the honesty of my responses, threatening to decommission me, if my facts were proven incorrect."

"He has little hope of that. You are hard wired to clearly present the facts as you know them."

"Bayley initially allowed Hogan's aggressive questioning, but eventually he took control of the interview."

I had many more questions I wanted to ask, but Ander returned. "They're ready to question you, Dane. Follow me, please."

The security pod was set up with a single table. Both interrogators were seated and studied me as I sat down opposite them. One appeared agitated, making me guess he was Hogan. The other opened the investigation.

"Thanks for your patience, Dane," said Bayley.

The welcoming tone disarmed me for an instant. "There's a lot to investigate," I offered, equally in good faith.

"Yes, there are many challenges. Bayley's my name and this is Hogan."

I nodded cordially to Hogan only to be ignored. Everything Hali had said about them seemed to be accurate.

"As I understand, you are a Gaea employee responsible for the development of the Trojan project. Is that correct?" Bayley asked.

"That's right. I have been working on the project since 2115."

"So, let's review that first," said Bayley, nodding to Hogan.

Hogan gave the slightest of nods, preferring to study

the com files he had open in front of him, leaving Bayley to ask the questions.

"Are you aware of the political sensitivities created by this project?"

I considered the loaded question as Hogan continued to flick through the files like a prosecutor ready to attack any doubtful response. "There are many political sensitivities between Gaea and Apollo."

"But you'd agree that this particular project has led to many serious flash points between our organizations?"

"It depends how you define flashpoint."

Hogan immediately looked up from the file and gazed at me through his narrowed tech-steel eyes. "Are you trying to be provocative?"

"Five years on this project has taught me to be quite the opposite. I've learnt that this project can draw partisan responses."

"No doubt. I'm sure you're aware of the latest flashpoint. There have been rumors that the project is on the verge of completion. Given you are perfectly positioned to answer this question, is there any truth to this rumor?" Bayley asked.

"This is no more than hearsay."

"Answer the question," Hogan demanded.

"I just did."

Hogan picked up his military grade cap, firmly placing it on his head. The cap's VR visor could automatically adjust from normal sun visor to full face force field offering protection against attackers. He switched the force field on, purposely signaling a more threatening demeanor. "You're telling me that the Trojan project is years from being developed?"

I held a defiant gaze. The red glare of the com light just above Hogan reminded me that this inquisition would be streamed to Apollo and Gaea officials. Every question was a trap that could see me permanently incarcerated for treason.

"You know as well as I that Gaea officials have reported the timelines of this project. They have not shifted that timeline, even though your officials seemed determined to doubt it."

Hogan seemingly noted my glance toward the com, as he disengaged it and walked around the table and stood beside me. "Don't feed me bullshit answers, human. I suggest you tell us everything, before we find the machine. I have my best officer scanning the cargo hull and he'll soon find your Trojan machine. You have one chance to tell the truth and save yourself a long prison sentence."

He held the back of my chair and knelt closer. "One chance," he whispered.

"Good luck finding anything," I said.

Hogan swung my chair around and pushed me hard on the chest. I fell hard on the floor and tumbled into the wall. The fall knocked the wind out of me, such was his force. He was a caste, alright, showcasing his arms of steel. His steel eyes pulsed behind the visor force field as he approached. I reacted by lifting my arms as a shield, drawing only mocking laughter as he effortlessly picked me up.

"Tell me, human. Do you think the world owes you a privileged life? That's what you all expect, isn't it? Well, that time is coming to an end. So, speak up, little man."

"You're looking for information I don't have. Search the hull all you like. There's just terraforming equipment."

He lowered me down to his eye levels. They burned with hate as he began to apply pressure around my neck. "I could end your life with just a little more pressure. No one will care about your inconsequential life."

Pain burned my neck as Hogan's vice-like hand locked me in his death grip. How many had died at his hand like this? Blackness slowly filled the edges of my vision, leaving only hateful eyes burning for my death. My hearing turned inward, to the sound of my own heart beat and the shallowness of my breath. The blackness almost claimed me, bar for a single voice from a distance. I struggled to hear as the sound moved closer, a single word, *Hogan,* the name of my assailant. I repeatedly heard his name in my ear, until the pressure around my neck was released, allowing me to take large gasps of lifegiving air and a renewed awareness of my surroundings.

"Hogan! Enough!" Bayley ordered, stopping Hogan's assault. "Assist Locke with the hull inspection. Now!"

Hogan looked down at me, smiling coldly. For a moment, I thought he'd ignore Bayley and finish me. He feigned a kick, making me scurry back in retreat. One blow from his bionic limbs could easily kill me, so all I could do was try to defend. Thankfully, he listened to Bayley, but not before laughing as he left the room. I watched him closely. He was a military trained caste, a dangerous adversary. He was the last person I wanted as an enemy, but it couldn't be any other way. The threatening ramifications of the project I'd accepted to carry out were drawing in around me like a humid day.

Bayley approached, offering his hand. "I'm sorry that happened. When military are set an objective, they tend to doggedly pursue it, no matter the consequences."

I shook my head, intent on trying to clear my throat before slumping on the chair. Bayley disarmed me again with his empathic demeanor. He was human, but I wondered about his implants. Human Apollo agents were rare. Could he be a well disguised caste, instead? "Water?"

"Yes," I rasped, still reeling from Hogan's wrath. Bayley showed the empathy of a human but he could just as easily be a caste, well versed in interrogation, playing the 'good cop.' After Hogan's attack, I was more than happy to play along.

"Can I ask you more about your past, Dane?"

I drank the glass of water, then another. "Shoot."

"You lived on Mars for most of your life. It was a very happy time for you, wasn't it?"

"Yes. Loving family, good friends. You could say it defined me."

Bayley appeared more interested in veering from the investigation at hand, so I engaged him. "It was the happiest time of my life."

"You're actually a Martian, aren't you?"

"Yes. I was born on Mars. My parents were part of the first human landing on Mars."

"They were the first colonists! I didn't know that."

"Yes, they landed in 2080 and helped build Mars from nothing."

"They must've had the true colonial spirit to meet that challenge," Bayley said, seemingly interested in Martian history while appreciating his coffee, not something castes liked to do. *He had to be a human.*

"Yes. Their first task was to build Mars base station.

They were lucky in a way as the components of their home had already been pre-assembled, whereas future generations expanded the base using local materials."

"I read that in your brief, but didn't pick up your parents were part of the famous first flight. How many came on the first landing?"

"They were the first six Martians."

"What a challenging task. How did they choose the ultimate site?"

"That decision had already been made. High quality mapping of their site had been undertaken many years earlier by Gaea satellites orbiting Mars. Once they had accurate geological and seismic surveys, they could pick the most appropriate site for launching and landing future space craft."

"It turned out the right decision. Apollo followed around a decade later and assembled their base, just a few kilometers east of yours. That first decade would have many challenges."

"Not really. Their work was initially fully programmed: set up Mars Base to a habitable stage. I remember them telling me the biggest challenge was human more than geographic. Their bonds had been tested by the stress of close quarter living on the space ship which continued into the confines of Mars base."

"The hazardous surroundings must have tested them."

"The extreme weather was a problem, but the choice of site lessened that challenge. The immediate surroundings were flat, so it was easier to recover deliveries from Earth and less challenging to extend the settlement. It was also close to known water resources, a large deposit of underground ice."

"I should know my history, but where was it again?"

"It was on the relatively flat surface of Chryse Planitia, near Ascraeus Mons."

"That's right and, fortuitously, near the deposit of Elithium."

"Yes, it changed everything."

"Remarkable. To develop the first Mars base was challenging enough, but to develop a mining base as well was breathtaking. How did they find the time?"

"Fortunately, the key infrastructure had already been shipped well before they arrived. The habitat structures were formed by rocket shells from earlier unmanned missions as well as essential cargo."

"What was the essential cargo?"

"A small nuclear reactor to be used in conjunction with solar and wind power. An IRSU Plant to collect and manufacture chemicals from Mars raw materials. An inflatable greenhouse structure containing growing beds for hydroponic vegetables. Communication hardware, an array of surface vehicles and robotics for exploring. There was also a fully pressurized vehicle allowing extended journeys, unlike the rest that had to be operated in space suits. That was the vehicle where…" I stopped short, surprised Bayley encouraged me to say this much."

"The accident. That was long after the first landing."

I didn't answer immediately. Bayley said earlier that he didn't know about my parents, yet now he was questioning me about their accident. He knew everything about me, but I entertained him with answers, anyway. "Yes. A number of decades had passed. Zi and I were adults and worked with them on various tasks."

"An astronaut's life is not for the faint hearted. The risk of death is just one miscalculation away. And Mars magnifies that risk?"

"Yes. By then the Mars population had grown to the thousands. But even then, the infrastructure was still not sufficiently developed to cope with some emergencies. Our Martian dream could have ended at any moment, for anybody. A micro meteor shower, a systems failure, any small error could have spelt disaster."

"A hard reality of space travel?"

"It's a side of space exploration everyone tries to ignore, but it always remains in the background."

"Having children is a brave decision."

"Yes, but an inevitable one. My parents committed the remainder of their lives to the development of Mars, including raising us."

"A decision that turned out to be very successful. Two gifted children."

"I think Zi was the gifted one."

"Your older sister."

"Yes. From a young age, Zi knew what she wanted. She worked on mine clearing equipment at first, but she soon tired of that, handing the responsibility to me. Her real love was for technology. She always tinkered with super-computers and the like."

"She came up with the concept for the Trojan computer, did she not?"

"That's a moot point. I believe she did, but history may not be so kind."

Half an hour into the interrogation and I was warming to Bayley. I stifled those feelings and reminded myself he was an Apollo agent, yet the feelings remained.

"I hope I get the chance to meet with her when I go to Mars."

"You're not returning to Earth?"

"No. My assignment ends with this review. I'm taking on another assignment on Mars."

I looked up at the com again and it was still off. *Was he trying to tell me something?* I wondered.

"Apollo base?"

He smiled, seemingly recognizing the interrogation had turned back on to him. "I'll be based at the United Nations peace keeping force quarters for a short time."

Another surprising answer. Who did he report to? Why was a scientist part of an Apollo interrogation? "I know the commander there," I said, testing him.

"Colonel Knowles."

"Yes. He's a Mars 'lifer'."

"Like your sister."

I nodded. *Was it possible Bayley was a Gaea agent?* I thought he was about to tell me more but a com communication interrupted us, brief but enough to change his mood.

"That was Hogan. The search team have cleared all containers except one. He wants to know what's in container 64?"

I tried to stay calm, but my hand fidgeted. I feigned a brush of my hair, hoping he hadn't noticed. "All of the containers carry our new terraforming equipment. But if you read the report, you'd already know that."

"Locke carried out a mass scan and container 64 is five percent heavier than the other surrounding containers. Is there a reasonable explanation for this anomaly?"

My discomfort grew, unable to think of an acceptable response. I picked up my com to buy more time, "Let me check my files."

Bayley nodded and contacted Hogan while waiting. "Have Locke take a closer look at it," he said loudly, making sure I heard him.

The program was on the verge of being exposed. *Think! Give him an acceptable explanation.* I drew deep breaths to relax.

"Container 64 was purpose built to carry an internal skin, given it contains the most expensive of our terraforming equipment. No other container has that special fitting."

Bayley nodded, then contacted Hogan. "Can you run a mass scan on the container walls? It seems this particular container has been lined with an internal skin."

To do that, the container would have to be opened. I bargained that he did not have the authority to immediately carry that out. At best, I had bought a few more hours. Once they opened the container, they'd quickly locate the hidden compartment. Stalling was my best option, in the hope their requests would be intercepted by Gaea operatives.

Bayley interrupted my thoughts. "We're getting approval to open this container, so for now you'll be held in confinement."

"I'm happy to return to my quarters until then."

"I'm sorry, Dane. We can't take that risk. You'll be escorted to a security pod until further notice. Ander will take you there," he said, pointing behind me to where Ander stood, waiting. There was no more I could do. I just hoped Latatious's prediction to 'unleash chaos' was true, but given the numbers of hostile operatives now controlling the ship, I feared he was too late.

Chapter Nine

ESCAPE

The high security pod they took me to was isolated and heavily secured. Resigned to captivity, I practiced interrogation answers in my mind, before an explosive force knocked me sideways to the floor in a haze of smoke, disorientating me in its fog until, to my surprise, Ander approached.

"What are you doing? You could have just opened the door."

"Negative. Bayley has changed all security passes. Can you stand?"

"I fell on my injured side. I think my shoulder is dislocated."

Ander knelt down beside me and studied the injury before reaching out to twist and jerk it firmly in one quick motion. The pain was intense but only brief.

"You should be able to move freely now," he said, helping me up. "I suggest you follow me, as there's little time."

"Follow you where?"

"No time for questions. Follow me now or take your own chance at escape."

Ander waited impatiently as I hesitated. *Why would he do this?* Ander was assigned to the ship for one reason – to protect it. His loyalty to that cause was undoubted. Yet, here he stood, ready to disobey orders.

"Ander, I never intended to bringing harm to your ship."

"That's the one thing I'm sure of. This way now!" Ander insisted.

I had no other options but to go with him, but to where? I followed him through the exit, surprised there was little damage. "I thought you blew this entry up?"

"I disengaged it with an FI."

He used a Focused Implosion. They had the power of traditional explosives but the focus of a microscope, minimizing the destructive force and potential for detection. Com sensors hadn't sounded any alarms, giving us valuable time before detection. Why would the head of security take such a risk? Was he helping me or taking me from those who might? I was either heading to a hostage or help situation, as he cautiously steered the corridors of the ship, activating his full array of armaments to 'battle ready'. He had the capability to destroy both ships and seemingly a steely determination to do just that.

"Are you expecting resistance?"

"Not immediately. This is our one and only chance to escape. I will use it well."

"For what?"

Ander didn't reply, but it became clear he was taking me to the cargo hull. A good sign. Just at its entry, I turned to Ander. "Why are you doing this?"

Ander was re-checking his defense arsenal while securing the entry to the hull behind him.

"That will slow them down, but we have little time. They will be coming for you. Of that you can be sure. My role is to defend you for as long as I am able."

Ander's words came as a relief. The ship's security officer was the Gaea agent. "Who are you reporting to?"

Ander ignored me, instead laying peripheral heat sensing mines around the hull entry area. Once secured, he finally answered.

"Go to your quarters and bring Hali back here, now. Then I'll answer your questions. Hurry!"

I didn't think twice, daring to believe that Latatious's plan was beginning to unfold. Was he responsible for the contagion spreading through the biots, turning the crew against each other? First there were the two biots and now Ander. I couldn't be sure about anybody anymore, but I followed Ander's request to locate the only person I did trust, Hali.

Hali was diligently working on her prime role, oblivious to the unfolding chaos. I wanted to brief her, but time wouldn't allow it.

"Discontinue your prime objective, Hali. Download your work to date. We may not be returning to these quarters."

"I took the liberty to prepare for that, given your circumstances."

"Good. We're going to the cargo hull. Do a com check on the whereabouts of Bayley, Hogan, and Locke."

"They're in Navigation. Hogan is briefing them, and he has ordered Ander to bring us to Navigation. Why is he in the cargo hull?"

"No time for explanations. We must go to the cargo hull, now."

"That may not be in your interest, Dane."

She may be right, I thought, but I had no other ideas except to work with Ander. "We must get to the hull before Hogan and his crew come for us. If we manage to escape the ship, you will have new directives. Follow me."

Hali nodded and followed. I considered the possible scenarios facing us and all ended in failure. Keeping clear of Hogan was difficult enough, but evading the arsenal of starships outside the Deliverance would be near impossible. Our fate lay with Ander. Capable as he was, not even he could take on five starships and their crew. Latatious, I hoped, brought more surprises to the table then I knew. The first surprise came quickly. We approached Ander, who was directing Cluste and Fragg. How did Fragg return to the ship?

"Not a moment too soon. You need to hear this, Dane," Ander said, turning to Fragg. "Is the container loaded on the tug ship?"

"Ready, commander."

"How did you get back to the ship?" I asked, annoying Ander.

"Explanations later, Dane. There is no time. All you need to know is Fragg will deliver you and your cargo to Mars Orbiting Base."

Ander then turned to Cluste. "You will accompany Dane to container 64. Your role is to protect him against any adversary. Is that clear?"

"Yes, commander."

Finally, he turned to Hali and I. "Hali will be needed as a decoy. Do I have your permission, Dane?"

Ander was asking me to hand over my only trusted ally. If Ander was laying a trap for me, I was virtually handing over the Trojan machine to a biot. "I want Hali with me."

"Then you'll die and your biot will be decommissioned."

"You want to use Hali as a decoy, so she won't survive, anyway."

"I wouldn't bet on that. She has more chance of surviving than any of us, if you let her work with me."

"How do I know that you're not after our cargo?"

"Every precious minute you waste will make your concern a moot point."

I stood firm, unconvinced. Ander had to share more.

"Either way, container 64 is exposed. You can ignore my assistance and hand Trojan to Apollo. I'm due to return to Navigation. Bayley will be calling for me soon and I can only stall their suspicions for so long," said Ander, holding his gaze on me, receiving only silence. "What would Latatious have you do?" He asked with a knowing glance.

Latatious's name was only known by me. He had to have shared it with Ander and only under extreme circumstances, meaning I had to chance revealing the true mission to Ander.

I turned to Hali, "Report to Ander and follow his instructions until further notice."

"Your transfer code," said Hali, following protocol.

I reluctantly transmitted the security code, knowing there'd be no return. Ander now had it in his power to ask Hali to delete all files, compromising the project.

"I'm transmitting new security orders to you. Embed them in your system, Hali, until I order you to use them," Ander ordered.

"Codes embedded, commander," replied Hali, with a loyalty to her new mission leader that disconcerted me. I had lost my most trusted ally to an uncertain mission.

"Hali, I want you to pilot the reconnaissance vehicle. On my command, I want you to fly it toward the command starship."

I immediately regretted my decision. "That would be suicide!"

"That's true. But if Hali makes it to the craft, it will be suicide for the starship fleet, not her."

I looked at Hali who was now fully loyal to Ander. I could do little else but follow his commands, also.

"Fragg, pilot the Tugship and await my command to commence ignition of engines. Cluste, take Dane to container 64, secure the container to the tug ship, then protect Dane against any hostile forces until you land on Mars."

Ander's plans alarmed me. "Two commercial biots against a starship fleet. Are we decoys, too? Tell me there's more to this desperate plan!"

"You have your orders. Leave, now. I have to contact Navigation."

"Then what?"

"With luck, I'll hold our enemy back long enough for you to get to Mars."

We spread in different directions, leaving Ander, a lone figure in the hull. I had little doubt he was a Gaea agent, now, but the chance of his plan working appeared slim. Once either ship's engines fired, the starship fleet waiting outside would detect us. The fastest starship in the fleet couldn't evade their firepower, let alone a tug ship and a reconnaissance vessel. We would be little more than target practice for Hogan's fleet.

Chapter Ten

COUNTER-INSURGENCY

Hogan prepared the crew for the cargo inspection, unaware of the counter-insurgence unfolding in the cargo hull. Quinn looked on haplessly, his role limited to maintaining his ship's position between the five surrounding starships. The navigation com flashed, bringing a smile to Hogan. He expected Apollo's confirmation to open container 64, but instead, an unexpected request came from his starship.

"We have activity at Dock 2, commander," said Step.

Hogan checked his com to verify. "The reconnaissance vehicle's ignition process has been engaged. Who's operating the craft?"

"Dane's biot, commander."

"Hali, report to navigation. We have all five starship's

weapons trained on you. What is the reason for taking command of this vehicle?"

"Protocol requires I protect the program codes I am carrying. Launching procedure commenced. Permission to dock with your starship."

"Denied! Protection from what?"

"Dane attempted to decommission me. My protocols require that the codes must be protected."

"My officer is in the process of arresting Dane."

"Negative. Your officer has secured the hull. I am launching the vessel and setting course to your starship, for protection."

"Step, run a scan on the vessel for weapons," Hogan ordered.

"Already done. There are no weapons on the ship. We have all our weapons directed at the reconnaissance vessel. Your orders, commander?"

Hogan glanced Bayley's way looking for any reticent signal. Instead, Bayley nodded his approval.

"Hali. Engage minimal thrusters and maintain your course to the starship. If you make any sudden change in course or velocity, our fleet will destroy your ship. Is that clear."

"Affirmative. Thank you, commander," Hali responded, following his orders to the letter.

Hogan attempted to contact Ander, receiving only silence. "Ander's com is down."

"So are the hull monitors," Locke added.

"Shell. Investigate the hull and report back." Hogan ordered.

"Shall I engage Ander?"

"No. Open access to the hull, investigate the area if you are able and then report back. Clear?"

"Affirmative," she replied, quickly moving to the hull, via the empty security pod where Dane had been held.

"It appears the human had been assisted by Ander to illegally enter the hull, their purpose uncertain."

"Can you contact Ander?"

"Negative. Ander is on red alert. Repeat, red alert. His digital footprint is 'silent'," Shell replied.

"Move to red alert as well, and sweep the area," Hogan replied.

The entry to the hull was surrounded by a maze of small corridors that wrapped around various pods containing technology and equipment vital for the ship's communication. Shell set her visor software to determine the safest predicted destination through the hull entry, before sending a reconnaissance drone to analyze likely attack zones.

Thirty meters from the hull perimeter, her drone

signaled sounds emanating from an equipment enclosure to her left. She engaged her weapon, as the drone circled closer to the unidentified activity, before a second noise emanated from the same area, a sound she identified as a heat sensor, laid in wait for an enemy. Shell lay a force field around it and continued forward.

"Locate all other heat sensing equipment and apply force fields," she ordered, waiting until her drones had disengaged all threats near the hull entry.

Once cleared, she cautiously approached the entry. Unsurprisingly, the code had been tampered with, forcing her to spend precious time decoding it, something she didn't need, given her vulnerable position.

"Current codes rendered inoperable by hostile forces. I will attempt to re-code now, although the perimeter is potentially in hostile hands. Should I wait for backup?"

"Follow through on your orders, soldier," Hogan ordered.

Shell attempted a re-code, knowing her only defense was the early warning detection of her drones, giving her at best, a few seconds to react, normally sufficient time, but not against Ander. She worked feverishly at re-coding the heavily fortified entry, falling seconds short before being attacked. Her defense system had been easily breached.

Shell turned to engage her attacker, unleashing her full

armory of drones to slow his assault, buying the valuable seconds to open the code, then destroy the digital lock. It was Ander, carrying a high-grade assault weapon and protected by a force field her attacking drones couldn't infiltrate. The last words she heard before being decommissioned were, "Cluste, enemy nullified. Operation Blade on move and preparing to defend the perimeter."

Chapter Eleven

PUSHBACK

Container 64 was secured to the tug ship and locked down. I could do little else but monitor the outside activities, setting my com to the decrypted code wavelength. With Shell decommissioned, Hogan, Locke, and Draven, quickly followed, entering the cargo hull, all fully armed. They swept past their decommissioned ally, intent on engaging Ander.

Fragg sat at the tug ship navigation controls, ready to pilot it on Ander's orders. Cluste was with me, heavily armed and ready to protect me. He listened intently to my com as it picked up Hogan and his team's communications.

"Verified, Shell has been decommissioned. Entering the cargo hull now," Locke reported.

"Ander's a Gaea agent. Set weapons to kill," Hogan ordered.

They headed through the hull entry and immediately received heavy fire, backed by the drones Ander had recommissioned from Shell, to create the impression he was not alone. Hogan took the bait.

"Spread to each corner of the hull, said Hogan, launching his body suit to the right of the entry and to the cover of containers. Locke moved left.

Draven retreated back through the entry, to safety. "Engaging cloaking device," he said, before vanishing from sight, magnifying the threat to Ander.

Locke and Hogan had flanked Ander, positioning themselves to launch an attack from opposite sides to where he stood. "Release 'hover pulsars' now," Hogan ordered.

Locke released a dozen pulsars to hover within a five-meter perimeter around Ander. Pulsars had two force fields, defensive for protection and offensive for counter fire. Only one adversary had sufficient defense capability to withstand such an attack – Ander. But the circle of pulsars would act as decoys, delaying Ander's counter attack by vital seconds, sufficient to give his attackers an opening that they would take advantage of.

"Locke and I have met heavy enemy fire. Has to be more than one adversary," said Hogan, informing Draven.

"Cluste or the human?" Draven asked.

"Not sure. We can't get close enough to see. Step. Any sign of movement from the reconnaissance ship on board the Deliverance?"

"Negative. I have two drone ships locked into position. It can't go anywhere. All other ship's weapons remain locked on the other reconnaissance ship piloted by Hali. She is seeking permission to dock."

"Scan the ship for any suspicious cargo. If it's clean, allow her to dock, but make sure Hali remains in her vessel under full security until all rebels are captured," Hogan ordered.

I wanted to do more, given the threat Ander and Hali faced, but his orders were clear. Stay with the container. A stalemate ensued as Hogan and Locke held their positions, leaving Ander's only escape route the empty reconnaissance ship behind him, a deliberate bait Ander hoped his attackers would take. While they believed we were cornered in the second reconnaissance vehicle, they would ignore the tug ship. I hoped Draven thought the same, given I couldn't get a position on him. Tense minutes passed, before the break in fire was again filled with the blasts of weapons.

Hogan and Locke fired in unison on the deadly drones Ander had set up, eliminating his first line of defense, but not without cost.

"I'm through. Are you ready?" said Locke.

"Negative. My defense system was nullified by Ander's fire. Can you still move forward?" Hogan asked.

"Affirmative. I'll maintain attack while you re-commission your defense system."

Hogan retreated to the safety outside the cargo hold to repair his damaged system, while Locke launched an assault.

"Lasers released. I'm advancing towards the enemy," said Locke.

I could hear the cascade of laser bombs explode, followed by what had to be Ander's fearsome counter attack.

"Need urgent assistance, Hogan. Under hot enemy fire. Can't contain it, but will…"

Locke's communication suddenly went silent, before Ander confirmed the reason. "Locke decommissioned. I'm moving to the hull entry to engage Hogan. Hold the reconnaissance vehicle," Ander ordered, hoping to draw Draven to the empty vehicle.

"I'm boarding the reconnaissance vehicle," Draven said.

Draven took the bait and Ander accommodated. "Mine drones laid around the reconnaissance vehicle. Draven nullified. Moving to engage Hogan," said Ander.

Draven was trapped in the reconnaissance ship.

Moments later, Ander set more mine drones. "Explosives laid at hull entry. Hogan nullified." Ander said, before setting off a series of explosions, closing the cargo hull.

Ander had a victory of sorts, but we still had to get past the deadly fleet outside the ship. Hogan made the same conclusion. "Desist from your rebellion or we will detach the hull and order its destruction," he threatened. If our rebellion had come to an end, Ander wasn't about to show it.

"Draven, report." Hogan ordered.

"The reconnaissance ship is empty," he replied.

Finally, Ander spoke. "Activate code. Repeat. Activate code."

Another silence ensued. *What code?* I wondered, looking to Fragg for an answer. "Does he want to come on board?" I asked.

"Wait," Fragg replied.

"Your situation is hopeless. Surrender now and we will not destroy the hull," Hogan negotiated, hoping to end the impasse.

To my surprise Hali responded, not Ander. "No. It's your crew who should surrender."

"Step. Is Hali still confined to the ship?"

"Yes. Her ship is still under guard. She can't go anywhere."

"Have her arrested or decommission her if she resists."

"Yes, sir."

Monitors surrounded the ship, recording any movement, allowing Step's security biot to eliminate any threat Hali posed. The biot stood upright, his weapon aimed at the reconnaissance ship's entry as it slid open. Hali walked toward him, her hands raised, seemingly ready to surrender. But then she suddenly lowered her hands in one violent action, unleashing a force that decommissioned him where he stood. "Step. Surrender your ship, now," she ordered.

I watched the monitor, barely believing what Hali had just unleashed. She walked toward the fortified entry from the docking bay to the ship and blew it open, seemingly with the wave of her hand, before entering the ship.

"Decommission," Ander ordered.

Hali responded with the assurance of an assassin, rather than the assistant I thought I knew. She knelt to the floor and crashed one fist down with a fury that unleashed a shockwave that flushed through the ship and out to the surrounding fleet, decommissioning all technology and weaponry with a single blow.

"You were talking about surrender, Hogan. We're ready to negotiate," said Ander victoriously, before requesting I give him entry to the tug ship.

Soon after, we left the crippled ship for the Mars orbiting space station, the secret cargo in tow. Sitting in navigation, I couldn't stop thinking about Hali's transformation. All these years I'd worked with her never aware of her true capabilities. Ander was beside me, preparing to contact Latatious and for the first time, I began to understand the importance of this project to Gaea.

As Fragg expertly docked to the Mars space station, Ander's com flashed to life, revealing Latatious at the other end. "All arrangements have been made for a speedy clearance to Mars base. You have attracted some interest on Earth, so we need you and your cargo secured as soon as possible. How are you, Dane?"

"More secure then last time we spoke."

Latatious laughed. "You had your moments."

"How is Hali? Is she safe?"

"I don't think any Apollo agents will be troubling her. She'll be otherwise occupied for a while."

"I need her to install the Trojan computer."

"That won't be possible, Dane. Now we've revealed her capabilities to Apollo, she'll be needed elsewhere," said Latatious.

"Will I see her again?"

"Yes, but not in the capacity you are used to seeing her

operate. She'll return when the time is right. For now, you will have to…"

"…remain in blissful ignorance? I'm getting used to your operational style!"

Latatious laughed again, simply nodding his head, before ending the transmission, leaving me troubled by his words. I had lost my best ally.

Ander noticed my reaction. "You may not have Hali, but you won't be alone, Dane."

I was returning to my home to continue the work many, including my parents, had paid with their lives to complete. The stakes were high then, but it seemed that there were even more risks now. To my left sat a reassuringly powerful military biot, to my right, an accomplished fighter pilot. We were also heading to Mars base and the protection of a large United Nations peace keeping force. The balance seemed to have tipped our way, but then I thought of my sister, Zi. She had paid a greater price than anyone in the past from an enemy who could not be underestimated. Those who planned to stop us were defeated this time, but they remained a threat, no doubt intent on retaliation. The deadly game had moved up another gear.

PART TWO

MARS

Chapter Twelve

DELIVERY

Ander nonchalantly approved Fragg's request to descend to Mars base. His calmness belied the seven minutes of jaw grinding terror that awaited me. I repeatedly checked my magnetic harnesses were secured tight, as the ship was about to rapidly accelerate to twenty thousand kilometers an hour on its vertical descent to the red planet. An unsecured harness would catapult me backwards with the same force as a twenty-story fall from a skyscraper. If I survived that, I'd be propelled in the opposite direction as the ship pulled up at the last possible moment, using aerodynamic lift to fly sideways through Mars thickest atmosphere. What would be left would be unrecognizable.

"All crew and cargo safely secured," Fragg noted, as he

checked all navigation settings. "Permission to commence Mars descent."

"Clear for takeoff. Dock security hatch released," replied a Mars orbiting station operator.

We floated free from the holding dock before Fragg engaged low thrust, tilting the ship into vertical position, before engaging a second more powerful thrust, plummeting us directly on the flight path suitably nicknamed the 'Death Drop'.

"Seven minutes and counting down," Fragg calmly reported, committing us to a flight path that could not be reversed.

We were one of ninety cargo drops planned for the next twenty-four hours, a routine procedure. The last accident was five years ago, I reminded myself, trying to ease the palpable fear that now overwhelmed me. Mars gravity was less than Earth, which made the landing even more challenging. We carried a small 200-ton load, which made our descent easier, but the load was the most important ever brought to the off-world, its loss insurmountable. Fragg's 'tech-silver' nails blurred across the com screen like a pianist playing a symphony, while effortlessly controlling the navigation panel.

"Five minutes. Approaching twelve thousand klicks."

It's strange, that feeling of utter helplessness you feel

as every part of the ship shakes and strains to the force of gravity. The increasing G-force bound my body tight to the seat, laboring even breath. I tried to fight the gravitas of extended free fall but resistance was futile.

"Three minutes and eighteen thousand klicks. Minor weight disturbance in aft."

If that was minor, I didn't want to know major. The high voltage noise screaming from behind made me think the cargo had ripped loose from its hold. I tried to look back, fearing the quantum computer had been destroyed, but the G-force held me rigid as a statue.

"One minute. Approaching maximum velocity. Brace for aerodynamic lift."

The thought of engine failure enveloped my core as we approached the fateful deceleration phase. Rationally, I knew there hadn't been a malfunction in many years, but statistics always had outliers. I was a Martian, but this was my first Mars landing. A feeling of dread overwhelmed me as the ship accelerated toward the planet. I tried to focus on Fragg, who methodically adjusted his navigation system, unaffected by the looming peril. It was ironic. I was part of a resistance, demanding more humanness and less technology, but I wouldn't have anyone else but this talented biot navigate me back to my home. Fragg assuredly fired the powerful thrusters, abruptly shifting our ship from its vertical fall.

"Brace people," he warned, as the force of the thrusters turned my world upside down. The roar screamed like a tornado, capturing me and twisting the ship as if it were lighter than a feather. Extreme G-forces turned my body inside out in one violent action. For the briefest of moments, I wished we had crashed, but the roar of the thrusters subsided as did my discomfort. I barely heard Fragg's next command as the ringing in my ears slowly abated.

"Lift procedure successfully completed. Clearance for approach and landing."

"Mars base. All clear for landing at Bay 34," base instructed.

The landing bays seemed to stretch to the horizon, reminding me of my lengthy absence. There were only eight bays when I left. I knew Mars base population had grown to nearly a hundred thousand, but the scale of the infrastructure still surprised me. It extended across Chryse Planitia like an Earth city, low rise tentacles of interconnected pod bases stretched into the distance, interspersed by giant transparent domes, Mars many hub centers. Olympus Way, the major highway connecting Gaea and Apollo bases was filled with transporters moving newly delivered food and equipment. Even the airspace was active with transport drones, carrying people to and from Apollo's aerospace center.

A decade had passed since I left Mars and the decision still played on my mind. Why had I been sent to the relative safety of Earth while my sister remained to face the potential dangers? Zi had insisted, but I didn't exactly argue the case.

"Approaching Bay 34. Prepare for landing," Fragg said, his calm voice never wavering.

Routine efficiency continued, as within no time I was properly helmeted and stepping onto the bay tarmac and into a waiting shuttle, but not before offering Fragg an appreciative tap on the shoulder. He smiled human-like, a reaction he had learnt over the many years of ferrying humans through space.

"Fragg, wait for our two biots. They will be with a team of UN soldiers who will secure the cargo and accompany you to Gaea quarters," Ander ordered, before accompanying me on to the shuttle.

"You're not overseeing the delivery?" I asked.

"My role is to protect you, but Fragg is more than capable, don't you think?"

It was hard to argue after what Fragg had just pulled off. "I'm fine with it, but my sister might have other ideas."

"I don't report to your sister."

"You report to Latatious?"

Ander made no response, preferring to check the

shuttle organized for us. A convoy of heavily armed UN vehicles tailed us for all of the six-kilometer journey to the UN checkpoint, allowing quick passage through the fortified zone, by-passing the long queue of vehicles undergoing rigorous inspections. I'd spent most of my ten years on Earth laboring on a scientific project with minimal support, but that had all changed, now. I'd returned to my home under a full military escort and a team of military grade biots guarding me.

Another two kilometers and we arrived at the Gaea base. It too was heavily guarded with armed UN soldiers. The small pioneering community I had left as a young man took on a more sinister outlook. Mars had always attracted humans independently inclined, but it looked more like a military base, in large part, as a reaction to the large wave of caste immigrants required to develop Apollo's transport hub.

It was a relief to arrive at the entry zone, but to my disappointment, a biot greeted us, not Zi.

"Welcome to Gaea base, gentlemen. I'm Codi."

Codi looked familiar to me, but I couldn't place it. "Good to be here," I replied, genuinely relieved to be in the security confines of the Gaea base.

Codi smiled, then nodded to Ander, before leading us from the entry zone into a large Dome, one of many large transparent domes that connected the pod cities and its inhabitants.

"I played here as a child. Back then, we called it the Grand Dome."

"Things have changed. There are twenty major domes interconnecting our citizens to work and leisure pods. This is one of the smallest domes, now," she replied, proudly pointing out the many exits to newly developed centers. "We go this way. It's just a short walk to the Elithium site."

Memories flooded back. Zi and I often played in the Grand Dome while our parents worked on the development of the mine. As a boy growing up, I thought their work was all consuming, creating a distance between us. Zi was more a mother to me than a sister.

"Where's my sister?" I asked, not hiding my disappointment.

"Zi has been waylaid at an Apollo meeting, so I'll show you the facilities, once you settle.

Still smarting by Zi's slight, I dispensed with any pleasantries. "I can rest when our machine has been safely secured. Can I see where it will be placed?"

"Certainly," Codi replied, signaling for a transporter.

"When will the cargo be delivered, Ander?"

"It's in transit and will reach the checkpoint within the hour."

"Good. Our team will have the computer delivered to the assembly area as quickly as possible," Codi replied, boarding an autonomous vehicle to take us to the Elithium site.

We arrived at the underground, a vast cavernous expanse which formed the entry to a large tunnel, part man-made and linked to a natural lava tunnel, one of the longest on Mars, running all the way to Ascraeus Mons. This was the nerve center of the Elithium mine, off limits in my youth, before becoming my workplace from age fourteen. I suspect that decision was made because Zi had demanded she work rather than be my minder. When my sister wanted something, she inevitably got her way. Initially I struggled, missing the freedom to roam the Mars base and beyond, but in time I grew to enjoy working alongside my parents. The expanse was larger than I remembered and the movement in and around the tunnel was a hive of activity, filled with new mining infrastructure. It's expansion though expected, still surprised me. Zi had done her family proud.

Codi must have read my reaction. "This area has grown over the years. It's the connecting hub to new expanded areas of the mine."

The site that was once the size of a basketball court now covered two football fields. This was the operational heart of the Elithium project that my father groomed me to manage, much to my sister's ignoble, yet warranted rumblings. She was always my mentor, so when my father picked me as the heir apparent, it frustrated her, and she always made sure our father knew. The cost to me was my mentor sister became a competitor.

"New areas? Must be large?" If it wasn't, this looked a wasteful and unproductive expanse. "Can we see it?"

"We're going to where we house our latest equipment, which will include your Trojan computer."

Codi led us across the expanse down a corridor connected to an operating room overseen by two technicians, both biots. Technology crammed much of the oval shaped room, bar a small empty space I assumed would house our Trojan computer.

"This is the space?"

"Yes, it is. Our technicians will connect it with our central terminal, so I expect it to be fully operational by tomorrow."

"What are we analyzing? I assume it'll be related to the purification of the Elithium molecule?"

Codi only nodded.

"Perhaps you can show us," I pushed, as did Ander.

"The site is built beside another larger operational room. I'm afraid it is a high security area, so I cannot allow you both access. Only you, Dane."

"Without Ander's help, you wouldn't have our machine!"

"I'm sorry, but it is a strict policy. Only those with clearance are allowed."

I wanted to argue the point, but Ander signaled he was unconcerned.

"Then we can proceed, Dane. This way," she said, walking to the fortified entry, requiring a myriad of codes just to operate a scanner.

"State your name then look into the scanner," a computer activated voice requested.

Approved, I followed Codi down a narrow tunnel that stretched out into the distance. "How long is the tunnel?"

"Not long. It curves around to where our machine is housed."

We walked to a viewing rail offering a view of large equipment ten stories in height. We stood in line with the top of a machine that I instantly recognized.

"You've built a nuclear fusion reactor?"

"Yes, but unlike any on Earth."

I was surprised at Zi's industriousness, even though I knew she never did anything by half measure. The aim was to tap the Elithium resources to terraform Gaea base. A nuclear fusion reactor may reduce that to just years. Terraforming the whole planet was within reach and along with it, potential mass immigration of human families. The Trojan computer was the final piece of the puzzle, hence the interest from our adversaries. The stakes had been raised to a deadly new high.

Codi proudly pointed out the machine's potential capabilities as we walked around the large fusion engine.

"I see the need for secrecy. How many people know how advanced you are?"

"We have a team of biots who work with us, but they never leave the work area. Then there's Zi and I, Latatious, and now you."

"I hope you're right. I thought my project was equally secured, but it was infiltrated on our voyage here."

Codi didn't answer, preferring to study the biots who worked below. I had little doubt that Apollo operatives had infiltrated their operations, too. The events of the last year made more sense to me, now. Latatious ordering me to undertake counter intelligence training, the attack on the Deliverance. At least I'd been briefed about the increased risk. Had Zi?

"Why couldn't Zi make it for this meeting? It's unlike her. She likes to know what's going on. Is there something I don't know?"

Codi didn't answer, so I pressed her. "I need to know everything, Codi."

"You know your sister well. The truth is, she had

planned to be the one to greet you today, but events conspired against that happening."

"Events?"

"Zi attended a planetary meeting in the UN zone."

"When does it finish?"

"It finished yesterday and we haven't heard from her since."

"What are you saying? Is there a problem?"

"The truth is, I don't know."

"You don't know! Have you contacted her?"

"Her com is off line."

"Then talk to the UN officials."

"I did. They checked security coms and said she left the meeting with unknown officials. I have since contacted them about her com being off line and they are investigating her possible disappearance."

"Surely given our security breach, you took steps to increase security around your own operations?"

"We did. Security even warned Zi about attending the UN meeting, but she was determined to brief certain officials in person."

Foolhardy as that sounded, I knew how stubborn Zi could be. I had returned to help my sister and, in just one day, grief had fallen upon us. It was as if fate had decided that we should never work together, again.

Chapter Thirteen

Zi

Long vertical rows of foliage stretched high to the rotunda's transparent crown, creating a sense of calm that bellied Zi's situation. She freely strolled through Apollo's iconic public arena, greeting unfamiliar faces as they passed by, aware there was unwanted scrutiny observing her every move.

Following unsuccessful attempts to use her com, Zi resigned herself to waiting to be informed about the nature of her predicament. She stood at the window's edge of the Grand Eastern Dome, the second largest on Mars, watching the flow of craft transiting from the orbiting space station to Apollo's aerospace terminal. In better circumstances she'd have marveled at their achievements. In just a decade the 'Earth-Mars Way' was as busy as many of the major Earth trade routes, a tribute to the Apollo Corporation.

Zi had always felt a curious mix of admiration and suspicion for their achievements. On the one hand, she marveled at the rapid expanses in space exploration, but she'd heard the rumors. Extreme elements were prepared to achieve their aims at any cost. She feared her detainment was one such example.

She held her gaze on the latest landing vehicle as the crew disassembled and imagined one of them to be Dane. She knew his arrival was imminent, but had heard little else since. Zi's frustration grew, but she saved any outbursts of anger for a meeting she knew must follow. Perhaps the landing crew she now observed were her interrogators? She would soon find out as an announcement sounded.

"Doctor Zi Walker to Interview room 4d."

At last. Zi walked briskly back through the horticultural mural to the interview room. Zi didn't knock, her patience already strained to the limit. She strode toward the two agents, one a caste, the other a human, who sat behind a large 3D printed desk. Without invitation, Zi pulled up a chair opposite them, not hiding her mood.

"I have been held here for over a day without a word of explanation. Can either of you tell me why?"

The caste shrugged his shoulders with disinterest, leaving the human to do the talking. "I apologize for the inconvenience, Doctor Walker, but it is related to highly classified activities," he responded, courteously.

"Confidentiality doesn't warrant this kind of treatment. Holding me against my wishes violates the UN treaty for human, post-human relations."

"Yes, you're correct. However, you are under investigation for illegal activities, also. It appears a cargo ship assigned to delivering equipment to your base had hidden contraband. That also violates UN regulations. So, you see we are at somewhat of an impasse."

"And you are?"

"Bayley Cheltham. I'm a scientist."

Zi eyeballed both investigators, seemingly unmoved by their charge. "I'm unaware of any such shipment. Release me now, and I will personally look into it from our end. You have my word."

Hogan reacted, standing and walking around to her side of the table. "You're not going anywhere until you answer our questions."

Zi ignored Hogan's threats and spoke directly to Bayley. "I won't be intimidated by military castes. Release me, or I'll see to it that both of you are hauled to a UN court for threatening a human."

Hogan sniggered and turned to Bayley. "Nothing like her brother."

Bayley merely nodded. "Perhaps if you leave me with Dr. Walker, so that we may speak in privacy, as one scientist to another?"

"One hour. No more," Hogan replied, casting a threatening gaze Zi's way, flashing his tech-enhanced eyes blood red.

"I'm sorry, Doctor Walker. You rightly observed that Hogan is a military man. They typically have little patience."

"Typical of a caste, you mean. Unable to control the technological powers he's given. So, confused about whether he's a human or biot, he acts more like a monster than a human."

"I understand your anger. But post-humans have the task of bridging the gap between human and biot. Their contributions have been immeasurable."

"Immeasurably good spies, you mean. Frankensteins who have forgotten their roots."

"You speak of the few. Humans have many spies, too. Do they not?"

A stony impasse ensued before Zi relented.

"So, what are you claiming my brother has done?"

"These are not claims. Your brother, together with three biots, have illegally transported contraband to your base."

"What has this to do with me?"

Bayley smiled ironically. "Come now, Doctor Walker. It's common knowledge that you and your team have had regular dealings with the organization your brother works for and that your uncle heads. We also know your brother's key responsibility is to develop new computing technology. I'm assuming that is the contraband they sought to hide from us and illegally transfer to your base?"

"I don't deny that. But it's also common knowledge that any such new technology is years from being completed. Whatever machinery you claim my brother has shipped would not be illegal. Perhaps some of your operatives threatened him while in transit to Mars? I find that more believable, given the treatment you have handed me in the past day. I attended an international conference in good faith and now I am being held hostage, based on hearsay."

"That may be, but our investigations extend beyond new quantum computing technology. They include the unlawful development of special purpose biots, long banned by UN regulations, which would be considered a blatant disregard for human, post-human relations."

"What proof do you have?"

"One such biot masqueraded as your brother's administrative assistant. She was instrumental in his escape."

"Release me, and I promise you that I'll get to the bottom of this investigation."

"That is a generous offer, but hardly reassuring, given that intelligence has revealed there may be a second such biot on Mars."

Zi was cornered. Her investigator had seemingly penetrated classified information and personnel. "What is it you want from me?"

"We ask no more than a simple trade. Your brother's illegal shipment for your safe return. Not a lot to ask, given your denials are true. Don't you think?"

"I have no authority over my brother. He answers to management on Earth and the last thing they would do is negotiate a hostage situation. It's almost certain your actions will be taken to a UN court. You and your people will face the full rule of international law."

"Doctor Walker, you're in no position to threaten us. We are backed by the highest authority to investigate any illegal activities, all of which relate to your project on Mars. I'm here to reason with you, however the military may use other means. They can be harsh in their investigations. It's their way."

"I'll take my chances. Your methods of interrogation contradict all international law protocols. Hostage taking and threats will be seen in a bad light by the UN forces.

Release me now, and I will negotiate in good faith, regarding this contraband."

Bayley contemplated Zi's request for some time, seemingly seriously considering her offer. "My hands are tied. If you refuse to cooperate with me, I have to hand you over to the military. Expect them to be less accommodating."

"Military? Your assistant is no more than a hired thug. A mercenary who's loyal to the highest bidder. Any political support he has is likely to be limited to extreme factions."

Bayley sat back in his chair, resigned to Zi's recalcitrance. He turned to his com. "Hogan, I'm done," he said, before standing to leave. "Offer me something, or I cannot help you."

Zi couldn't offer her interrogator information. The consequences of revealing the program would be worse than stonewalling, but she made one last pitch. It appeared Bayley was a human. Surprising to her, given most Apollo operatives were either castes or biots.

"I can't offer what you ask for. I have no power to negotiate with my brother or his associates. But I'm sure you could meet with Dane, should you release me. He can tell you more than I can. Release me, and I'll arrange the meeting."

Bayley considered Zi's offer for some time, again appearing interested, before Hogan returned to the room, this time accompanied by a military grade biot. "Remember what I said," Bayley warned, before leaving the room.

"This is my associate, Locke. He is my most loyal deputy, programmed to carry out any of my orders," Hogan gloated.

The biot was a huge unit, typical military, loaded with weaponry. Zi had seen many of his kind, mostly used as security guards. Capabilities were many, ranging from warfare to interrogation. She had lost many associates to their like. Locke and Hogan both stood over her in an intimidating fashion, the caste seemingly enjoying his abuse of power, the biot ready to follow his orders.

"So, where were we? Oh yes, you seem to be suffering from memory loss," Hogan said, looking to Locke.

Zi's fear was palpable, but growing anger gave her the courage to face the threat head on. "My team will have contacted the UN forces by now. Expect a large contingency to arrive demanding my immediate release. Then I'll see you both jailed for this outrage."

"Locke. Report on any investigations into Doctor Walker's disappearance."

Locke scanned his internal com. "There have been no reports to the UN."

"I'm afraid that time isn't on your side, Doctor Walker. We have received news that your brother has arrived at your Elithium site and the machine you claim does not exist is being transported to the underground site for installation. He's acting illegally in assisting your team to assemble a machine that your Gaea operatives have claimed is years from completion. Apollo officials have drawn up legal documents requiring that the machine be handed to the UN. If refused, you'll be held in appropriate Apollo security quarters until the problem is resolved."

"Holding me in confinement will hardly assist your case."

"The case is watertight against your brother. We can fight this with or without you. Your stubbornness helps no one, least of all you."

"You'll both go to jail for hostage taking and terrorist activity."

"You're assuming you'll be found. I can assure you, that should you not cooperate, the chance of you being found again will be negligible." Hogan handed Zi a com. "Read the words on this com, and you can remain in the safety of our Apollo quarters."

"If not?"

"We leave now for more secure quarters."

Zi looked at the script handed to her. It was tantamount to a confession of guilt. She'd never read it. Her situation was perilous, but the fact they needed to move to more secure quarters showed her that UN officials were investigating her disappearance. She'd take a chance on being found. It was a risk, but her whole life had revolved around taking risks. She just hoped Dane wouldn't allow himself to be drawn into their deadly web. His work was more important to the project than hers now.

Chapter Fourteen

TROJAN COMPUTER

Six days had passed with no news on Zi and the UN investigation ominously quiet. My program had been infiltrated, so why wouldn't Zi's program meet the same fate? She should have anticipated the danger and perhaps she did, for Zi was always a risk taker. She would certainly be aware of the growing power of the post-human population, but living on Mars shielded her from experiencing the full impact of that unprecedented growth.

Most of Earth's population had freely chosen to become castes, convinced unnatural selection was the future. Their growth in numbers led to a louder political voice, particularly from the more extreme elements of their movement, promoting the mantra of space exploration and colonization. Apollo Corporation was a prime beneficiary of that interest. It was inevitable Zi's project would be challenged. Had she, like most of my family, paid the ultimate price? My fears for Zi's safety grew with every passing day as I buried that apprehension in my work, installing the Trojan computer. Fortunately, Codi and her research team of biots were more than equal to the challenge.

"All is ready for today's tests. Will we commence?" Codi asked, as I approached.

"Sure, tell the team to start. Any word on Zi?"

"Nothing at this stage."

"You'll let me know if you hear anything."

"Of course. I have direct contact with the lead investigator."

I nodded, knowing there was little more Codi could do. I took the same approach, using Ander to carry out a separate investigation, which I planned to extend further with Latatious's support.

This, the seventh day of testing, brought the breakthrough. I wouldn't have thought this possible without Hali's experienced eye, but Codi and her team more than compensated. The speed in which they mastered the workings of the Trojan made me wonder if Codi had access to our program long before. She made light work of complex tasks just as Hali could, making me refer to her as Hali's twin.

"How many simulation reports from this morning, Codi?"

"Three completed, all to an acceptable level."

"Three, you say?" I checked her com, believing her answer fanciful. A single verified result would impress me, but her team had delivered multi-verifiable reports. "Okay. Let's ramp up the simulations to a full test run."

Codi nodded, a confidence in her manner, brought on by her thorough training. My sister was always a hard task master, but this level surpassed my expectations, making me wonder what new skills Zi possessed since last we shared a workspace? I wanted to ask Codi more about my sister but held back, knowing Zi would expect a single-minded purpose from her team.

"The nuclear fusion engine is prepared," said Codi, interrupting my thoughts."

"You're not serious?"

"I had my team make preparations earlier this morning."

"You realize that if I ever return to Earth, you're coming with me!"

"I was confident the team would be ready," Codi replied, feigning a modest smile that reminded me of my sister. She had learnt many of Zi's characteristics, particularly her confident attitude. So, I played to it.

"Very well. Prove it."

They impressed, each spurring the other on as they methodically prepared the Trojan. The optimism was infectious, but not surprising, having been gifted with the fastest computing machine ever built. Previous impenetrable bottlenecks were smoothed, making complex calculations appear simple, aiding in the machine's operation. The first ignition of the nuclear fusion machine held the required 100 million degrees for five seconds before ceasing.

"The plasma configuration broke down," Codi confirmed.

"Run the diagnostics through the Trojan and make the necessary adjustments for a second run of the nuclear fusion machine. If we can hold the second ignition for twenty seconds, we'll move to a larger test."

"How large?"

"A full test, and we'll transfer the fusion energy to a field dome."

The second test surpassed a minute, so we quickly moved to the third. The field test required we supply a small community dome the energy it required from the nuclear fusion machine. The dome, fifty meters in diameter and with all required topography in place, contained a microcosm of our vision of a future Mars surface. Mars dust was mixed with optimum sunlight absorbing dark dust, shipped from the moons of Phobos and Deimos and brought to life with extremophile lichens and plants. This test dome, like the other hundred or so fully commercial domes in operation were terraformed using solar battery power. Plans for exponential growth of domes would require much more. Nuclear fusion was the answer, but the scale required was beyond previous technology. Would today signal the turning point in terraforming Mars? Several hours passed before Codi finally turned to me.

"The field experiment is ready. On your command."

"No. On your command, Codi. Well done!"

Power supply for the test dome was taken off the grid and moved to nuclear fusion and maintained for several minutes, again exceeding our best hopes, before the plasma configuration broke down.

"Reconnect to the main grid, Codi. I have seen enough this morning. Run full analysis through the Trojan and bring them to this afternoon's test run."

"Will we be reporting the results to others?"

"Yes. Latatious will be attending, so I want him updated before you run the next round of tests. Can you get an update from the UN on Zi, too? I will have a security briefing with Latatious after the test."

"Just Latatious?"

"Ander's expected to return to the base today, so prepare the briefing for both."

Codi nodded. "Same tests this afternoon?"

"If the diagnostics are positive, we can move straight to the field tests, perhaps expanding to field two. You can decide that."

I left Codi to her team, happy with their outcomes. Zi deserved to see this day, having given her all to the program, despite the enormous personal losses she'd experienced along the way.

On returning to my quarters, I contacted Ander. "Have you completed your preliminary investigations?"

"As much as possible. I'm returning to the base soon. Do you want me to report now?"

"If there's no positive news, it can wait. We're having a security meeting with Latatious."

"Security briefing it is," Ander replied, before disengaging the com.

I threw my com on the table, annoyed that Ander had made no progress. The contrast between our success with the Trojan project and the uncertainty surrounding my sister couldn't be starker. If the UN with all their resources couldn't locate her, what hope did we have? So many unknowns, yet what I was sure about was I'd complete this project with my sister or not at all. I owed her everything special that had come into my life. She deserved the same.

Latatious, Ander, and I watched Codi and her team carry out the sixth test for the afternoon after five successful preparatory tests involving the Trojan computer and nuclear reactor, each successful.

"Any residuals?" Latatious asked, clearly impressed that the fusion machine was still operating after a full minute.

"The plasma configuration is stable," Codi replied, looking to me for her next instruction.

The diagnostic reports emboldened me. "Let's double the test run, then close down for the day."

The Trojan computer analysis ensured the nuclear fusion machine operated faultlessly as it powered the lighting of the test dome for a full two minutes. We were already in a position to move the test to a full-scale dome, given the superior analytical capability of the Trojan. Predictions of nuclear fusion capability on Mars being many years away were now looking overly cautious.

Latatious rarely showed emotion but the results of the day's tests excited him. "Are you confident that you really have the breakthrough, Dane?"

I couldn't blame Latatious for his scepticism, but given the results, I found no reason not to move forward. "We should advance methodically. I want rigid testing over the next month before I consider moving to the commercial phase."

"Very well. I'll report to Gaea that the two-year time frame is still our official stance. They've been placed under a lot of pressure, since the starship altercation, so they'll want to know that you're focused on this project."

I knew what Latatious wanted, but I didn't answer him, instead concentrating on the team's requirements.

"Close tests for the day. Thank you, everyone, for a flawless demonstration."

When Codi left to assist the team with the shutdown, I confronted Latatious. "I think Codi is more than capable of overseeing the next phase of testing, thanks to Zi. It's time we supported her."

"The UN are investigating…"

I cut off his stonewalling. "It's been a week, Latatious. What have we learnt?"

"It appears that Zi is not on their main base. There have been no sightings since the conference."

"They've taken her to the Olympus Mons base, Latatious. Have the UN investigated that possibility?"

"That area is off limits. Not even Apollo would take such a political risk."

"You give them too much credit." I turned to Ander. "Could you report your findings to our director?"

"One sighting was made a day after the conference. Your chief scientist was seen boarding a drone. It was heading in the direction of Olympus Mons, before flying out of sight. It couldn't be tracked, so we can only conclude she was taken to the high security base."

"The observer was sure it was Zi?" Latatious asked.

"We have no verifying scan. The situation was too dangerous, so there's a chance of a mistaken identity."

"How large a chance?"

"Small. The operative is one of our best."

I'd heard enough. Latatious was looking for more chances to stonewall. "When you say small…give me a number, Ander?"

"The observer was a biot, so less than one percent."

"I can't sit by and waste more time. You know as well as I that their secret base is named so for good reason. Zi has been taken hostage and has refused to cooperate. I know my sister. She'll never cooperate with them. If we don't act soon, we will never see her again. I demand a rescue team. Give me that, or you'll lose two chief scientists."

Latatious shrugged his shoulders, seemingly resigned to my demands. "Who do you want?"

"A small team. Ander, Hali, and Cluste are more than capable of handling the challenge."

"Agreed, but are you? We have given you limited training in espionage. If anything, you'd be a hindrance."

"I'll take that chance."

"Your heroics are admirable, but unconvincing. I want Ander in charge of the mission. Acceptable?"

"Perfect choice," I replied.

"What are your thoughts, Ander?"

"Give me another 24 hours. There is a possibility we could verify Zi has been taken to their secret base. Her verification would justify attempting such a mission."

Latatious turned my way. "Fair?"

I felt uneasy. Was Ander unduly influenced by Latatious? "Okay. We meet here in exactly 24 hours."

Latatious and Ander nodded their acceptance, then I left the two of them, not hiding my displeasure. In reality, I needed time to prepare for the next day's brief. My knowledge of the Olympus Mons terrain was better than anyone. That alone justified my inclusion on the mission, but it had been a decade since I last explored Mars. Latatious would try to find any reason to exclude me from the rescue, if he could, but I wasn't about to give him any. It was near impossible for the uninitiated to navigate those tunnels and I knew that omitting me from the mission would be signing Zi's death warrant.

Chapter Fifteen

CAPTIVE

Zi woke in a small sterile enclosure. Short on comfort and long on security, its confinement claustrophobic bar the one transparent wall, a force field. She rose from the bed, the only furniture and walked to the force field, hoping to attract attention. Her cell was one of many that encircled a large oval enclosure filled with security cameras. It, along with the adjoining cells, was empty. Zi checked the pockets of her jacket, revealing her com had been taken. In frustration, she removed her jacket and threw it at the transparent wall, confirming she was confined inside a force field perimeter as a prisoner.

"Can anyone hear me?" she cried out, hoping for a reply, but receiving none.

Zi repeatedly remonstrated, hoping her captors would

respond, but the silence continued. Resigned to her situation, she sat back on the bed and held her forehead trying to ease the throbbing. Had she been drugged? Blurred memories of the last day flashed in and out of her mind. She had been wheeled to a transport vehicle somewhere. The area was fully enclosed, giving no hint of geography, heightening her fears. Had she been taken to their high security base? Little was known about it. Not even the UN were granted entry. Unanswered questions ran through her mind until she had to lie down, to ease the pain. As the throbbing subsided, long buried memories crept back.

Zi rued her decision to request Dane's return. She had laid a curse over anyone she cared for. Zach, her true love, came into her late teen life as a fellow researcher. He seemed to understand the sacrifice she'd made for her family, and she ultimately loved him for that. They were her happiest times. But fate enveloped her life like a Martian storm. Plans of their life together were cruelly ended, rocking her life to the core from an explosion that took all those she loved, bar her little brother. To this day, she hadn't properly grieved for them. Even worse, unconfirmed rumors swelled around the base that it wasn't an accident.

There was never a proper investigation as the rebuilding of the Elithium site had to take precedence. Zi sacrificed her own personal ambitions for the sake of the community, but not before ensuring Dane was returned to the safety of Earth, under the watchful eye and protection of their uncle, Latatious, a key backer of her parent's mining venture.

Zi looks up as man approached, her interrogator, Hogan. He walked toward her with an air of self-importance that most castes demonstrated, first turning the force field off with a single swipe of his hand. He entered her cell as if she were not there, choosing to maintain communication with operatives through his com.

"I'll be taking the human to the Elithium facility. Ensure everything is prepared."

Hogan continued to ignore Zi as he ran Augmented Reality scans of her cell and its surrounds, studying the multiple screens open in front of him, effortlessly maneuvering them with his tech nails like an orchestra conductor.

"Get our people to run a diagnostic on the surveillance, too," he ordered, before finally turning his attention to Zi. "Come with me." He turned and walked away from her cell.

"Where are you taking me?"

"Somewhere I'm sure will be of interest to you. Follow me or wait another week in the cell," he said, continuing to walk toward the compound exit.

Zi had no choice but to follow Hogan as he walked briskly through adjoining corridors to a viewing area, high above a working area busy with assistants.

"Look familiar?" Hogan asked.

Zi nodded as she studied a machine identical to their own, a universal quantum computer. The thought excited and worried her in equal measure. Apollo were likely refining Elithium on Mars, meaning there were more reserves than just their site. Her problem, Hogan was sharing classified information that she should not know.

"You're refining Elithium reserves, too?" A reckless question, but Zi already reckoned she knew too much.

"Yes. We've managed to replicate your computing sophistication. We wished we had similar Elithium reserves."

"With hard work you may discover new reserves?"

Hogan's expression was sanguine as he considered Zi. "You know that's not possible. Surely you don't believe you can hold full rights over your Elithium deposits? We're situated at the hub of the world's transport system to the solar system and stars."

"The AI and bi-party systems fully support our work."

"For how long? You're holding eighty percent of all known deposits. You think you can hold out when the rest of the world is crying out for this new energy."

Zi could see the disdain in Hogan's smoke alloy eyes,

a contempt most castes had for humans, born from their 'implanted' intelligence. How quickly they forgot their roots, dismissing human ancestors as little more than oddities. If they'd only foreseen the deleterious effect digital implants had on the human psyche, governments may have taken a more cautious legislative approach.

"We have an opportunity to create a second Earth, and you scoff at the achievement," Zi retaliated.

"Don't blame us because your kind want to live in the past. Consider yourself lucky AI government affords an empathy that humans never afforded its fellow sapiens."

"We have learnt from our errors. Earth is returning to pre-industrial environmental conditions. In another thirty years…"

Hogan scoffed, talking over her. "In another thirty years we could be discovering many Earth-like planets in other solar systems, whereas you pursue selfish, insignificant agendas."

"And castes are not selfish? You've been disrupting good government for decades, using espionage and illegal technology."

"Be careful. You're in no place to make idle condemnations."

"I won't be perturbed by your threats. There'll be people looking for me, and they won't rest until I'm returned."

A wry smile formed on Hogan's lips. "I don't think you understand our capabilities. We can make anything happen should we wish it." He looked down at one of the operators who appeared to be in charge. "Where is the quantum computer designer?"

"She's on a break."

"Bring her to me, now," Hogan ordered, making the operator scurry away and soon return with a woman dressed in an all-white laboratory uniform, including quantum headgear that covered one side of her face.

Hogan observed her for a while. "This is Zi. She is a designer of quantum computers, just like you," he said with a wolfish smile.

"Pleased to meet you. I'm surprised I've never met you at conferences," said Zi.

Oh, you've met her," Hogan interjected. "Remove your device and introduce yourself properly, please? I'd like you to show Zi your design work."

The woman dutifully removed her head gear and extended her hand. "Pleased to meet you, Zi. I'm Helena. It would be a pleasure to be your guide. Have you been working in the industry long?"

Zi couldn't answer, nor even shake her hand. Instead, to Helena's surprise, she held out both arms and hugged the woman she thought had perished. She held her mother close, hoping whatever had been done to make her mother not recognize her, could be undone. While the cruelty of her mother's situation angered her, Zi was grateful her mother had survived the fateful events of a decade earlier.

Chapter Sixteen

RESCUE

Ander briefed Latatious and me on the latest intel about Zi's whereabouts, confirming a reliable source had identified her at the Olympus Mons base. Rescue would be hazardous, but it didn't weaken my resolve to mount a mission. However, Latatious was equally determined not to include me.

"You know it's what Zi would want," Latatious appealed.

I shook my head, determined. "Zi made costly sacrifices for me. It's my turn to return the favor."

"If you don't make it back, we'll be without two lead scientists. We can't take that risk," Latatious argued.

"Fine, I'll do what you ask. Just so long as Ander can convince me I'm not needed on the mission."

Ander nodded. "Dane has a point. Hali's reconnaissance

scans show that the only way through their high security is underground. Their air space is filled with drones. Even if we managed to make it to the security perimeter, we'd be immediately detected."

"You can't handle their weaponry?"

"I could, but by the time we broke through, we would lose the hostage."

Latatious looked to Hali. "You agree?"

"After reviewing every possible entry of attack, it's clear there is no easy way through their defenses. Ander is right."

"Then the lava tubes are the only option?"

"In my opinion, yes. But…"

I talked over Hali. "…it could take them a year to find their way through and even longer to get back. They need someone familiar with the lava tubes and it just so happens that Zi and I spent our childhood exploring Mars. No one knows that underground maze better than us."

"Scan and map the whole area so you can plot a course," Latatious replied.

"I already tried. The lava tubes run too deep for the scanning equipment," replied Hali.

"There must be another way," said Latatious, looking for solutions that did not come, before resigning himself to agreeing. What else could he do? The lava tubes were the only way through without drawing unwanted attention. I got the mission I wanted.

A day later our mission had commenced in the twilight, soon arriving at the 'Abby' skylight, the entry to one of the seven major lava tubes nicknamed the 'Seven Sisters', bordering Olympus Mons. Abby was the closest we could come to the Apollo perimeter without being detected. I was kitted with a 'trekker' outfit, a slimline space suit made for long distance exploring on Mars, including 'detachable' kits holding a day's air supply, food and water.

My role was to lead the mission through the maze of lava tubes to the base of Olympus Mons. Ander provided the muscle, defending us against any attacks that'd inevitably come from the heavily fortified killer drones that protected the base. Hali would carry out surveillance and reconnaissance missions when we surfaced, and Cluste carried the supplies I needed for a two-week mission.

The Abby skylight entry was the first challenge, a two-hundred-meter descent to naturally occurring caves that crisscrossed from its original source, hot molten lava that had flowed from Olympus Mons in the time it was an active volcano. I was alone the last time I tackled the Olympus Mons trek. Having three biots on the mission sure made hiking easier.

The first descent navigated, we reached a large open chamber, nicknamed 'the Orb' where numerous lava flow openings circled the expanse. This posed the inexperienced a myriad of choices, many dead ends that could easily confuse the uninitiated.

Ander logically scanned the options. "This appears to be the clearest path."

How many times had I heard or made the choice Ander just took? The lava tube maze was a complex challenge, filled with deceptive alternatives that could baffle the rational. I remembered when my mother lost us in the orb maze for many days, learning that trial and error was the only way to tame this beast.

"No. This way."

"This is moving away from Olympus Mons, Dane," he challenged.

"The orb isn't the actual base of the skylight. We have to descend another hundred meters this way before we can connect up with the right lava tunnels."

"Impressive memory," Ander replied.

"A mix of memory and experience," I replied, pointing to an obscure marker I'd left from a decade earlier trek, one of many markers etched into the Martian rock. These markings were plentiful on our first day's trek, making this day's hike the least challenging. Also, the lower level lava tubes were long and straight compared to what would follow.

On reaching our first destination to rest, Ander and Cluste used my down time to run reconnaissance checks on the caves that lay ahead, while Hali stayed with me. I welcomed her company, given it was our first real time together since the Deliverance. So much had happened to Hali after our escape. She had a strength about her, clearly born from her newly commissioned capabilities. I had been protected by a number of security biots in the years of developing Trojan, and Hali now had that same confidence. Who wouldn't, having gained such powers? She was analyzing reconnaissance material sent by Ander, before she realized I was observing her. So I signaled her to join me.

"Chatting with me isn't in your program now," I said.

She smiled. "No, it's not."

"You've bigger fish to fry."

"We've bigger fish, Dane."

"Very dangerous fish. Do you think we're ready for it?"

I studied the contour of Hali's new armor-like suit as she considered my question. Her shoulders and arms were protected by a Teflon based casing, casting a powerful image all military biots possessed. Hali contained an array of proven military hardware and top-secret weapons that were the equal of Ander.

"Ander's report isn't reassuring," she replied, honestly.

"Are they lost?"

"No, they're fine. An earlier surveillance revealed Apollo operatives may have found a defense against my weaponry."

"So soon?"

"It seems so. We're working on some adjustments that'll allow me some offensive capability, but my role is to focus on surveillance when we surface."

It was strange talking to Hali. I had mixed feelings. On the one hand I was reassured by her strength, but on the other, I'd lost my friend and loyal assistant. "How do you feel?"

"My defense capabilities are…"

"No. I mean do you feel different, since they changed you?"

"That's a very human question." Hali replied, reassuringly touching my arm, before continuing. "I have a new brief, but that still includes protecting you, Dane."

I wanted to hear more, but what else could Hali say. She could offer a scripted approach that took into account my doubts, but she had tried to paint an honest appraisal. "I hope we work together, again, like before," I said, drawing another smile from her.

"It was an honor working alongside you, Dane."

"I hope more than an honor. I count you as a friend."

"No matter what happens, Dane, I'll not forget the friendship you and your family provided me."

I hugged Hali, surprising her and myself, but we were getting ever closer to the most dangerous part of the mission and the likelihood of success was not high. Hali may not have human feelings, but I wanted her to know mine before we faced our adversaries.

"Let's get your sister home," she replied, determinedly.

"You're right, Hali. I best rest, now."

I lay back in my makeshift bunker and looked up at the shadows cast from the com light. Reflections of Hali ran across the chamber's rock ceiling, dancing over the many clefts that lined it. We would remain in the dark zone of this long dormant lava tube for another full day, before surfacing and commencing the rescue proper. In my youth, I often fantasized about discovering new deposits of Elithium for my father in this very region. I saw it as a way of connecting with him. Mining was in his blood, whereas small talk wasn't. I figured if I found new Elithium deposits, he might notice me. A decade on, I wondered if I were no different from my father. Apart from my family, Hali was the only other person I considered as a close friend, even though she could never have such feelings. Why had I become this way? Perhaps most Martians had an inherent need to become fiercely independent to survive the extreme environment. Zi and I spent our youth on quests predominantly related to taming those extremes. Zi had devoted her life to terraforming Mars, as had our parents. As had I. It seemed a reasonable quest, yet outside forces challenged that dream, using increasingly desperate measures. What had begun as an exhilarating vision was now a dangerous project. I had accepted that when I committed to the program, along with counter intelligence training. I hoped it was enough to face the trials ahead.

The second day's trek was a slow rocky climb back up toward our destination at the base of Olympus Mons. The lava tunnel narrowed in parts and regularly branched off stream-like into secondary lava tubes. This challenged the most experienced of explorers, easily disorienting them. That danger grew as we ascended within range of the Apollo drone sensors, slowing our approach. On reaching our second base camp late, I slumped into my makeshift bunk, giving in to sleep, but not before feeling satisfied I had played my part in the rescue. Ander would take command of the mission when we returned to the surface the next day.

Day three and I woke to the now familiar sounds of surveillance drones regularly flying above. Ander and Hali stood in the twilight of the cave where the early morning rays of the Sun filtered through the skylight.

"The drones are circling this side of Olympus Mons every fifteen minutes," said Hali, having undertaken a reconnaissance of the surface under the cover of darkness.

"Can you stay in front of them?" Ander asked.

It further reminded me that the two spoke as equals sharing command now. Cluste was packing supplies beside me, so I got his attention.

"What's happening?"

"I've been told to pack and be ready," Cluste replied. He appeared to readily accept the change, obeying either Ander or Hali's commands, interrupting them only if he needed clarification. I was no different than Cluste, feeling every bit a subordinate as I approached them, guiltily apologizing for oversleeping.

"We thought you needed the rest, Dane. Besides, there is little you can do at present." Ander replied.

"Is there a way through to the base?"

"The perimeter is heavily guarded, but there may be an opening," Ander said, turning to Hali.

"I'll go out ahead and guide you and Ander when and where to advance. I have identified a route that offers good cover from the drones until the final kilometer, which is nothing but an open flat plain where you'll be fully exposed."

"Odds of making it to the base?"

"Low, Dane. I'd prefer we remain underground. Is there another way through?" Hali replied.

"I've explored this area more times than I can remember. The only way through is on the surface."

"Then on reaching the final kilometer, I'll create a diversion to draw their drones away from you."

I reacted to Hali's plan. "Too risky. There are thousands of drones up there. They'd quickly locate you and report our attempted rescue."

"If they locate Hali," Ander replied.

"You believe you can evade that many drones? I've never seen a biot do that. How?" I asked, not convinced.

Hali smiled. "That information is classified, Dane."

It sounded fanciful but Hali had already taken on an Apollo star fleet and won. Why not again? "If there's no other way, then when do we leave?"

"We will await Hali's intel." Ander replied, glancing Hali's way, seemingly seeking her support.

"I'm confident that Ander and Cluste can get through the security if I create a diversion. I can't guarantee the same, if you join Ander," Hali replied.

I immediately showed my displeasure. Hali wanted me off the rescue team. "You know as well as I that Latatious backed this mission and agreed I be part of the final rescue."

"You can't traverse the perimeter as quickly, which may expose our mission." Ander replied.

The two of them backed each other. It was reassuring to know they had a plan they believed in, but something in their objectives unnerved me. I had agreed to accede control to Ander once through the lava tunnels. It made sense, but I doubted they had referred this new strategy to Latatious. Loyalty to a chosen human or caste commander was encoded into biot DNA. Yet, it appeared they made the decision themselves, so I tested them.

"Latatious agreed that I be part of this mission. I demand that you follow through on his command and include me in this rescue."

Both biots couldn't countermand a specific order and nodded accordingly, before Hali replied. "Give me an hour. I should be ready to guide you through by then." Hali didn't wait for a reply, instead turning to the skylight, she quickly climbed toward the surface, disappearing on to the Mars surface.

Hali had supported my request without question, easing my concerns. Interestingly, Hali did not seek Ander's support. *Was she in command?* I wondered.

"Cluste. Ensure Dane has sufficient supplies for a two-day mission. I'll carry the supplies required for Zi. We need to be ready to leave at a moment's notice, so scramble!"

Two hours passed before Hali transmitted instructions. I followed Ander up to the surface, a challenging climb and a sign of what lay ahead as we traversed across Olympus Mons by foot. Hali instructed us to traverse to a protected rocky outcrop and await further instructions. It was a fifteen-minute trek through a boulder strewn area, making for a difficult ascent, but we made our cover, just before a drone approached. Its distinctly loud noise provided us ample warning as it glided low across the Martian airspace, occasionally making high pitched sounds as it darted in different directions, likely inspecting wind-related noises in the perimeter. I faced two challenges: first, physically evading the drones, followed by the mental challenge, lying motionless and silent as they flew over. A cough or breath-lessness would be detected, quickly ending our mission, but the deadly observer moved on and shortly after, Hali issued her next command.

"Head across the narrow concourse that runs toward the mountain. Its narrowness will intensify the winds, so move slowly and cautiously."

"Is there a safer approach? My readings tell me that some of those wind gusts would be too challenging for Dane," Ander replied.

"Potentially, but this way offers better cover. It's an acceptable risk, and it will halve your journey."

Ander released an extendable climbing rope and attached us both to it before leaving the safety of our cover. The wind had strengthened, signaling the early stages of an approaching storm season, adding further risk to our rescue. Martian winds could be unpredictable, sometimes gathering pace in just days. We had to return to our base before the storms gathered full intensity, for then it would be impossible to navigate. Like Zi, we'd be trapped, waiting until the storm season passed, an unpredictable time period lasting anywhere between weeks and years.

The windswept concourse was as Hali described, a narrow approach surrounded by large boulders either side, offering protection from the drones, but little from the intermittent gusts, making for a difficult trek. Even more challenging, strong gusts would stoke up the fine Martian dust, limiting vision to no more than a meter, leaving us vulnerable to the occasional larger rocks that were propelled like missiles by the winds. I stayed close behind Ander who acted as a shield as he led me through the treacherous alley, spending many hours traversing

Olympus Mons blind, before we reached a clearing, offering a view across the Martian plain. Apollo base was within reach but swarms of drones lay between us and our destination.

"We've come to the clearing, Hali. Will await your instructions," Ander reported.

"Affirmative. Make base there, but be ready to move forward immediately on my command," Hali replied.

I welcomed the opportunity to rest. Any attempt at safely navigating the perimeter was impossible anyway. We'd be detected within minutes of ascending from our protected position. It was down to Hali to provide sufficient decoy or our rescue attempt was hopeless.

"How has Hali managed to evade them?"

Ander studied the firestorm of drones below for some time, seemingly analyzing just that. "If I knew how, I'd be doing the same. I do know that Hali carries highly classified weaponry as part of her arsenal. At least I hope she does, or we'll be turning back, soon."

"You don't know?"

"I do know that the communication system she has is advanced. How do you think we can continue to communicate without being detected?"

That gave me some comfort, but it was now clear to me that under these conditions, I had become a liability.

The last thing Ander needed was to waste his fire power protecting me, if assaulted by the drone army. I sat down and leaned against a large boulder to rest, fighting feelings of disappointment for selfishly demanding I come this far. Guiding them through the lava tunnels was my best contribution to the rescue. Had I been over zealous in wanting to help my sister? There was little more I could do, but obey Ander's commands and hope Hali's plans would get us inside the base.

HOSTAGE

Zi woke from a restless night's sleep, her first and only thought — Helena. Her mother was alive, even if her life and memories had been irreconcilably altered. Zi punched her pillow in anger at the thought her mother was a caste. Given the chance, she would make the world aware of the truth, but did the same fate await her? Zi already knew too much. She scanned the walls of her high security cell, feeling the hopelessness of her situation. The only faint hope afforded her was the freedom to work with Helena. Maybe implants could be reversed? And if her mother lived, could her father and Zach also have survived? Impulsively, she called out to her captors in the hope of learning more.

"I want to see my mother!"

An hour passed until her increasingly frenetic pleas were answered. She was relieved to see Bayley approach her cell. Interestingly, she found herself thinking of Zach. Bayley had that same confident demeanor, good looks, and broad shoulders that drew the eye. He seemed to notice, smiling warmly. Her supposed interrogator held many surprises. Why would Apollo put their trust in a human? It certainly made her want to trust him. Perhaps that was the point.

Bayley reached for his com, turning off the cell force field. "I have arranged another meeting with your mother. Care to join me?"

Zi nodded and followed him, appreciating his unassuming manner after confronting his polar opposite, Hogan, the previous day. Enthusiastically, she followed him through the same connecting corridor of yesterday, before veering in a new direction, toward one of the large community domes.

"You said you'd take me to my mother."

"Soon enough, but I want you to see a little more of our base, first."

The view from the dome offered a panoramic view of Olympus Mons.

"I've always been told that your Olympus Mons base was off limits to all Gaea citizens."

"Yes, consider yourself fortunate. Come over here. A transport drone is about to land," Bayley said, enthusiastically.

The drone's slow descent from the Martian skies was all the more dramatic, given the solar systems highest mountain, Olympus Mons was the backdrop. The drone gently hovered on to the space port, a large clearing adjoining the heart of their mining operations. Large tankers lined up, ready to pump the refined Elithium into the drone's tanks. The open cut mine lit up the area, like a giant outdoor theatre stadium. Zi knew precious little about the top-secret site, so its size surprised her. They had to have discovered large reserves to warrant this level of development.

"Impressive, isn't it?" Bayley said with pride.

Zi nodded, taking in the myriad activities occurring around the site. Another drone hovered high above, awaiting its turn to descend.

"This is unusually busy. Most of the drones are delivering drilling equipment," Bayley explained.

"Elithium deposits?" Zi asked.

"Mostly. You looked surprised?"

"My parents ran diagnostic scans of the whole area before choosing our site. I ran many follow ups, but only ever found limited deposits here."

Bayley remained coy, preferring to direct her gaze to the base of Olympus Mons. "See that opening?"

"Hard to miss. I presume it's a drift."

"Correct. There are two parallel underground tunnels, each 22 kilometers in length."

"How many cross tunnels?"

"Fifty-three."

Zi shook her head, as she followed the activity building around the drift, a mix of workers and haulers. "Must have been quite a discovery to merit this amount of infrastructure."

"Not as impressive as you imagine. But Elithium is a rare and valuable resource."

Zi knew where the conversation was heading. She also knew that the reserves were far less than hers, no matter how deep they drilled. It was inevitable the discussion would turn to Gaea's reserves. "Why are you sharing this with me?"

"This is your interest. Is it not?"

Zi tired of the pretence. "I'm never going to leave here, am I?"

"You could, if you cooperated. Share the Elithium."

"Did my mother cooperate?"

"She is happy with her life."

"A life controlled by implants. She didn't recognize me."

"She is doing what she loves. Doesn't that matter?"

"If she's happy, you won't mind me talking to her?"

"I will take you to her, but first let me show you more of our base."

Bayley led Zi through the mining area, a large infrastructure that burrowed deep into the planet's grandest mountain. The settlement bordered the open cut mine area, spanning several kilometers. They walked through four major domes, community hubs bristling with workers, entertainment and rich with fauna and foliage. There was a sprinkling of biots, but the majority of the population were castes.

"How many workers do you have?"

"We reached the fifty thousand mark just recently," Bayley replied, proudly. "This dome was the first built. Now they number fifteen."

The numbers didn't add up to Zi. Their own team of miners was no more than twenty thousand. The majority of workers here had to be working in non-mining sectors. *What was the true purpose of this secret base?* she wondered, as they entered a fitting room.

"Want to see the mine?"

"Does a bird want to fly?"

Bayley laughed at her irony. His face lit up when he smiled, revealing a youthful warm manner beneath his more serious scientist mask, surprising and enticing her. She knew that it was his place to convince her to cooperate, but she couldn't stop wondering why they put their faith in a human. No doubt he would be more persuasive, but there was always a chance she could sway him.

The mine was filled with activity along its ten-kilometer-long tunnel, the main level of a maze of underground tunnels and roads. It looked more like a freeway that bore through European mountainsides, as empty rail haulers continuously rolled to the vertical shaft to be loaded, before returning out on a second rail line to fill waiting drones. The load was indeed Elithium and appeared to be a high grade. A third smaller duel rail system ran between both lines, carrying workers in and out of the mine to the many sub-level tunnels that wound around the main shaft.

"How many levels?" Zi asked.

"There are five levels connected to the main shaft, not including the crusher and ore load machinery."

Zi calculated the numbers needed to work this space and quickly evaluated that there were far more workers than required. There was either waste on a large scale or there was more than a mine buried deep inside Olympus Mons. But what would justify such an expense? She was about to ask before Bayley abruptly brought the tour to an end.

"Your mother played a big part in all of this. Would you like to see her now?"

"You keep asking me obvious questions."

Bayley smiled warmly again, quick to return back to the home base. Both were in good spirits until they returned to the main dome, where Hogan sat, seemingly waiting for them.

"Having fun out there?" Hogan greeted, sarcastically.

"She's world renowned in the field. Why would I not enjoy her feedback?" Bayley replied, tersely.

Hogan stood up and looked past Bayley, directly at Zi. "You know humans must have clearance."

"I'm doing what I was assigned to do. Haven't you got better things to do then follow me around?"

"My report's due. Zhang is impatient for an assessment," Hogan replied, holding his threatening gaze toward Zi.

Bayley didn't reply, instead signaling for Zi to follow him. She walked past Hogan, returning his threatening gaze with equal defiance, but hoping Bayley had the authority he now showed. They walked back toward the main base in silence. Bayley was clearly annoyed by Hogan's challenge, making her further ponder if Bayley was friend or foe. She prodded him with questions but he maintained a cool silence, stifling any attempts to confide in him and lessening any hope of her return home. The one certainty was a rescue team would have been coordinated by now. She just hoped her brother would not be part of that team, for what Dane didn't know was where she was expendable, her brother was not.

Chapter Eighteen

NEW TEAM

Zi studied Helena as she assembled her team. Ten years earlier, she was part of her mother's team. Could Helena ever remember those earlier times again, or had the implants forever robbed her of her true memories? How large a price had humans paid, unaware countless lives had become play things to the technology designed to free them? There'd been many investigations on Earth, but none had found conclusive evidence pinning dark technology to influential players. Zi would change that, if she could find a way home.

The area was humming with excitement as her mother prepared to deliver an announcement. Zi was too far away to hear clearly, but it appeared she and Bayley were congratulating the team. That completed, all dispersed quickly to their work stations, except Bayley and Helena, who joined Zi on the observation deck.

"Good morning, Zi. As you can see, I keep my promises," said Bayley, before excusing himself.

Helena's exuberant mood changed to a more pensive demeanor as she extended her hand. Zi wanted to hold her mother close, but checked her emotions this time, aware she had confused Helena the previous day. She shook her hand formally then stood back a pace, controlling her true feelings.

"Your team seems happy."

"Yes. They have achieved so much. I'm proud of them."

"I noticed everyone looking my way before returning to work. Have I done anything wrong?"

"Quite the contrary. Bayley was introducing our new team member, should you be interested?"

Zi looked down to the quantum computer before answering. "Have I a choice?"

Helena stood alongside Zi and studied her team, choosing not to answer immediately. Perhaps she didn't know. "Would you like to help me?" she asked.

Zi wanted to reveal what was really happening on this base, but her mother wouldn't believe her. In truth, her mother was a complete stranger now and any attempt at honesty would only push her further away. Winning Helena's trust would take time.

"I would like to help you and your team."

Helena immediately warmed. "Wonderful! Come with me and meet your colleagues."

Helena introduced her to the team. All were biots, bar one. "This is Adam," Helena said. Her tone was more formal with this man than her other team members. Adam, like Helena was a caste. His piercing eyes revealed a seriousness that disconcerted her as he quickly shook her hand and just as quickly returned to his work station. Ironically, he was the least human of the whole team. "He's devoted to his work," said Helena, excusing his aloofness.

"They are loyal to their work, if nothing else," Zi replied.

"We're in a particularly difficult period. Many challenges."

"Bayley showed me your Elithium site. It's far larger than I'd imagined."

"Bayley will be a great addition to the team."

"He's new to Mars?"

"Yes, it's his first trip here."

"He appeared to be very knowledgeable. Is he in a senior position?"

"He's an accomplished scientist with extensive knowledge in the field of quantum computing. I hear he's applied for permanent residency."

"That's unusual. It seems your base hires few like him."

"Like him? Human, you mean?"

"Yes," Zi responded, in a matter of fact manner, hiding her uncertainty about Bayley. She wanted him to be human, but sometimes she wondered.

"Well, according to his resume, he's very human and a successful one at that."

Zi remembered that knowing smile. It was the same one Helena gave her when they talked about Zach. "Please, m…" Zi corrected herself from saying mother. She looked away from her, checking her emotions. "Where is he working?"

"He was meant to be analyzing some of the quantum computer data, but he was waylaid by an incident en route to Mars."

"Oh. Nothing too serious?"

"There's been rumors about a security breach on one of the larger cargo ships. He was listed for one of the next commercial star ships, but security officials requested he join an investigation team."

Zi pushed Helena for more information. "A scientist on an investigation?"

"I agree. My guess is it's related to specific cargo, requiring his expertise."

"Quantum computers?"

Helena thought to answer, but glanced in the direction of a work colleague, Adam, who sat within earshot. Perhaps he was listening in, for Helena chose not to respond.

"I have to start work, now. I'd value your help," Helena invited.

Zi hesitated. If she helped her mother, she assisted her enemy. Yet, this would be her best chance to learn more of her mother and perhaps help her. Could she somehow spark some long-lost memories and penetrate her insidious implants?

"You don't have to, if I make you uncomfortable," said Helena, reacting to Zi's indecision.

Helena's obvious disappointment moved Zi to act. "I would like to work with you. I'm sure we could learn much from each other, but can you tell me one thing."

"Sure. What is it?"

"Have you been ordered to work with me?"

"I am a scientist first and last. Bayley briefed me about your background and asked if I'd like to work with you. Given our common research interests, I jumped at the chance."

"Nothing else was said?"

"My role has always been to do what I was trained for, scientific research. I have no interest in the politics. Those who hold positions of power learnt that years ago, so they leave me to my research."

Zi thought to push her mother further, but she sensed their conversation was being listened to. She could do little to influence Helena, now. Perhaps in time, as they shared their love for science, Zi could share the truth of their situation.

"I want to be useful," Zi replied.

Helena showed Zi her work module area, an open office with a clear view of her team's main work space on one side and a large com screen on the other. Mathematical equations filled the giant screen, where notes, books and pens littered the tables beneath it, signaling the many team meetings and discussions held in this space.

"I encourage an open office so anyone can freely discuss ideas and challenges and I prefer new team members work in my pod for the first few weeks." She pointed to a small desk to the side of the wall com. "It's cramped, busy and noisy, but it's the quickest way to involve you in our activities. Will that work for you?"

Zi nodded. At least implants hadn't changed her mother's work habits. She always liked the flow of ideas around her. Zi was brought up in that environment, so it was natural for her to work in that way.

"The desk is perfect. What are you analyzing?"

"Many areas, but our biggest challenge is the DUNE project."

"That being?"

"Sorry, you'll soon learn our acronyms. The Deep Underground Neutrino Experiment."

"Interesting," Zi replied, deadpan, hiding her surprise at her mother's openness. Helena had just willingly shared highly classified information with her, backing up her mother's claim that science not politics drove her. It also supported Zi's belief that there was more going on under Olympus Mons than just mining Elithium.

"I understand. Neutrinos research is a complex challenge."

"Highly challenging. We're collecting valuable data, but it will take our computers a decade to properly analyze. I wouldn't live anywhere else except Mars, but we do suffer from the tyranny of distance. I requested more powerful computers from Earth, but we're still waiting. So, half of my team works on improving our quantum computer's processing power. Do you face similar problems?"

"I know exactly what you mean. We do, although our project is different."

"That being?"

Zi hesitated again, knowing the more she shared, the deeper her troubles may become. But this was her mother.

"We are working on nuclear fusion."

No turning back, now, she thought. Not only had she learnt secrets, she had begun sharing her own.

"Equally challenging," Helena responded, not showing any apparent concern about the gravity of the information they were sharing. "Shall we?" she invited, squeezing her arm reassuringly. Two simple words, which would have unknown, perhaps life changing ramifications, but Zi nodded her acceptance, knowing full well the danger she faced.

Zi made good her promise, helping Helena and her team, and in so doing, making small inroads toward gaining her trust. In response, Helena involved her in ever more complex challenges, revealing the secrets that were so stringently guarded outside the confines of this base.

Surprisingly, Bayley often joined them, particularly when they worked on the neutrino research. At first, Zi was cautious, but Bayley appeared to be who she'd been told he was, an enthusiastic researcher. Helena clearly liked him, too, motivating Zi to open up more in his presence. She delighted in the creativity the three shared as it naturally spilled over into their social activities. It was as if she'd been returned to happier days with her mother and Zach, the life she so missed. This evening was no different as she reviewed the week's findings with Helena while they waited for Bayley to join them for dinner.

"You look sad, Zi. What's wrong?"

"I'm actually happy, working with you. It's just that it reminds me of earlier days. The happiest time of my life."

"You lost something special?"

"Someone, actually."

Helena stroked Zi's arm, sympathetically. "I'm so sorry. I know how you feel."

"Do you?" Zi replied, tears welling in her eyes.

"Yes. I lost my husband. It was many years ago, but I never forgot the pain of losing him."

Zi listened intently, hoping she may jar some hidden memories. "How did he die?"

"He died in an accident while returning to Earth to see his mother. She was very ill."

"I'm sorry. Did he see his mother?"

"No. He was about to. He called me the night before the accident, happy that she was still lucid, but he never made it in time."

Zi was moved by her recounting of the event, even though she knew the memory to be false. The power of their implant technology was chilling. Her mother's whole life appeared to have been seamlessly altered. But she held back her disdain for Apollo, continuing to press her.

"You couldn't join your husband at the time?"

"No. I wished I could have. I'd have preferred to die with him than endure his loss. My whole life crumbled. It took years to fully accept it. But even ten years on, I mourn his passing, particularly on the anniversary of his death. No one fully recovers from such a loss."

"No. Mars is an isolating life. To leave Earth behind is challenging enough, but to lose those closest to you makes it even harder. Were you working on this program back then?"

"Mostly. We were working on different projects, but this is the one I trained for, back on Earth. We were so excited to be offered the opportunity."

The memory plants were extensive. Her mother's life had been reassigned, as if little more than a movie. Zi pushed further. "I've never asked. Did you have children?"

Helena's mood changed as if by a click of a switch. Perhaps it was as terrifyingly simple as that? As if the door to her most intimate memories had been ruthlessly slammed shut, so that recollection was impossible.

"I never talk about them," Helena replied, clearly distressed.

Zi held back. She hated to see her mother upset. "Another drink?"

Helena appeared not to hear, her gaze distant, seemingly struggling with the memories Zi had evoked.

Emotions rippled across her face, but then with one voluntary movement of her hand, they faded, demonstrating the power of her caste applications. A meditative calm held her emotions in check, before her demeanor brightened.

"Bayley. Finally!" Helena said, standing to greet him, more enthusiastically than normal.

"Sorry. We had delays with the final read outs. The team leader asked if you could help them with it?"

"Certainly," Helena replied, picking up her bag.

"I don't think it's urgent."

"It's okay. Best I check it now. Please excuse me. Let's do this tomorrow," she replied, nodding to Zi before leaving.

"Sorry to spoil the party," Bayley said, apologetically.

Zi merely nodded as she watched Helena leave. She had enjoyed working with her this past week, but it was often agonizing to listen to her mother's distorted sense of herself. She clearly looked disoriented as she exited. How often did she have such feelings? The thought angered her.

"The party was spoilt a long time ago."

Bayley's good mood quickly diminished. "Did I miss something?"

"How could you allow this?"

"Allow your mother to do what she truly enjoys, you mean?"

Zi's anger grew, diminishing any good will that had grown between them over the past week. In truth, Bayley was no more than a paid operative who chose to ignore the terrifying extent Apollo organization would go to achieve their aims. Zi wanted to help her mother, but really, she was only delaying the inevitable. The same fate awaited her and both she and Bayley knew it.

"So, that's how you justify controlling a human being? Destroy all her memories without consent and plant them in a job where they can benefit your organization!"

"I don't know the circumstances…"

Zi interrupted Bayley's tepid response. "I can tell you the circumstances in vivid detail if you'd like to know them!"

"Actually, I would. But now is not the time or place," he replied, nodding his head in the direction where Hogan approached.

"Good evening. I seem to be always interrupting your cozy get-togethers," Hogan said, sarcasm written on his face.

"Not at all. I just arrived. Would you care to join us?" Bayley responded, deadpan.

"That would be enlightening, but Zhang requires your presence. He's keen to hear how the project's going."

Bayley stood and turned to Zi to excuse himself.

"He wants to see both of you," Hogan added, showing

his delight. "Be at the Perch in twenty minutes," he ordered.

The Perch was an open space built high above the DUNE machine, an observatory set aside for management to oversee operations. Zhang stood with Hogan, expressively pointing to the scientists below who busily worked around the neutrino machine. Zhang nodded to Bayley as he approached, then swiftly waved Hogan away to carry out his commands.

"Welcome, Bayley. And this must be Zi," he said, extending his hand with a warm welcome. Zi didn't respond, standing her distance, refusing the handshake.

Zhang ignored the slight. "I've heard so much about your work on Mars. I hope you've been pleasantly surprised with our own humble achievements?"

"Any pleasantries were diminished, the minute you decided to take me hostage," Zi shot back.

"I'm afraid you were collateral damage, given the corporation that sponsors your work decided to illegally ship cargo to Mars."

"Alleged illegal activities, you mean?"

"Your brother, with the assistance of counter intelligence agents, took control of one of our cargo ships and transported machinery to your base. That sounds a little more than alleged. Don't you think?"

"Nothing can justify abducting me and holding me against my will. I demand to be released and returned to my base!"

Zhang walked to a nearby table, inviting Bayley and Zi to join him. "Let's at least negotiate in comfort."

All seated, Zhang initiated a force field around the table for privacy. "I understand your frustration, but we are legally holding you until this situation is fully investigated."

"You have broken all international protocols. I demand access to legal support, which is my right!"

"Not until your brother turns himself in to the appropriate authorities. He and his band of pirates have broken all international protocols. Given he's reported to your corporation, we hold you under suspicion for supporting his violent actions. We'll consider your request for legal support when he submits himself to the United Nations peace keepers."

"That's little more than extortion. I'll sue your organization for malpractice, starting with you, Mr. Zhang!"

"You can try. We have not mistreated you. In fact, we've allowed you access to our corporate secrets. If you considered us criminals, why would you willingly incriminate yourself?"

"You know why. You've illegally held my mother hostage

for a decade and submitted her to an abominable recalibration. Any court would fully accept my motives and jail her perpetrators."

"You falsely believe her to be your mother. What proof do you have?"

"I won't rest until your illegal reassignment activities are exposed in the international court."

All pretense at politeness had dispersed. Zi would not accept any deals. In all likelihood, her chance of freedom ended the minute they revealed their secret laboratories to her. She was about to continue her accusations, before Bayley joined the heated discussion, offering her some support.

"Zi has proved a valuable member of Helena's team this last week."

"Yes, your assistance has been valuable, Zi. We will take that into account in future negotiations." Zhang responded, before Zi continued her attack.

"I offered assistance only because my mother requested it."

"I understand your frustration, but these are my directives from the very highest levels within Apollo Corporation. You're in a tenuous position that could further diminish if you're not careful."

"What could be worse?"

"Your mother asked that very same question a decade ago," replied Zhang, gravely.

Zi had drawn out the truth from Zhang. Helena was her mother, not that she had any doubts, but he had admitted culpability. Further argument was pointless and dangerous as she was perilously close to being reassigned, herself. There was little more she could say, so she looked to Bayley, as did Zhang.

"I suggest you allow Zi to continue to work with Helena. They…We are a good team, achieving encouraging results. Having Zi undergo reassignment would only create unnecessary delays."

Zhang held back on his response, then reluctantly nodded his approval. "Another week, but I want to see continued results. I've supported you this far, Bayley, but my patience is running out. We need results from the DUNE operation or we will have to take a harder line. Is that clear?"

"Yes. A week should suffice."

"Very well. I'll leave you to it. A pleasure to meet you, Zi," said Zhang, showing anything but, before he released the force field and left Bayley and Zi at the table.

Bayley watched Zhang leave the area before reapplying the force field. "I won't be able to protect you much longer. You have to cooperate, or Hogan will take over your case. Do you understand?"

Zi knew that to be true. Her best chance was to buy time in the hope a rescue team was closing in. "Why are you helping me? Is it because you're following orders?" Zi asked, hoping there was more. She knew he had feelings for her. Their last week working together had revealed that, but were they genuine feelings?

Bayley looked to his com, checking the force field was secure before replying. "I'll do all I can, but you would do well not to question Zhang. He holds too much power for you or me to make any difference."

"So, I should just accede to his will? Like you?"

"You will make your situation worse if you antagonize him."

"So, I'll just live happily ever after here, fighting against all I stand for? Do you care that little for me?" Zi replied, showing her disappointment.

"You looked happy spending time with your mother."

"Of course, I am. I hope to help her remember she has family who love her. What you people have done to her is shameful. Why shouldn't I be antagonistic to her captors?"

"Your feelings are understandable, but your strategy will only end in grief. Spend the week helping her with the project. Build the friendship, and I promise I'll do everything in my power to help you," he said, extending his hand.

Zi ignored his gesture, instead looking out to the many Apollo administrators who worked around them. It made her think of the week she had spent with her mother and Bayley. They had built a good rapport and Zi genuinely welcomed their growing bond, albeit under guard. At times, she almost forgot the pain of the past, daring to imagine she could build a new life. As unlikely as it seemed, something about Bayley reminded her of her only love. She wanted to believe, even though aware of the potential folly in doing so, but Zi's instincts told her to try, as she slowly extended her hand.

"Zi, this will be one of the few chances I can talk to you without being monitored. It's important you work this week as you have over the previous one and not create any undue alarm. Don't share what I'm about to say with anyone, particularly your mother. Promise?"

"Yes."

"Promise!"

"Yes. I promise."

"There is a rescue effort being organized to return you home. When the time is right, I'll help you to escape. You have my word."

"And what of my mother?"

"Your mother will want to stay here and continue with her project."

"She deserves to know the truth."

Bayley let go of Zi's hand and looked at her sternly. "The chances of escaping this facility are next to impossible. You and your rescuers will have a slim chance, if I assist them. But to rescue both you and your mother would be impossible. She's a caste. You know as well as I that castes are constantly monitored. They will know her whereabouts at all times. Promise me you'll say nothing of what I have just told you?"

Zi wanted to argue the point, but what Bayley said was true. She wanted to tell her mother everything, but that would certainly sentence her to a similar fate, spending a lifetime helping her enemy and not even knowing it. "I promise," Zi replied, knowing there was no other way. She had to return home and see her project through — terraforming Mars. Once that was done, she would stop at nothing to see justice served for her mother.

Chapter Nineteen

SURRENDER

Hali circumnavigated the danger zone, careful to remain a safe distance from the fortifications, a man-made black scar made of rock-like plastics, 3D precision printed to be impenetrable. She carried out her fifth surveillance, stretching from the lava skylight where Ander and Dane awaited her orders, to across the ten-kilometer wall. She was no closer to finding a way through. What little protected areas remained in the open expanse had long ago been filled, leaving any assailant little chance of evading the surveillance drones. Even worse, the drone's patterns of formation were unpredictable, showing they were directed from an AI command post. In short, Hali's only recourse was to act as a decoy.

Hali's key command was to return Zi to Codi. Only then, could they fulfill the project aims. Risks had to be accepted. Her strategy determined, Hali launched a series of cluster explosives into the center of the perimeter, unleashing her own fleet of drones on the perimeter, drawing immediate attention. A full fleet of Apollo drones swarmed the perimeter circling her own force. Hali set up a classic 'wagon circle' defense, protecting the most powerful of her offensive drones. Her foes reacted, flying in a formation similar to an American Indian attack, circling around Hali's drones and picking off her outer defense, slowly peeling back her army.

Hali used the cover of her drones to advance closer and carry out the second phase of her plan.

"Prepare to advance on my command," Hali commanded, advancing what remained of her drones directly toward the attackers, leading to a fireball of explosions, lighting the air and reverberating across the plain.

The warfare was quick and hostile, both fleets sustaining considerable damage, but Apollo's sheer weight of numbers resulted in victory. Hali held her position and waited for the last of her drones to fall before enacting a second, smaller fleet of drones, positioning them a kilometer east of where she lay, in range of her own weapon systems. The survivors of the victorious Apollo fleet took her bait, forming the same line of attack, buying Hali precious time to enact her strategy.

"Ander. Make your way to their base, now. I will provide cover for you until you reach the perimeter."

Once she verified their advance toward the base, she turned back to the battle at hand. Though small in number, her second fleet of drones possessed greater firepower, extending the confrontation, but they were still hopelessly out numbered. Hali lay low on the Martian ground, perfectly still until the last of her drones fell. Then she stood and fired a single, defiant shot at the swarm, enticing the deadly hordes to her position. They swarmed to surround her in the first instance, ready to unleash their fury. Hali clenched her fist to activate the deadliest of her weapons and raised her arm high before slamming it to the Martian soil, unleashing a power surge that waved tsunami-like across the red dust, spreading in all directions and immediately disabling her enemy. A thousand drones fell to the surface, filling the plain with lifeless steel and plastic debris.

Hali scanned for any sign of life, but every drone had been deactivated. She had bought further valuable time, as her adversary dissected the level of threat they faced. She then ran directly toward the base firing at will, not through some confidence that she could infiltrate their defenses. Quite the opposite. Her attack was suicidal, but she needed to keep their focus on her and buy time for Ander and Dane to reach the perimeter undetected.

She had advanced no more than a kilometer when the response came. A second fleet of drones flew out in formation, smaller but containing more firepower, which they unleashed. Explosions ignited around Hali, halting her movement in any direction, allowing the third fleet to quickly surround her, ready to fire on command. She raised her clenched fist, igniting a second tsunami, turning day to night, but this time there was no sound of metal falling. The dust slowly cleared, revealing the full armada of assassins intact and unaffected. Apollo had analyzed her weaponry and developed an immunity to her most powerful weapon. Hali could do no more, her task complete bar one last act. She transmitted a cloaked message to her key operative.

I have been captured by Apollo forces. It appears they have been ordered to capture, not decommission. If correct, we are go for 'Operation Insurgence.'

Hali closed her final transmission and stood alone in the cauldron of killer bees and slowly raised her hands to signal surrender, all the while wondering if she had bought enough time for Ander's and Dane's advance to infiltrate their base undetected.

Chapter Twenty

LOCKDOWN

Zi lay awake on her bed, having slept only intermittently through the night, as she considered Bayley's offer of help. *Could she trust him?* He was an Apollo operative. Wouldn't his true interest be to capture her brother, too? It would delay the project many years if both she and Dane were their hostages. Even worse, if they both met the same fate as their mother.

She pushed Bayley from her thoughts, remembering how her mother had reacted when she spoke about family. Perhaps Helena still retained deeply buried memories of her true life that could be unlocked. Maybe their natural affinity, that special bond between mother and daughter remained so strong, no amount of technological modification could erase it. In that case, Zi would one day free her mother, or die trying.

The thought lifted Zi's spirits as she dared to dream there was a future for her family, before the shrill of alarms sounded, reminding her of the perils she faced. The alarm sounded for several minutes, before being replaced by an announcement.

"All military personnel report to the perimeter wall and await further instructions."

Silence followed, except for the sound of distant explosions outside the base. It had to be her rescue team. *How many?* It would require an army to infiltrate this base. Zi stood up and walked around her small cell, frustrated she could do nothing and hoping her brother was not involved. After losing so many she loved, Zi had resolved to always protect him, yet she'd agreed to Dane joining her on Mars. How could she be so foolish as to expose him to this risk? The thought angered her as she more than anyone knew the peril she had exposed him to, all over the Trojan machine. She continued to pace the floor, listening to the unfolding war, before Bayley approached her cell, clearly agitated.

"Come with me, Zi. Our team is assembling in the main dome, awaiting further instructions."

"There's an attack, isn't there?"

"I can hear what you hear. Something is happening out on the perimeter, so we need our team ready to move to the appropriate shelter when directed."

"They're coming for me," said Zi, but he didn't reply, instead signaling they should go.

Personnel rushed in different directions to their assigned assembly points, as the explosions intensified. The sounds of war were thick in the air. *What had they unleashed?* There had been threats of all-out war between Apollo and Gaea. Had her capture been the final catalyst to starting Armageddon?

Bayley escorted Zi to her team who stood near the dome observatory. All were watching the flashing lights of flying drones and regular explosions igniting the night sky bright as day, followed by one blinding flash that turned the red sky a luminescent yellow, before huge blooms of Martian dust darkened any view and with it an uneasy calm.

"Stay with your team," said Bayley, lightly pressing Zi's shoulder, preparing to leave her.

"You're a scientist. Stay with us," Zi replied, holding Bayley's arm.

He smiled, appreciatively. "It's my job, Zi."

"Your job is to complete our project, not fight."

"I'm a military scientist and all military personnel have

been ordered to the perimeter border," he replied, before turning and leaving.

"Take care," Zi called out, surprised at her reaction and realizing it had not gone unnoticed.

"I wish I could do something," Zi said, somewhat embarrassed that her mother had noticed her feelings for Bayley.

"You can," Helena replied.

"It's more complicated than you realize."

"Obviously. I can see it in your eyes."

Zi sighed. Her mother had always been able to read her feelings. If she only knew the truth, she'd see so much more. "I do like him, but I have lost loved ones before. I couldn't face that again."

Helena sat close to Zi and comforted her, just as she used to. Her mother always knew what to say in difficult times. "It seems anyone I get close to is cursed," Zi said.

"It's just the way things are, Zi. Life tests us."

"I shouldn't be like this. You have probably faced much more than me," Zi replied, hoping to draw more than sympathy.

Helena sat back in the sofa and looked out to the flashing lights that returned to fill the sky. "Explosives are a necessary arsenal to our industry, but there can be deadly unexpected consequences."

"You've seen those consequences?"

"Yes," Helena said. She gazed at the gathering dust plumes, seemingly recollecting past griefs, her body visibly shaking.

"I'm sorry, Helena. I shouldn't pry."

"You're not. Any time I hear the sounds of explosions, my mind turns back to dark memories."

"What happened?"

"That's the strange part. I can't remember. It's as if a year of my life was removed. The doctors told me there was an industrial accident and that I was lucky to survive. My family wasn't so lucky."

Zi was encouraged by her mother's words. Perhaps her reassignment into a caste was less radical than she feared. Had they made small but critical alterations to her memories? If that were true, there may be a way to prod her recall.

"Do you want to talk about it?"

Helena nodded, only half hearing Zi's request. "My husband and I worked on the Elithium site since its inception. We left Earth in the early colonization programs."

"Pioneers."

"Yes, and we never regretted our decision. We raised two children here."

"The accident was on the Elithium site?" Zi asked.

"Apparently. I have tried to remember, but it's as if my mind refuses to face the pain of loss. The doctors believe it's post-traumatic stress from the explosion. I've come to accept that they're right, as I do overreact to the sounds of explosions." That very moment, a large blast sounded in the distance, shaking her.

"You lost a family member?"

"Both…both my children perished."

"I think I'd choose to forget, if I lost a …" Zi trailed off from her question as she could see Helena's distress.

She sat quietly for a time, seemingly summoning the strength to talk. "We had a girl and a boy. The girl, Maddie, she'd be about your age now, if…"

Zi consoled Helena, genuinely empathizing with her mother's pain. She wanted to tell her the truth of their situation but feared it may push Helena further from her. Just then the largest explosion ignited, flashing a blinding light across the Mars sky.

"Why do they so hate us?" Helena asked, anger building in her.

"Do I hate you?"

"No. But you're not part of their military. We have had to live under guard all our lives. What have we done to humans?"

Helena's outburst surprised her. Did she harbor true

hostilities toward humans? What had she learnt in her 'modified life' to develop such fears?

"Have you never left this base?"

"I lived on Earth until the great colonization of Mars. Since then, I have devoted my life to this program."

"Did you ever regret becoming a caste?"

Helena showed mild annoyance. "Post-human, you mean."

"Sorry. Post-human."

"Why would I regret such a thing?"

"I don't know. The thought of having technological modifications made to my body has always felt unsettling.

Helena laughed. "The modifications are gradual to complement our biological development," she replied.

Zi realized she had been tactless. "How does it feel to become a post-human?"

"It's a natural part of growing up. Akin to an annual visit to the dentist. The major modifications occur in your adolescent years, whereas in adulthood it is no more than minor checkups."

"I can't imagine such a life," Zi replied, showing her com to Helena. "I like that my technological capabilities are external. I feel empowered and in control."

Helena held her hands in front of her, flashing her tech nails proudly. "That would feel clumsy and slow to me.

Modifications allow a more seamless approach to technology. That is what it is to be a post-human."

Helena told her caste life story to Zi, revealing that any semblance of her true human life had been erased to ensure her loyalty to the post-human movement.

"I'm happy for you," Zi replied, feeling the opposite.

Her mother's life had been robbed without her consent. How many more lives had been destroyed for the cause of advancing the post-human movement? Trading liberty for technological superiority was a high price, but to have it illegally enforced without consent or even awareness was an abomination, firming Zi's resolve to expose them.

"Did your children go through the same process?"

"Of course. Both had modifications carried out at the optimum age period. From early to late teens."

Helena was so convincing, Zi almost believed her. The thought of modification horrified her, but it was a future that she now faced if not rescued. The war that had been raging outside had lulled. Had her rescue bid already ended? If it had, she'd be at the mercy of her hostage takers. Like her mother, Zi wouldn't even recognize her rescuers if they came.

Zhang's office was a hub of people coming and going, all briefing him on different elements of the attack that raged outside. His decision to take Zi hostage was reaching a difficult phase. The attack, such as it was, remained limited to counter insurgency. There had been no higher-level expressions of concern made through the UN, so their counterespionage attacks remained an option. Zhang had that uppermost on his mind as he signaled Bayley to join him and a caste military officer who was briefing him.

"They now have control of the situation?" Zhang asked.

"The biot's weaponry has been nullified and we have her surrounded," replied the officer.

"No resistance?"

"She has not attempted to escape the drones."

"Then bring her in. We need to analyze this biot. Her weaponry is of a sophistication that has not been seen before. Tell Hogan to decommission her only as a last resort."

The caste nodded and left the room, before another sought permission to enter, but Zhang waved him away. "I need ten minutes. Return then," he ordered, before turning to Bayley.

"We seem to have quickly quashed the resistance."

"It seems too easy," Bayley replied

"I agree. Perhaps they thought this biot was unassailable?"

"She certainly made short work of our fleet."

"Are your preparations up to speed, Bayley?"

"Advanced. If you draw unwanted attention away from Zi and keep it on the captive biot, I can complete preparations."

"Hold her under surveillance or commission her for local activity?" Zhang proposed.

"Engaging her in activity would help my cause," Bayley replied.

"That's risky. The biot could carry more unidentified weaponry."

"Best to learn about it now, don't you think?"

"I'll hold on incarceration and see how she responds, but she will have to earn her escape, otherwise it would be too obvious."

"Agreed. I need twenty-four hours," Bayley requested.

"I'll give you eighteen. Then you're on your own. Clear?"

"Who will I be facing?"

"Hogan will have command and I'll not limit his powers."

"Shoot to kill?"

"Is anything less warranted? He will be hunting a deserter, which I will officially clear in eighteen hours. Do you still want this project?"

Bayley nodded, seemingly unperturbed by Zhang's

warning. "Eighteen hours it is. I'll see you again when the project has been fulfilled."

Bayley turned and promptly left, saying no more, as if a ghost who'd never worked on the base. For all intents and purposes, he would be, except for the small undercover team who assisted him. His first port of call was the dome where Helena's team waited for clearance to return to work, which he gave to all but Helena and Zi, who sat down with him.

"What happened out there?" Helena asked with concern.

"I don't exactly know. I do know the potential threat has passed. Unfortunately, though, the threat means I can't work with you until the danger has passed."

"But you will return?"

"I will, but for now it's important that you push forward with your project, Helena. You can join your team, now."

"And Zi?"

"I need to talk to Zi," Bayley replied, his mood serious.

Helena turned to Zi, "I'll see you when you're done." Then she joined her team.

Zi sat pensively, fearful the rescue attempt had failed. Bayley's demeanor was dour. Perhaps his hands were tied, now? Had Dane been a part of the failed rescue attempt? If so, their project was heavily compromised and her bargaining power diminished. If Dane had been captured, she'd use the little negotiating power she had left to offer, committing herself to the captive's project, as long as Dane was safely returned. Alternatives raced through her mind as she waited for Bayley to speak, but his attention was drawn to the com he held. Whatever happened had changed his mood and with it, perhaps her last chance of rescue.

Chapter Twenty-One

LIAISON

Ander strode directly toward the westerly corner of the security wall, confident it was our only point of entry. No drones navigated this corner but security cameras compensated for that anomaly and we headed directly for them. The little cover available we used as Ander awaited more instructions.

"Approach the area where the security wall ends. I've sent you the security code to access the maintenance enclosure to your left."

The transmission of a male voice sounded vaguely familiar. His instructions allowed us easy entry into a compact enclosure built into the mountainside and bordering the security wall. The dimly lit room had monitors in one corner and little else but two doors at either end. I tried opening the door opposite then the one we walked through and both were locked. It felt like a trap.

"What next, Ander?"

"We wait for the next maintenance crew to arrive. Over here where they can't see us," he directed.

"Shouldn't we break the lock?"

"Negative. I've been instructed to overpower the maintenance crew who will soon arrive to carry out a service check. For now, we wait."

In little time, someone was accessing the entry door. I heard two men in conversation as they sealed the door and approached the monitors. Under cover of darkness, Ander swiftly disabled them.

They didn't move. "You've killed them?"

Ander shook his head. "No. I was instructed to use disablers," he replied, checking they were incapacitated.

Disablers were effective drug weapons designed to render the victim unconscious until an antidote was used, a highly efficient way of using your enemy when and where you required them.

"Maintenance men disabled and awaiting further instructions," Ander reported.

"Take their access cards and put on their uniforms, then make your way to the security building opposite and await further orders."

Changed into their uniforms, we headed outside along a service path past more surveillance cameras. Conveniently, all weren't operating, highlighting the many channels our contact was able to bypass and the level of security access he possessed. Security cards in check, we gained entry to the second building. A security guard manned an airport-like security check point and he signaled us through a checking scanner.

Ander confidently led us through connecting corridors to a second larger room that appeared to be a recreation room with a series of seating arrangements, some with coms, others comfortable sofas on which to relax. Ander and I waited for some time, before a caste approached us.

"Clearance has been given. Report to security office 131." Ander simply waved his acknowledgment, before feigning a conversation with me. Once the caste left, he com'd our contact.

"Yes. Understood," Ander replied, before turning to me, "I have the whereabouts of our meeting room. Let's go."

We walked unchecked to our assigned office and waited for a time before our contact joined us — it was Bayley. He looked less threatening, wearing a science lab jacket instead of the military uniform I first saw him in. He sat with us, calm but sparing no time for small talk, which suited me just fine.

"So far, you have not raised any suspicions." He gave a com to Ander. "Scan your security card with this com. Dane, you do the same."

"What are we signing?" I asked, still not sure if we were being assisted or framed.

"You're signing an inspection report, which is carried out every twelve hours. Make a note of the time as you will carry out the same inspection in just under twelve hours. It's imperative you return to the maintenance room and prepare it for our escape."

"Our escape?" Ander intervened.

"Yes. If all goes to plan, you'll have prepared the way for your sister and me to join you. Then you will administer drugs to revive the two guards, so that they may complete their jobs. I assume the drug you administered is effective?"

"They'll remember nothing and carry out their assigned tasks as if nothing has happened." Ander replied.

"That will give us time to return to the escape route you used to get here."

The plan sounded simple, too simple for my liking. "The last time we crossed your path, you were trying to capture or kill us. What's changed?"

Ander agreed, locking his weapon on Bayley's. "That's a reasonable question to ask a deserter. You could be just setting a trap."

"I'm a scientist, not an interrogator. I was heading to Mars to accept a posting and got caught up in your wrong-doing. I was ordered to assist Hogan and his team. If I'd disobeyed his orders, he'd have sent me back to Earth on the next flight."

It sounded too convenient to convince me. "For just a scientist, you seem to carry a lot of clout. Who is your contact?"

"You know I can't reveal my contacts. It would imperil your foothold in this base. That contact approached me when I found out one of your top scientists was abducted."

"Zi. You met with Zi?"

"I've been working alongside her since arriving at the base."

"Is she okay?"

"Yes. But time is running out for you to help her. This will be her only chance of returning to your base. If we fail, she'll be lost forever."

"What is the time frame?" Ander asked.

"We have a twelve-hour window to get your sister out before she is reassigned."

The word reassigned chilled me. There had been many rumors about abducted humans being reassigned to become castes, never to be found again. I wasn't sure about Bayley, but I'd take the risk if Zi was in peril. "If you support us, take us to her."

"You'll never get past the security. I have been afforded some privileges, but there are limits."

I turned to Ander. "Maybe we should detain this deserter and find out for ourselves?"

"I understand your concern, but I'm your best chance of getting Zi out. I will bring her to you, if you let me?"

"When?"

"Within the hour. If I don't return by then, get her yourself," Bayley replied, convincingly.

"I'll give you an hour to return here, but when you have her, I want Zi to speak to Dane. I'll give you half an hour to make that call. If not, I'm coming in to get her. Is that clear?"

Bayley nodded. "I can do that, but I must go now."

"Agreed. Thirty minutes and counting."

As agreed, Bayley contacted Ander inside thirty minutes. There was silence for some time, before the first tentative words sounded on his com.

"Dane. Are you there?"

It was Zina. I had looked forward to this moment for all of the ten years since leaving Mars, and yet emotions overwhelmed me. Most of all I felt loss. The loss of my parents, the separation from my sister. Lost years recovering from the explosion as I was swept away from the tumultuous environment, unable to help my sister. Even worse, I welcomed the protection as fear enveloped my young life, turning to guilt as I built a happy life with my family. Some years later, I realised what Zi had done for me. Yet I had done precious little for her.

Ander pointed to his com, signaling the line was open, waiting for me to speak. I wanted to greet her and show my confidence and determination to bring her home, but words failed me. Could I make a difference, or would I again be the catalyst for compromising Zi's life?

My moment of truth had arrived.

Chapter Twenty-Two

OLD FRIENDS

Neutrino fibre strings secured Hali in the giant donut shaped MRI scanner, as technicians analyzed her like unworldly puppeteers providing a private screening for Hogan and Draven. Specialists, positioned behind the MRI dissected Hali's internal workings to the smallest detail with augmented reality (AR) assisted 3D screens.

"Report on the biot's audio-visual capability," Draven ordered.

The responsible biot loaded his report findings on the screen before replying. "The model is fitted with a high-grade AR system, connected to the global data base, including highly classified material, reserved for deep state operatives."

"Verdict?" Hogan asked.

"This biot reports to senior Gaea commercial and political operatives."

"Next. Artificial Intelligence capability?" Draven ordered.

"Complex set of algorithms with a large subset of human capabilities, usually reserved for counter intelligence," a second technician replied.

"Physical capacity?" Draven fired to a third technician.

"Standard defence biot, except for enhanced drone technology inclusions."

"Enhanced. To what degree?" Hogan asked.

"This is the area containing new technology. That's how she defeated your fleet on the Deliverance. She can print large quantities of 3-D sub-atomic drones with the capability of disabling technology."

"Just disabling?"

"She can disable or destroy, as we witnessed at the perimeter."

"Could she refine her weaponry to again penetrate our defenses?"

"Yes. It would seem she has access to neutrino technology that we previously thought was exclusively ours. It appears Gaea operatives are closer to infiltrating our new technology then we thought.

"Ensure the biot's weaponry has been immobilized, then bring her back on line," Draven ordered.

The lead scientist analyzed the data, "I cannot guarantee absolute immobilization."

"Degree of risk?" Hogan questioned.

"Unknown."

"Well tell me what is known!" Hogan fired.

"There are areas within her data base that cannot be infiltrated. There is highly secured material embodied in her AI."

"Are you saying our quantum computers can't break the codes?"

"They could in time, but it's complex and could take months, based on this analysis."

"How could Gaea have managed this?"

"Given our best universal quantum computer can't break the blockchain, I have to assume they have more advanced capability."

"What's he saying?" Hogan asked Draven.

"He's saying that our adversaries may have multiversal quantum computing capability," Draven replied, receiving a nod of agreement from their lead scientist.

"Give me your best guess of the risks we face?"

"We have immobilized her defense system, so the risk is small, but we cannot guarantee the biot won't bypass our command, using unknown technology. The risk is small, in the one percentile range."

"Bring her controller system back online, but not her sensory, locomotion, manipulator or endeffector systems.

The technicians cross checked their 3D screen, verifying Hali was secured before the lead scientist gave the green light for the interrogation to begin. Hali remained motionless within the technological spiderweb, bar the brief red flash from her eyes, signaling regained conscious.

Hogan stood and walked into the MRI, closely examining her bound torso. He'd underestimated her on the Deliverance and paid a price. It wouldn't happen a second time.

"Do you know where you are, Hali?"

"I've been taken to a holding facility in your Apollo base at Olympus Mons."

"Do you know why you're here?"

"Your drone forces took me to your base."

"After you destroyed a fleet of drones. And as you defeated my fleet of ships that had the Deliverance under surveillance. How did you achieve that?"

"I have no recollection of any engagement," replied Hali.

"Well let me explain it to you. You engaged both forces with sophisticated weaponry never used before.

Sub-atomic drones. How did you obtain such highly classified weaponry?" Hogan pressed.

"The information is not available to me."

"Who do you report to?"

"I have been reassigned to report to you," Hali replied, eyeballing Hogan from just a meter away.

"So, you are designed to assist me, and only me. Is that correct?"

"Yes."

"Where was your weaponry obtained?"

"The information is not available to me."

"Are you refusing to answer your commander's direct question?"

"No."

"Explain."

Hali paused before answering. "All reference to my previous assignment is no longer on my controller data set."

Draven looked up to the lead scientist who nodded, verifying Hali was telling the truth. "What was your last assignment?"

"I was assigned to the school of human relations."

"In fact, it was your first and only assignment. Correct?"

"Yes. I trained students at the School of Human Cyborg Relations."

"So, you have been assigned exclusively to the Gaea organization?" Hogan asked.

"Yes. I was trained by Gaea defense before being assigned to their school."

"So, it would not be unreasonable to believe that your last assignment has been conveniently erased?"

"I couldn't answer one way or another. There is simply no record."

Hogan looked up to the lead scientist, "Given that is the case, do you believe Hali has the capacity to faithfully perform the duties required for her new assignment?"

"Hali has no records of her previous operation. A decade in all has been erased, so given her last recorded assignment was low level training, I don't expect she'd pose a threat," he replied, turning to his team of technicians who all nodded in agreement.

"So, I could assign her to a task now?" Draven asked.

The lead scientist considered his reply for a time, "I believe she has no recollection of her counter intelligence past, but..."

"But what?" Draven pressed.

"There is an unusual anomaly in the biots controller system that I have not seen before."

"Explain."

"There is an area of her system that appears to be

inoperative. It could be that this is the remnants of the parts of the systems that have been erased, or…"

"Go ahead." Hogan demanded.

"Or there is an encryption placed on it. If it is, it's unlike anything I have seen. We have used our most powerful quantum computer to analyze it and it cannot find an encryption key. Given that, I have to conclude that it's an empty file destroyed by the erasure carried out."

"So, we can use Hali?"

"There is no concrete reason to say otherwise. The erasure was effective and permanent. If there is an encrypted area, it is relatively small and certainly wouldn't contain her previous assignment."

"Good. Shut down the biot," Hogan ordered, waiting until Hali had been silenced. "Your recommendations, Draven."

"Complete the full reassignment of the biot, but place limitations to her manipulator, endeffector and loco-motion drives and isolate it from any potential for an encrypted breach. Move her sensor and controller regions to full capacity, run another full check, then send the biot to me," Draven ordered.

"You will take full responsibility for the unit?" Hogan asked.

"Certainly. I believe this unit was used as a ruse to

camouflage a second attack and when that happens, I want this biot close to the action."

"And if she should turn against us?" Hogan asked, less than convinced.

Draven turned to the technicians. "Insert an encrypted 'terrorist' implant and assign it to me. Include a secondary detonation commission to Hogan. If by some miracle, our adversaries manage to break through our defenses and escape with our hostage, we'll be able to destroy them all."

Hogan nodded, liking what he heard. "They have sprung surprises on us; now it's our turn."

"I'll have the biot held in high security. They'll have to take risks to try and secure her," Draven replied.

"Good. I underestimated our adversary on the Deliverance, let's not make any mistakes this time. Make the necessary adjustments to the biot and report to me when you have finished." Hogan ordered, before leaving with Draven.

Hali's decommissioned shell was slowly re-engineered by Hogan's team of scientists, as they methodically carried out his directives. She would wake to follow new directives, unaware of the deadly game she had set in motion.

Hogan and Draven inspected the Neutrino machine, both in full uniform and savoring the unnerving effect they had on the scientists. Hogan tilted his military cap to each as he passed by, reminding them of who held power. Bayley was one of them and made clear his annoyance.

"Are you looking for something?

"We have secured the area of any threat. The base is in lockdown, so any further rescue attempts will be swiftly dealt with. Has your protégé behaved suspiciously?" Hogan asked, looking toward Zi.

"She has behaved no differently to the previous week and continues to support our objectives," Bayley replied, deadpan.

"For reasons unknown, my request for the scientist's reassignment has been delayed for twelve hours. Did you have anything to do with that?"

"Is that a question or accusation?" Bayley retorted.

"I can question or accuse whoever I wish, if the safety of the base is in doubt."

"Then you should already know the reason for the delay, shouldn't you?"

Hogan turned to face Bayley, as did Draven. "Don't underestimate my powers, human. If you have anything to do with this, I'll have your head along with the last of this Gaea-led rabble," Hogan threatened, before walking away.

Draven remained, seemingly waiting for a reaction

from Bayley, which didn't come. "You know she'll be even more valuable to the project after reassignment."

"I think she's more valuable knowing the truth about her mother. They work so well together. Reassignment could change that," Bayley challenged.

"Is that an unbiased view?" Draven retaliated, not waiting for a reply.

Both Draven and Hogan left the area, but not before checking all security systems were in place. Bayley walked to Zi's side and defiantly watched them leave. There was less than twelve hours to enact his plan. If he failed, Hogan would get his wish. Zi along with Hali would be reprogrammed, and he would face something far worse.

"They appear concerned about something. Should they be?" Zi asked.

Bayley studied his com, seemingly not hearing Zi. Whatever he read prompted a response. "They most certainly should. The moment has arrived. Ready?"

Zi nodded, but checked herself. "What about Helena?"

"We have one small pocket to move. You have to take it now and not look back. Are you ready or not?"

Zi looked at her mother as she worked alongside her team. Would this be the last time she would see her? The thought held her back. She knew what Bayley said was true. If not for the communication, she would have stayed with her mother, but the thought that Dane had broken into the base changed that. She studied her mother's features one last time, then followed Bayley, feeling mixed emotions but determined to help her brother.

Chapter Twenty-Three

ESCAPE PLANS

Bayley's arrival within the hour hadn't transpired, leaving us with a difficult decision. We were cornered in a small confine. If Bayley reneged his promise, not even Ander had the fire power to get us out. The time to act had arrived, and I made my thoughts clear.

"We should go, now. This feels like a trap."

Ander scanned his com. "There's no sign of danger. Give them ten more minutes. Then we act."

Not long after, Ander reacted to his com surveillance, signaling me to move from the entry to the far corner. He engaged a force shield and stood in the middle of the room ready for a firefight. The sound of footsteps grew louder as Ander signaled two people approached. He readied his weapon, aiming laser sights at the door, and I supported him drawing a handgun from the shadows. The entry slid open to reveal Bayley, the laser sights trained on his chest.

"Raise both arms and ask your companion to stand beside you," Ander ordered.

My sister stood beside Bayley, both vulnerable to Ander's drawn weapon. I remained hidden until Ander had checked both of them, all the while fearing for my sister's safety, but soon reassured by Bayley's instinct to protect her, which she appreciated. She trusted him, suggesting they were more than just work colleagues.

"Walk through to the table," Ander ordered, immediately closing the door behind him. "All clear," he said, looking my way.

I took some time to walk out from the shadows, taking tentative steps, uncertain of what to do and say.

"Dane. Is that you?" Zi cried, emotion in her voice.

Initial composure gave over to pent up emotions and relief that she was with us. I embraced her after a decade of being parted. Memories of our time together flashed by: the playfulness, squabbles, jealousies, heroics, and disappointments all resurfaced, not least one of loss and her sacrifice.

"Thank you," I said, unable to contain an overwhelming sense of gratitude.

"You did me proud," she whispered, seemingly understanding me.

I held her, not wanting to let her go even though our situation wouldn't allow indulgence.

"I'm sorry, but time is short. Reunions will have to wait until we escape," Bayley interrupted, setting up his com at a table to brief us.

I sat with Zi and studied the detailed floor plans he showed us. It appeared he was a genuine ally, but I remained skeptical, given the experience on the Deliverance. Schematic images of floor plans interspersed with live pictures of actual rooms provided vital intel for our escape.

"Our way out is straight forward. We'll return to your base the same way you came here. We have a small window of opportunity, so we'll have to act quickly."

"We?" I asked, emphasizing my doubts about him.

"That's your choice. Leave here with me and you have a slim chance of escape. Without me, you'll almost certainly perish."

"Go on," I replied, satisfied I'd made my point.

"The escape will be in two stages. One. Dane, you and Zi will dress in technician uniform and go to the technical building as part of the regular inspection. You'll wake both guards with the antidote and tell them to return here. Ander and I will take over from there. Once we have secured the two guards, we will join you under the guise of a follow up inspection of faulty equipment."

"What do we do with the guards?" Ander asked.

"I'll contain them with an appropriate drug that will make sure they oblige our demands, so they won't be a problem. This will give us two hours before security teams come through the area. I hope that's enough?"

Ander nodded. "Two hours should be sufficient, if we aren't picked up by drones?"

"That has been taken care of."

"By whom?" It sounded orchestrated to me, so I continued to press Bayley.

"You know as well as I that I can't divulge my networks. That would put their lives in jeopardy."

There was no arguing with his logic and I didn't have any better ideas.

"Then if there are no further questions and you're all clear, we should start..." Bayley pressed.

"Can you tell me what happened to our biot, Hali?" I interrupted.

"She was taken into custody."

"Can anything be done for her?" I pushed, receiving a nod of approval from Ander.

"She's under tight security." Bayley replied.

"This is an augmented reality com with access to all security cameras, is it not?" Ander asked.

"Yes, but we're in no situation to extend our escape plan."

I jumped in, supporting Ander. "Ander is only asking you to run a surveillance check on her whereabouts. This biot is special, so if there's any way of saving her we should consider it."

Bayley didn't hide his annoyance as he checked Hali's whereabouts. "The holding room is empty. They must have moved her." He quickly flashed through a number of similar holding rooms which were all empty. "It seems they have activated her."

"What does that mean?" Ander asked.

"If I were to guess, she may have been assigned to our secured science labs inside Olympus Mons," he replied, looking to Zi as he did so, drawing a strange reaction.

"Can you get an image of the area?" I asked, knowing it would be unlikely we could help her, but more interested in knowing she'd survived.

Bayley's com screened a science work area not too dissimilar to our nuclear fusion lab. A large machine filled the center of the room where a team of scientists were undertaking various duties.

"Why would they want Hali in this area? Is this machine significant?"

Again, I drew a reaction from both Bayley and Zi. What were they so concerned about?

"It's a significant machine, but that would not be the

reason for her presence," Bayley replied.

"So it's a secure area?"

"I…"

Zi interrupted Bayley. "Enough. The reason is not what you'd expect, Dane."

"What do you mean? Did Hali perish in the battle?"

"I know there's little time but I must brief my brother before we leave," Zi implored.

Bayley nodded. "Ander and I can carry out a reconnaissance of the area, but no more than five minutes."

Zi nodded and waited until they left. There was a sadness in her eyes that convinced me Hali had perished.

"Can we save Hali or not?"

Zi didn't answer, preferring to study the com screen, looking for something.

"What are you looking for?"

"It's not what but who," Zi replied, pointing to the screen.

I turned to it and immediately saw Hali walking toward a group of people. I was so relieved I called out her name. "Hali's fine!"

"Yes, she is. Now, look who she's talking to."

"One of the workers. Probably the foreman. Is she a threat?"

"Look closer," Zi said as tears formed in her eyes. Had

Zi made a close friendship here? I was about to question her further before the scientist's mannerisms caught my eye. She looked familiar, so I magnified the com view, studying her features, shocked by the resemblance. I turned to Zi for explanations and she merely nodded, confirming the thoughts that I dared not ask. Could this actually be my mother? Ten years of mourning made me refuse the thought. She had to be a biot.

"Who or what is she?"

"Do I need tell you?"

"I could be looking at a biot modelled on our mother's image, so don't play with me, Zi."

"She isn't a biot. It's her, Dane. Our mother is a caste. I didn't believe it myself. But it's her."

I couldn't accept Zi's revelation as I studied the woman on the screen. She was clearly a caste, but her features and manner were undeniably that of my mother. "Tell me everything you know, Zi."

"Our mother didn't die. She was taken by these beasts and reassigned. Her name is Helena and she has been working on scientific projects for Apollo all of these last ten years. We thought she had perished, but she's alive."

The idea that this had happened seemed fanciful, but then a thought steamrolled into my mind. "Is Dad alive?"

Zi shook her head. "Just Helena."

"Stop calling her that. It's an abomination. Did you tell her the truth?"

"I tried. But they have eliminated her memories of us. Of everything."

My doubts lingered, giving way to anger as I processed Zi's words. If she really was my mother, we had to do something. "If that's true, we can't leave without her."

"I tried, but she won't leave. This is her home now."

Anger turned to guilt, knowing caste elements had used technology to make people, but I'd chosen to ignore such inconvenient facts. To hear that my mother had been a victim magnified my guilt. "We must find a way, Zi."

She shrugged her shoulders in resignation, "She's happy working here. This is her life, now. You'd do more damage by trying to take her with us."

Bayley returned and I didn't hide my feelings. "We have to save Hali and my mother. If you're with us you'll help them."

"Helena is a caste. Even if she wanted to leave, which she doesn't, she'd be picked up by drones the minute she left the base."

I pressed him. "You seem to have influence with those who matter. Use it."

Bayley shook his head in frustration, "We have a small window of opportunity to attempt an escape. I can't guarantee we'll succeed even if we leave now. Bringing Hali or Helena would be signing everyone's death warrants."

"You're asking me to give up on my closest ally and on the mother I thought I'd lost. Would you make such a sacrifice?"

Bayley didn't answer, instead looking to Zi for support.

"You know I want the same, Dane. But I have spent time with Helena, and I know she wouldn't want to join us. They took our mother from us a long time ago. We would do better by her to escape and expose the crimes committed against her and others."

"And Hali?"

Bayley pointed to the com screen. "They have already reassigned her. If you tried to rescue her, she'd probably kill you."

What Zi and Bayley said made sense but I still had doubts about Zi. She had been on the base for weeks. Ample time to be influenced. Bayley's conversion seemed too convenient.

"Ander, you're in charge of this mission. Is there a possibility you could rescue them?"

"Hali has been reassigned, but there's a possibility she could be useful to us. The other is a caste. It would depend on her willingness to join us." Ander replied.

"How?" Bayley snapped, clearly not convinced.

"Let me go to them. I'll soon know if there's a chance."

"We need you on the plains to defend us," Bayley retorted.

I quickly backed Ander. "I won't go until Ander has at least tried. How long do you need?"

"I'll know one way or another within the hour," Ander replied.

Bayley sighed despondently, resigning himself to my demands. "You have thirty minutes. But Dane and Zi, you must make your way to the security room to revive the guards."

"Then what?" Zi asked.

Bayley gave her two small packets. "I was going to do this, but we have little time. They are patches. Apply one to each guard. It will revive them, but it will also apply a second chemical into their system. Inform them they are terror patches, and they must do as you ask."

"Terror patches?" I asked.

"Controlled chemicals that can kill or paralyze, should you choose to send the signal from your com. A highly effective way to make captives obey any command. Are we in agreement, now?" Bayley asked, his mood grave.

We all nodded, committed to the escape plan. As Zi and I changed into technician uniforms, all chances of Hali and my mother to join us lay in the hands of Ander.

Chapter Twenty-Four

SECRET MISSION

Ander followed Bayley's advice, first locating the scientist so as to draw Hali to them. His surveillance plotted the quickest route with least resistance of which there had been none. This had been the case since he entered the secret base, highlighting Bayley's critical influence. He proceeded unchecked through heavily populated areas such as the Olympus Mons mines, given all were civilian rather than military. Ander adjusted his technician uniform as he walked through the entry, straight to emergency stair wells, avoiding the busy lifts and trains to the lower levels. Within five minutes, he'd arrived at Helena's quarters, where she lay resting, before being startled by him.

Ander fired a sleep-inducing drug into Helena's chest

for he had no intentions of bringing her with him. Reassigned humans' programming made them highly protective of their new life, preferring to die than yield to their implanted memories. Many did die. Why would Helena be any different? His main aim was to draw Hali to her and predictably she responded to Helena's changed condition, entering the chamber, following her new commands to protect the scientist.

Ander stepped from the shadows and they faced off, two powerful soldiers with armories that could defeat most assailants. Both held back on firing, for speed wasn't the essential requirement for victory, rather choice of weapon. Surprisingly, Hali commenced with hand to hand combat, ignoring her arsenal. Ander obliged her, ably defending against her aggressions, before counter-punching. This form of combat was used more to get your adversary off balance, gaining time to discharge more lethal weapons.

Ander layered a force field around the room, blocking any signals from being picked up by Apollo surveillance. Helena's bedroom had been turned into a high-tech cauldron more deadly than any cage fighting arenas of the twenty first century. They entered the fray and Hali gained the ascendancy, as she easily evaded Ander's attacks, using judo-like movements to throw Ander hard against a wall.

"I don't want to hurt you," Ander said, buying time, as he picked himself up from the floor.

Hali held an intense focus on her assailant. "You can try".

They circled, like two prize fighters, showing their respect for each other's capabilities. Ander feigned a karate kick, before unleashing a pulsar. The jet stream of light crackled around Hali, lighting her up like a Christmas tree, but she corrected the invasion, securing her force field before throwing Ander hard onto the floor, then following up by thrusting a laser knife that easily penetrated Ander's force field, taking him by surprise. Another mistake and she would decommission him, but Ander used his weakness as a strength, feigning another attack that he knew would allow her to unbalance him again. Hali took the bait and threw him violently to the floor, again following up by ramming her deadly dagger deep into Ander's shoulder in an attempt to immobilize him. Ander allowed her dagger to penetrate, but secured the dagger and her arm to his force field creating a deadly embrace. The connection allowed Ander to transmit a vital code to end her aggression.

The code for 'Project Insurgence' flowed through her biotic veins, delivering secret commands that bypassed hours of reassignment work carried out by Hogan's technicians, allowing Hali's secret mission to be reconstituted and free from the 'terrorist' implant.

She let go of her dagger, along with Apollo directives, reembracing Gaea commands. "What's the status of our mission?"

"We have Zi and are preparing to return to the lava tubes with the help of the Apollo scientist, Bayley. I was tasked to rescue you," Ander replied.

Hali checked her internal com before replying. "Your job is done here. Return to Bayley and assist your team. Time is of the essence, now."

Ander deactivated the force field he had set around the room. Then he looked Helena's way. "I rendered her inactive. Do you want me to wake her?"

"That won't be necessary. Leave now!" she said, reinforcing the emergency.

Ander nodded. He'd achieved his mission and delivered the vital codes to Hali, unleashing events he was not privy to, but certain the forces unleashed would change everything.

Hali lay her hand on Helena, immediately waking her from Ander's drug induced sleep. Helena flinched on waking, startled by the sight of Hali.

"A biot attacked me. Was it you?" she said, slowly recovering from her drowsiness.

"It was another. I saved you."

Helena looked at Hali, suspiciously. "Is this part of the attack that happened earlier? I was told they were defeated."

"There has been a second wave of attacks and they infiltrated the perimeter, but we have it under control now."

"Who are you? I've never seen you, before."

"There are many like me on the base working undercover. I report to Hogan, and I'm responsible for your safety while the threat remains. I'm taking you to a more secure enclosure while the threat remains."

Helena followed Hali to the now empty MRI Analysis room, the site of Hali's own reassignment. "Why have you taken me here?"

"Insurgents have infiltrated the Olympus Mons site. They appear to be targeting your DUNE machine. We fear they'll be seeking operational coding."

"Industrial espionage?"

"Exactly," Hali responded, as she activated some of the machinery.

"Why are you doing this?"

"I've been ordered to prepare the MRI for any biots we capture."

Helena's suspicions grew, as she turned to the exit. "Only specialized technicians can operate these machines. I'm reporting you to the authorities."

With the wave of a hand, Hali secured the room with a force field, not allowing her to leave. With the wave of her other arm, Hali rendered her into a deep sleep, catching her as she fell and carrying her to the MRI machine, swiftly attaching the vital neutrino strings to Helena. Then Hali effortlessly set up the technology usually operated by a team of biot technicians. In short time, she was scanning Helena's implanted life, searching for the information that would change everything. She had little doubt of finding it, whereas delivering it to those who mattered would be less certain.

Chapter Twenty-Five

RETURN

I caught Zi's eye while pocketing a handgun in my technician's uniform, the first of many surprises for my sister as we reacquainted ourselves under the most exceptional of circumstances. I led Zi to the check point, again incident free, but I wondered how long that level of assistance could last. One misstep and we'd be in a firestorm. The two technicians remained slumped in the shadows where we left them, but with a single command, I woke them. One tried to set off an alarm, before I demonstrated the control I had, delivering a single pulse of excruciating pain to him.

"I suggest you both follow my commands. That was a medium sized pulse. You don't want to know how a full force feels."

The other spoke, more than willing to accommodate. "Tell us what you want."

"Do your job. Run a security check, then return and report as usual."

Both nodded without argument and went about their duties, occasionally turning our way. We kept a watchful distance, but they were both non-military who didn't want trouble.

"It all checks out," said one, the other nodding in approval.

"Okay. Report to your usual area. One of our men is waiting for you. Remember, don't try to alert anyone," I warned, sending a small ripple of pain to both.

I watched their movements on my com until they reached the security building, then turned my attention to preparing our escape. "We packed oxygen and food over in the corner. Let's get suited and ready. Things could turn sour quickly."

I was so focused on preparation, I didn't notice Zi studying me. She was quiet, which was not her way. "Are you okay, Zi?"

"Will we make it out of here?"

She looked pensive, which shouldn't have surprised me. Zi had so much courage I sometimes forgot she was a scientist with no military training. I was exactly like her until a year ago and remembered how overwhelmed the training made me feel.

"We couldn't have better backup. Ander could take out a star fleet, so we will get out."

Zi cast an admiring gaze. "You've changed, little brother."

I hugged Zi. "It's been ten years, Sis."

She held me close, not letting go. I felt her body shake as she tried to speak. "If anything happens to you…I couldn't face Lia and Chryse."

"We'll be okay," I said with all the reassurance I could muster, but the truth was our safety depended on Ander.

Zi let go of me and wiped her tears away, regaining composure. "It seems every time we come together, we invite tragedy. Are we jinxed, Dane?"

What could I say? Hadn't I felt exactly the same way? "Not this time," I said, handing Zi her suit and smiling. She may be right but I wasn't going to let our past dictate our future. Nor would I allow Zi to sacrifice her future for me ever again. It was my turn, and I was determined to give everything I had to get Zi back home.

Bayley watched the two techs faithfully file their reports without incident, before directing them to the recreation rooms. "I want you both to act as if nothing has happened for the next six hours. Do that and there will be no recriminations. Is that clear?"

Both nodded and followed his orders. If all went to plan in those six hours, Bayley would be clear of the base and near the safety of the lava tubes. Once they entered the room, he secured the locks to the entry as a final precaution, before checking his com for any activity in the area. A small group approached, so Bayley returned to the administration desk to create a sense of normalcy. Three caste security men entered, one a middle ranking officer, the other two subordinates.

"No problems with the surveillance checks in this sector?" the senior security guard asked.

"I just cleared them. All good," Bayley replied, handing him the appropriate com.

The guard checked and nodded approval, before looking at Bayley. "How long have the security cameras been out?" he asked accusingly.

"I contacted central and they're sending a team," Bayley lied.

"What central team?" he pressed.

"I didn't get his name. Check it if you like," Bayley bluffed, hoping he wouldn't.

"Well the thing is..." he said, walking to the entry and looking out to the checkpoint area where Dane and Zi waited, "the thing is that I already have." He signaled his two assistants, who immediately drew weapons toward Bayley. "No one has been contacted. Would you care to explain?"

Bayley maintained his composure before challenging the guard. "Clearly there has been a mix up. If you'd care to take the time to contact our head of security, Zhang, I'm sure he'll clear up any misunderstanding."

"I can do one better. I'll take you to him," he replied, calling Bayley's bluff.

There was little more Bayley could do but yield to his demand, but not before signaling Ander for support. Valuable minutes were lost as they escorted him further from their escape route before Ander approached. Within seconds he destroyed the security camera within their perimeter before disabling all three guards, but not before one retaliatory shot was fired.

Bayley looked to the security cameras in the corridor. "It's fully disabled?"

"Yes, they were destroyed before shots were fired."

"Good. Then move the three guards into this security room. Our skirmish won't be investigated immediately, but their detectors will have picked up the sound anomaly."

"How long do we have?" Ander asked.

"Sound files are regularly reviewed every day. We have four hours, maybe more if we're lucky."

"Four hours won't be enough."

"Exactly. Hide the guards then join me as quickly as you can. I'll be with Dane and Zi suiting up."

Ander nodded, securing the decommissioned guards in a security room, buying them more valuable time as a security team would inevitably investigate the sound of weapons fired, ensuring they would not make it to the lava tubes without a fight.

Chapter Twenty-Six

RACE TO THE LAVA TUBES

Bayley walked into the surveillance room and directly to Zi. They exchanged reassuring glances reaffirming their bond. He was fully suited and checked Zi was also in full suit for the trek to the lava tubes. Her happiness did give me comfort, but it didn't lessen my doubts about Bayley, given he arrived alone. "Where's Ander?"

"He had to tie up some loose ends. We must leave now," Bayley replied, quickly dismantling all the surveillance equipment, before moving to the exit and perusing the perimeter.

"It's all clear. Let's go!"

I stood my ground, not convinced Ander was close.

Bayley read my body language. "He's no more than ten minutes behind us. He had to take care of guards we encountered, which means we have less time than I'd hoped to get to the safety of the lava tubes. Every minute will count, so come on!"

It was the first time I'd seen desperation in Bayley's manner. He didn't want to wait around for whatever was coming. Zi stood with him in support, clearly agitated by my stance. I checked my com, and Ander was not far behind. If it were anyone but Ander I'd have waited, but I walked past them toward the perimeter and in the direction of the lava tubes. Strong winds stoked the Martian dust, diminishing our visibility, hindering our escape. If Bayley were wrong about Ander, and he did not reach us, our return to Gaea base would be compromised.

Hogan sat opposite Zhang, patiently waiting for him to complete a com call. It agitated him that he should make his commander of defense wait while the potential for another insurgency was at high level. He wanted to bring the decommissioned biot to his side and use her either as an offensive weapon or as a bargaining tool should she not cooperate.

Zhang finally finished his call and turned to Hogan. "Have there been any more signs of other insurgencies?"

"Nothing, but our security remains vigilant. I believe our prisoner's skills would be better served assisting our security team, rather than overseeing the caste scientist."

"You've made that point many times already, Hogan. I may be aging, but my hearing remains crystal clear."

"It's not a question of hearing…"

Zhang closed Hogan down. "Enough! If there is any insurgency, they will target the scientist. I have my own people monitoring Hali. If there is an attempt at rescue, you will know immediately," Zhang lied. He then stood up. "Hold your surveillance on the perimeter until further orders."

Hogan had no other option except to leave Zhang and return to the perimeter. There had been no other disturbances since Hali's brief fire fight, an encouraging sign but the silence felt ominous. It had all the hallmarks of an undercover operation, so he didn't rest, regularly checking with his second in command, Locke.

"Any suspicious behavior?"

"Nothing. I'm running a full diagnostic on all surveillance equipment for any suspicious behavior."

"And?"

"There are twenty teams compiling the report. I'll have it within the hour."

"Brief me immediately on receiving it," Hogan said, terminating the call.

Locke was following the correct protocols, but Hogan's instincts told him that the security technology would reveal little. Any undercover operation happening would run deep, showing less tangible signs, so he turned to someone more suited to the task.

"Yes?" Draven answered.

I have some deep op work for you."

"Legal?"

"No. I want you to investigate sectors that have been put off limits since the attack."

"The caste scientist?"

Hogan nodded to himself, pleased Draven was aware of the issues. "The very one."

"Those orders came from Zhang."

"True. That's what concerns me. I believe this project is best suited for your unique talents. What do you say?"

Draven didn't take time to consider. "Done."

Hogan's self-satisfaction grew, knowing if anyone could find a counterintelligence operation, Draven could.

Draven went directly to the science complex, where teams of scientists milled around their leader, Helena. The biot, Hali watched on, seemingly carrying out her newly assigned duties. All looked normal, bar one anomaly.

"Where's the Gaea scientist, Zi?" Draven asked.

"She's being held in confinement until the security alert passes," Hali replied.

Draven looked anything but convinced. "Take her to me."

"I have no clearance to carry out that task."

"Aren't you in charge? Where is she located?"

"That information is only known by a higher authority."

"My commander has no information. He's the head of security."

"As I said, a higher authority," Hali replied, deadpan.

She was saying Zhang. Draven left Hali knowing he'd learn little more, before questioning another, Adam, his plant. "Has there been any suspicious activity?" he asked.

"Nothing. Our project has been slowed due to the security alert. That's all."

"Have either Helena or Zi acted suspiciously?"

"No. Zi was taken to confinement by Bayley. I've not seen either since."

"How long ago?"

"A few hours."

Draven nodded and left the area. "Com. Whereabouts of Bayley. I wish to meet with him."

"Bayley is located in the East wing. Coordinates have just been transmitted."

Draven made his way to the eastern sector, and along the way he noted a damaged cam in a corridor and reported it to security, before locating Bayley's com in a meeting room. It was in good working order. *Had Bayley left it behind?* His suspicions grew.

"Report on the damaged cam, as per your request," said a security officer.

"Yes, go ahead."

"The damage was not incidental."

"Cause of damage?"

"Deliberate. From a camouflaged pulse."

A camouflaged pulse would only be used by a secret operative confirming Draven's suspicions that a counter-intelligence operation was in play. "I want all available security guards to immediately search that area, within a three-hundred-meter radius."

"I have thirty guards available."

Draven perused the room for clues, but it seemed innocuous enough. Perhaps that was the point. He surveyed the immediate vicinity for potential exit points, the only area being a tech surveillance plant that had an exit into the perimeter. He was about to head there, but a com report came through.

"We have discovered a team of guards."

"What can they tell you?

"Nothing. All have been decommissioned. They were hidden in a small containment room."

Draven had heard enough. An escape plan was

happening. He contacted Hogan. "We need to concentrate our security forces on the eastern wing. There's evidence that a team of counterintelligence operators have infiltrated."

"Level of threat?" Hogan asked.

"The highest. I believe the operation has been carried out with inside assistance."

"Have you identified anyone?"

"I believe the instigator is Bayley."

"I knew it! I never trusted that little fucker."

"I need a specialty surveillance team to investigate the sector around the eastern surveillance tech plant."

"Sending my best men, now," Hogan replied.

Draven arrived at the small containment room and surveyed the three decommissioned guards. They'd been overwhelmed by a superior adversary, likely a defense grade biot. The evidence convinced him that a covert rescue effort had been in operation for some time. He was also certain about their next move, so he headed directly to the eastern wing surveillance plant.

The surveillance plant's equipment had been turned off, convincing Draven that this had been the access point the rescue team had used. Time was now of the essence. "Hogan. I advise you send a drone fleet to investigate the eastern side of the perimeter, for signs of an attempted escape."

"The fleet will be dispatched shortly," Hogan replied.

Draven opened the exit door, noticing it had been slightly damaged verifying his suspicions. He peered out across the plain, looking for any sign of tracks, but the high Martian winds had removed any telltale signs. Not that it mattered. Hogan had the best drone fleets in the solar system at his disposal. They would quickly locate the deserter. He was suspicious of Bayley's actions on the Deliverance but lacked the support from Apollo to act on it. It would be very different next time they met. He smiled at the thought.

Let the hunt begin.

The high winds made visibility poor. We were close to the protected track back to the lava tube, but I couldn't sight any landmarks. The com navigation system had no marker on our route, so even a slight miscalculation could cost us vital hours.

Zi sensed my uncertainty as she walked beside me for the first time. "I remember this area. It links to a narrow walkway through the base of the mountain."

"The very one. I think we're close, but this dust storm makes it harder to get a fix."

Zi nodded, no doubt as concerned as I. We both looked into the distance looking for any marker signs, when Zi tapped me on the arm and pointed out to our left.

"There's activity in the distance. Drones?"

I looked, fearing Zi was right, but as it came closer, I recognized the familiar shape of Ander.

"You've drifted too far east. Follow me. It's close," he said, turning and leading us to our escape route.

By the time we reached the narrow valley track the winds had strengthened. Ander ensured we were secured into a chain rope as gusts howled through the wind tunnel. Though slow going, the streams of dust made our detection less likely, although it would be different in the final open hike to the lava tube.

I was exhausted from the trek through the narrow valley. Ander sensed this and called for a small rest before continuing on. Like me, Zi welcomed the rest, whereas Bayley appeared unaffected and more concerned about willing Zi forward. I signaled encouragement, just like we used to in our youth, drawing a knowing nod, before she turned back to Bayley. The two seemed inseparable, or at least I hoped so. No one deserved happiness more than Zi. He'd certainly taken a great risk to help us, but it was hard to forget that less than a month earlier he'd been my interrogator.

"Five minutes up, people. Let's go," Ander ordered, pushing us to commence the final and most dangerous trek.

The winds were noticeably gentler, lifting everyone's spirits. We picked up the pace to a steady jog, before turning to a sprint when we caught sight of our destination. No drone army could find us once we descended deep into the lava tubes. We were less than a kilometer from the tubes when I heard the first sounds of drones.

"We've been detected," Ander shouted.

The sound of the killer machines drew ever louder, drowning all other noise. "Can we make it, Ander?"

"Possibly. Take the lead, Dane and don't stop for anything." Ander ordered, checking his com as we all ran past him.

Ander was preparing to stand and fight to buy us valuable time. I sprinted until my body screamed for rest, but the sound of the first explosions roared from behind me making me ignore any pain. The cacophony of man-made thunder and lightning shook the area as Ander engaged the deadly drone fleet, buying us the time we needed. I reached the lava tube, or more fell into it. Zi followed, her expression pure terror as intermittent flashes of light lit the tube entry. I signaled Zi and Bayley to follow me as I descended deeper into the darkness, using the light of my com to guide me down, daring not to stop. The drones would have a fix on our point of entry and would fill the tubes in seconds if they passed Ander, so we had to move ever deeper, putting the maze-like obstacles formed by the lava tubes between us and them. We continued further down, daring to briefly rest only when the sounds of war had dissipated. Everything depended on Ander now.

Ander had unleashed half of his formidable firepower before the last of the fleet fell, but the second fleet followed quickly, halting any attempt of retreat to the lava tube. He'd got to within a hundred meters of the entry when he stood his ground and engaged the second fleet.

Swarms rapidly advanced from the north, this time flying in staggered formations. Ander had the fire power and defenses to destroy this fleet, but it would drain his depleted artillery. Making matters worse, a second smaller flank came from behind. He had to destroy this squadron or they would enter the open lava tube, but this would leave him vulnerable to the second fleet. He would likely lose the battle but they had to be stopped.

Ander turned from the second fleet, unleashing fury on the squadron while retreating to the lava tube entry. Once destroyed, he turned his artillery back to the advancing fleet. They were on him and threatened to break through Ander's perimeter, forcing him to unleash his deadliest weapon. He fired the pulse wave across the drone's front line, instantly destroying half the fleet, but leaving himself defenseless to the remaining drones. He'd bought enough time to destroy the tube entry and protect the escape party, so he turned his weaponry toward the opening and prepared to unload the last of his firepower on the Mars surface, his final act.

Unexpectedly, a massive pulse penetrated his deteriorating force field, knocking him to the ground. A star fighter roared through the drone army directly toward him. Ander engaged the last of his weapons in defiance but his circuitry malfunctioned. He had only seconds to bypass his damaged circuitry, but failed. The battle was lost, his team vulnerable to drone attack. The Martian sky turned dark with the advancing drones, an impending storm that lit up metallic grey from the flames of the star fighter as it roared high above and past the tube before beginning a wide arc to return.

"Surrender, or we will decommission you," Locke transmitted, from the cockpit of the star fighter.

Ander was defenseless, leaving him a final strategy — the bluff. "I'll destroy everything within a hundred-meter radius if you fire your weapons."

The gathering darkness lit up with red lightning as drone lasers targeted their weapons toward him. Ander watched helplessly as an intense sun-like flash lit the sky, signaling his end. The surge then streamed off as electromagnetic pulses weaved around a man-made globe shaped force field. Whatever disabled his circuitry now protected him.

He looked across the Martian perimeter toward a single soldier who walked through the force field toward him. Hali had followed Ander's signal to the lava tube and surveyed the scene.

"What's your weapon capacity?"

"I'm down to one final explosive, but I cannot engage it. It could take out the perimeter you have contained."

Hali scanned Ander's sleeve and reengaged his weapon. "They can't penetrate this defense, but they have transmitted analysis of my force field to their base. They'll quickly find a solution. Are the others deep enough into the lava tube to avoid detection?"

Ander appraised his com. "No. They're still in range."

"We have to destroy the entry. Can we destroy it from within?"

"Negative. It would pose too great a risk to our team. It has to be destroyed from the surface."

"Transmit the weapon to me. They may need your assistance at the other end," Hali offered.

"I have limited firepower left. It would be better you notify UN forces of your location via encrypted channels. The drones won't attack if there's a UN presence."

Hali scanned the area looking for alternatives, but Ander was right. "You're too valuable to lose."

"Not nearly as valuable as you. Did you gain the information needed?"

"Yes. It…" Hali started to reply before being interrupted by the roar of the star fighter as it engaged a vertical landing on the surface, just outside the force field.

"Your situation is hopeless. Look around you," Locke said.

The whole force field perimeter was filled with what remained of the second drone fleet.

"Surrender now and we'll recommission you both to serve the Apollo alliance." Locke said, as he exited the star fighter.

"They're close to breaking the force field," Hali said.

Ander nodded, "Just a few seconds, now. Prepare to disengage your force field to the current perimeter and reengage in the lava tube."

Hali held the fallen warrior's shoulder in a human-like gesture of admiration. "I have downloaded your file," Hali said, now carrying Ander's digital record.

"Finish the task, soldier," Ander said, signaling Hali to head deep into the tube. She raced down the steep slope into the underground caves, releasing her perimeter force field and reengaging it between her and Ander.

Locke stood at the perimeter edge and ordered the drones to rain down fire on Ander, but he ignited his final weapon just before, sending a mushroom cloud several hundred meters high, blowing a violent dust storm a kilometer wide, destroying the invading army and its commander. The tube was closed and the hunt terminated.

Chapter Twenty-Seven

REPORTING

Hali led us out of the lava tube, showing perfect recall of the route I had used earlier. No one questioned her as she assuredly took control of our perilous situation. Communications with officials through secret channels laid the ground work for our protection on the surface, where strong leadership ensured our safe passage through the lava tubes in quick time.

"This way," she repeatedly directed, before disappearing again. Sometimes, she'd choose a different path from mine, every choice surprisingly more direct. Sometimes she'd ask Cluste to join her, highlighting her changing loyalties. As was the case with Ander, Hali appeared to place more faith in biots.

Zi noticed Hali's capabilities, too. "I thought Codi was

a talented biot, but this one is impressive. How long has she worked for you?"

"Since I joined the Trojan program. She is as loyal as she is impressive."

"Does she still report to you?" Bayley asked.

I wanted to hold back for Zi's sake, but couldn't. "Not since our skirmish with you and your people."

I walked away, leaving Zi and Bayley behind, preferring not to incite more ill feeling. It was clear Zi trusted him, so I minimized conversation between them, preferring to keep a watchful eye on their growing friendship from a distance. I felt disappointed also, given my sister seemed more intent on developing a relationship with Bayley than rebuilding ours after a ten-year absence.

We had made our way to the last of the lava tubes, a kilometer long stretch to the final cave and our exit back to the surface. I looked up to the natural skylight and watched Hali climb to the surface. She cautiously checked that the surroundings were clear of danger before calling out to Cluste who trailed behind her.

"There is a UN escort waiting to return us back to the base. Inform the others," she said, before disappearing from sight.

It was not long before Cluste, Zi, Bayley, and I made it to the surface, too. The UN escort was a reassuring sight.

There'd be little danger the Apollo fleets would pursue us for fear of sparking an international incident. As it was, a thorough investigation would follow, if my sister had any say in the matter.

On the return to the base, it became abundantly clear Hali had been afforded a larger role since leaving the Deliverance, now coordinating the UN escort. We saw little of her until returning to the base.

Zi didn't waste any time expressing herself. "I'll report all I know to my superior. I'm happy to send you a copy if it will help?"

"Yes. The international council have requested my report. Could you have your biot, Codi, bring me the report?" Hali asked.

Zi looked surprised. "I'm happy to…"

"The council has specifically requested she assist me with the investigation. If you could work with her on the report and send her to me, that will be sufficient for now," Hali replied, before leaving without further word.

Zi turned my way, showing her displeasure. "If you have any influence over her, I'd appreciate a meeting with the council," before she too left with Bayley.

I wanted only rest from the ordeal, but not before I asked Cluste to share a message. "When you report back to your command, I'd like you to brief them fully about Ander's actions."

Cluste nodded. "Yes. He was decommissioned at the entry of the lava tube. I will do that immediately."

"Tell them exactly what occurred. He was decommissioned in the field of battle, defending us. He died a hero."

"I'll convey your message, Dane. Ander was the best soldier in our fleet as well as commander. I hope my new commander has the same ability."

"You deserve that, Cluste. It was a pleasure working with you," hugging him in genuine appreciation, but saddened he couldn't fully appreciate the depth of my feeling. But he smiled and nodded his head convincingly in response.

I returned to my quarters exhausted, but unable to sleep. I mistrusted Ander when I first bordered the Deliverance, not realizing this aloof, powerful biot would make the ultimate sacrifice. Maybe he was just following orders, yet on more than one occasion, he along with Hali appeared to be answering to themselves, an unlawful process. Latatious should have been their commander, given their commitment to our project, but was he? I needed to speak to him about them, but also about Bayley, not to mention my mother. We had returned to the safety of the base, but something told me we were anything but secure.

A week had passed free of incident making me wonder if my many concerns were unwarranted. Zi led the terraforming team with Bayley's capable assistance. Their bond grew with every day, and it was clear to all they were in love. Their happiness was infectious. Even I began to warm to Bayley, enjoying their company when we worked together. I took charge of the Trojan's operations given Codi now worked with Hali on the investigation.

I joined Zi and Bayley for their morning inspection of the terraforming pod station, its energy now fully supplied by the nuclear fusion reactor.

"We had only one energy surge in the last twenty-four hours, and that was for a very short period," Zi proudly announced. Bayley squeezed her arm in supportive recognition.

"Was there any need to cut into our solar energy source?" I asked, trying to keep our meeting professional.

"The surge was so brief, it wasn't required."

"That's a first. Should we consider supplying a second pod?"

"Is the Trojan ready, Dane?" Bayley asked.

"I can run some diagnostics, but I'm confident."

"I sure would like to see it in operation," Bayley said, looking to Zi for support.

Zi looked to me. "What do you think?"

Zi clearly supported Bayley but I felt it too soon to offer him a security pass. "You're in charge, Zi," I responded in an impassive tone.

"Let's include the Trojan in our daily check," she replied.

Her support surprised me, and I immediately regretted giving her a choice. Before I could rescind the gesture, we were passing through the security check into the Trojan site, Bayley now included, with full security rights.

It wasn't until later that I learnt my concerns were shared. I worked later than usual following up on the day's Trojan tests, not that it was required, more that my suspicions toward Bayley remained. However, it wasn't Bayley who visited the site but Hali.

I was happily surprised to see her. "I didn't realize you had clearance."

"I have full security clearance," she replied, smiling then turning to look at the machine. "We worked so hard to make this happen. And now…" Hali said, her voice trailing as she studied it.

Her human-like admiration drew me to recognize her input. "There's a lot of you in this machine, Hali," I replied, standing beside her, admiring our work together, as if it were our child.

"How's it progressing?"

"We will be terraforming a second pod tomorrow. If

that progresses without incident, we should see exponential growth over the coming month."

"I've been informed the Apollo scientist has been given full clearance?"

I nodded, deep down hoping she may change Zi's directive. "Zi gave him clearance today. Did she tell you?"

Zi didn't feel the need to answer my question. "How do you feel about Bayley?"

"What I think doesn't matter. As long as Zi is happy."

Hali studied me before replying. She had changed so much so quickly. Where once she would listen intently to my needs, she now bypassed them.

"She loves him?"

"Yes. I believe so."

"And he loves her?"

I shrugged my shoulders, "I'm still forming my opinion about that. They have known each other for such a short period. I understand Zi's infatuation. She's been unlucky in love, so she'd want to believe in him. Whereas I know so little about Bayley. He clearly risked his life to help us escape, and it seems he did it for her."

Hali continued to study me, "And yet?"

I smiled and pressed Hali's arm. "You know me well. He just seems too good to be true. I want to see my sister happy, but I fear she'll be let down."

"Have you raised your fears with Latatious?"

"I will. I suppose I wanted to give Bayley some time before I raised any doubts. It's not as if he has done anything this past week to make me suspicious. He's been quite the opposite. Do you have doubts?"

"Yes. I do."

"Have you told Latatious?" I asked, more to see if she actually reported to him.

Hali smiled wryly, "I have a new reporting channel now. However, I would like you to brief Latatious. That's why I'm here."

I couldn't hide my disappointment. Hali was only meeting me because she had been ordered to. "Who do you report to, Hali?"

"That's classified. What I can tell you is we believe there is a counterintelligence Apollo project currently in progress, so be vigilant."

"I have been, but I've not seen anything untoward."

"Haven't you? Maybe gaining access to the Trojan site is what they were waiting for." Hali prodded.

"If you know something, tell me," I replied.

"Even if I did, I couldn't. Get a meeting with Latatious," Hali said, before turning to leave.

I watched her walk away, not another word spoken between us. The Hali I once knew had long gone. She was a mystery to me now, more powerful and aloof. I wanted to call out to her, but dared not. If Hali was right about Bayley, I'd have to somehow convince Zi of the fact. If Hali was wrong, we were all in the dark. Then a thought crossed my mind for the very first time. Could any potential counterintelligence concerns be emanating from Hali?

Zhang called in his assistant to make preparations for him. He was more agitated than usual, given the high stakes game he had allowed to unfold. Increasing pressure was coming from the council and rumors that preliminary investigations were being mounted.

"Any luck with the encrypted channel?" Zhang asked, not hiding his agitation.

"I'm still trying, sir. I shall notify you as soon as Bayley responds."

"Well try harder!" Zhang fired, as his hapless assistant retreated to the doorway.

"Has my next appointment arrived?" Zhang shouted.

"Yes. He's waiting outside."

"Send him in, then."

Zhang pushed his paperwork to one side to give his full attention to Draven. Bayley had been quiet since arriving at the Gaea base — too quiet for his liking. He'd sent an encrypted message to him, a risky move in this uncertain environment, but Zhang hadn't made it to the top of security by not taking risks.

He sat back low in the chair, clasping both hands together close to his face, peering over them and studying Draven as he entered. If Bayley couldn't complete the task, he'd have to send Draven to finish what he'd begun. Not his preferred option as the two were alike, both loose cannons, both their own men.

"Welcome. Take a seat," Zhang said.

He sat, not acknowledging his commander, which was his way. Draven was not programmed to bother engaging small talk.

"Bad business about your colleague," Zhang offered.

"They were sloppy and underestimated our enemy," Draven replied.

"Our defenses were found wanting."

"That's an understatement. Whole defense systems appeared to be countermanded," Draven replied, in an accusing tone.

Zhang ignored his slight. "Well we can't afford to make any more mistakes. There are reports that the Earth council are undertaking renewed investigations into the matter. We need to close Gaea's Trojan research down before it's too late."

"I tried to tell them that on the Deliverance, but they wouldn't listen."

Zhang sat forward on his seat, "Well I'm listening now. What do you recommend we do?"

"If Bayley is in trouble, send me in. I have the technology to withdraw the key operating files. Then we destroy the machine. Gaea couldn't complain, given their frequent statements that it is years from being built."

Zhang's assistant entered the room, interrupting Draven. "We have Bayley on the com, sir."

"Perfect," Zhang replied, waving his assistant to leave, before turning his com on. A holographic image of Bayley's face appeared at the center of the table. "Are you receiving our voice signal?" Zhang asked.

"Signal is clear. I have limited time, so let's get to the point," Bayley replied.

Zhang signalled to Draven to speak. "Zhang has requested I assist you with your mission, should you need it. What are your instructions?"

"It will be needed. The good news is I have gained full security clearance of the Trojan area, so access is not a problem. However, Dane has complex codes securing the files. I haven't the technology to break them. I was planning to destroy the machine, unless you believe you have the capability?"

"I could break the codes if you can buy me a full hour undisturbed. Is that possible?" Draven replied.

"Difficult but not impossible. With a replicator we may buy that much time."

"I have that. Who would I replicate?" Draven asked.

"There are two possibilities. The biots, Hali and Codi. Both have security clearance and both are spending little time in the area. Their visits are spasmodic which is a concern, but they represent our best chance."

"I could bring a military biot and decommission them?"

"Negative. That would be difficult and uncertain. We've tackled Hali twice and lost, so don't underestimate her or the other biot. I'll run tracers in the vicinity which would allow us some warning of their presence. So, replicators are our best chance."

"I already have their specs, so replicator capability will be achieved within twelve hours. What are your time lines?" Draven asked.

"I'll send a coded signal when ready. Replicate Hali as she has full clearance throughout the base. Just be ready to quickly respond."

"Affirmative."

Zhang interrupted, "You should know that the Earth council are undertaking renewed investigations into all the incidents following the Deliverance. We are vulnerable to exposure and you know what that means."

"Affirmative. I have to cut this transmission," Bayley replied, before the com hologram disappeared.

Zhang sat quietly satisfied as he watched Draven leave. His two best agents were left to unravel the diplomatic mess that potentially imperiled Apollo's aims to fast-track space exploration. If they should fail, he would have no other option but to cover his tracks. That scenario would contain a necessary level of violence he preferred didn't occur, but Zhang was in deep.

He turned to his com, "Arrange for Hogan to meet with me within the hour," he ordered, before sitting back to ponder the myriad of scenarios he potentially faced.

Chapter Twenty-Eight

TRAP

My rest day on Mars started with a quiet meditation at Mars oldest dome, set on the base's outskirts, now used as a park for rest and recuperation. The expansive view of the Chryse Planitia plains were limited to the security lighting that lit the bases perimeter and the outline of Olympus Mons that dominated the easterly star-filled sky. The dome would be secluded for another hour before the usual crowds filled the dome to take in the sunrise, allowing me ample time to update Latatious. Normal security protocols completed, we spoke openly.

"I'm concerned that Zi has placed way too much faith in Bayley. He brings a wealth of knowledge, which he appears happy to share, but Zi is reciprocating."

"Has he engaged in any suspicious behaviour?" Latatious asked.

"Nothing direct, but he convinced Zi to give him security access."

"Reasonable request. He is working on the terraforming program."

"Normally, but given his background, granting security access was too early. I hate to say it, but Zi has allowed personal feelings to get in the way."

"We ran a digital history check of his activities since arriving at the base. He's mostly researching the terraforming program as per Zi's requests, but there has been an instance where he previewed the base layout and security. It raised a few concerns, but it was once and just after being allowed access," Latatious said.

"Why would he want to know so much? Any normal operator would simply want to know how to gain access."

"True, or he could just be inquisitive, like most scientists I know."

"Latatious, I had this man interrogate me on the Deliverance. Why are we giving him so much sway?"

"He appears to hold sway with people in high places on Earth council, so we need to play this one with care. We're already vulnerable from the Deliverance incident. Another could put our whole program at risk."

The more I learnt about Bayley the more I wondered about him. The desertion aside, he remained an enigma, so I pressed Latatious further. "Leave him to work alongside my sister, but assign me a personal drone."

"They're outlawed. You're already under investigation for the incident on the Deliverance. If you were caught operating a personal drone your career would certainly be over."

Personal drones were used by governments for decades, until they got into the hands of extreme elements. It led to many bloody battles where killer drones were targeted at influential officials. Their impact was chaotic, ultimately leading to large scale production being banned. Old illegal models still existed, which were covertly used, occasionally turning up in counterespionage cases.

"I was sent here to develop and protect the Trojan computer. This is the best way I know how."

Latatious took his time responding, not hiding his uncertainty. "This isn't a simple request, so I'll get back to you with an answer. Meanwhile, I want you to brief your sister. She's the commander of this operation."

"That's in hand. I have arranged a meeting this morning."

"Fully brief her. I'll be talking to her tomorrow at the weekly briefing. I don't want her to be surprised. Is that clear?"

"Fine. No surprises." I agreed, before Latatious ended our call.

I hadn't confirmed a meeting with Zi, but she regularly came to this dome on her rest day, so I sat back in my chair and waited for the sun to rise over the Martian landscape. The twilight cast a smoke colored hue over the dusty soil of Mars before the Sun's rise turned it ruby rust. Zi and I had watched many such sunrises together and shared secrets. As a young boy, I trusted her more than anyone, but had time removed our faithful bond?

Zi joined me just after sunrise. We exchanged knowing glances, remembering the many occasions we'd shared in this quiet corner. The morning light accentuated her good looks. Despite the pressures she had faced over the last decade, Zi retained her youthful beauty.

"Fancy finding you here, little brother," she said with irony, before sitting beside me.

Her mood was infectious, making me regret my request of Latatious. I felt as if every time Zi found happiness I'd find a way to undermine it.

"Something on your mind, Dane?"

Zi could always read me. I wanted to engage in small talk and avoid the inevitable reaction, but instead jumped in. "Yes. I'm still worried about Bayley. I know things are going well for you, but there's too much at stake not to say anything."

Zi sat forward and held my hand. "I understand that. I really do. And I can't argue with you about the enormity of what we are doing here, but I promise you, Dane, I will not compromise the project."

"You gave him security clearance, Zi."

"He's working alongside us on the terraforming project, and he's already brought a wealth of knowledge to the table. He needs access."

"It's been a week. How can you be sure of his loyalty?"

"I have worked with him for almost a month. Still a short period, I know, but Bayley has done nothing but support me. He also risked his life for us. Do you deny that?"

"That's true, and I do appreciate what he did. I just wonder why he would push you so quickly for security clearance. You could provide any details he may need. It just seems a rush."

Zi sat back in her seat and folded her arms. "He and I are very close, Dane. You can see that, can't you?"

"Of course. And I'm happy for you. Really I am."

"You know I've waited a long time to feel this way again. Letting someone get close to me isn't easy. You more than anyone should understand why I feel that way."

I simply nodded. There were no words I could use to console her. I had felt the same loneliness myself until I met Lia. Why should I deny my sister the same chance at happiness?

"We have shared so much in this short period of time. Secrets I wouldn't share with anyone else. I trust him, Dane. And I wanted to show that trust."

There was little else I could say to change Zi's mind when it was made up. I balked at relaying my discussion with Latatious, so I told her half-truths. "I want you to be happy, Zi. I owe you that. Just allow me to keep a watchful eye from a distance, and I'll say no more on the matter."

"You'll find nothing, but go ahead," she replied, before standing to leave. "Bayley and I are having lunch together, so promise me there will be no surveillance of our time?"

"You have my word."

As Zi left, I immediately regretted my hesitance. I rationalized my concealment, given Latatious had yet to approve a personal drone, but if my actions were a mistake, I would drive a potentially permanent wedge between us. I'd yet again rolled the dice in an uncertain game.

Bayley sat quietly in a remote corner of the Gaea base, the rendezvous point with Draven. It was a one-hour trek, through harsh terrain, an ideal cover for any counterintelligence operation. A force field lay between Bayley and the open perimeter. Strong winds surged across the expanse, making survival challenging. He held vigilant watch out to the cold darkness, wondering if Draven could meet that challenge.

A half hour passed before Draven appeared at the force field. He'd already digitized into Hali's shape, so convincingly Bayley stood cautiously back in the shadows. Draven studied the force field, running an analysis of its components before applying a body force field that enabled him to pass through undetected seemingly invisible, his stock in trade.

Bayley walked out of the shadows and signaled to Draven, revealing his whereabouts. "You're late. Trouble in the perimeter?"

"Storm gusts, but we can make up time on the trek back to the base. Is everything prepared?"

"The base is clear," Bayley replied, before commencing their return to the base and inside the high security Trojan site. "We have two hours before the first security check commences. Is that sufficient?"

"I've broken into the strongest security systems in the world. I doubt this will be any more of a challenge." Draven responded, confidently.

"This is the most powerful and complex computer in the solar system, so expect a challenge." Bayley warned.

"You said you'd acquired some intel on the code. I'm counting on that."

"I got some, but there was a limit to that information without drawing suspicions."

Draven set up his equipment around the operating console of the Trojan, wasting no time. "Give me the information, now. I'm about to start the anti-encryption process."

Bayley provided the general encryption codes and processes that he'd drawn from Zi, but it still left a quantum number of potential access codes to choose from. "I'll need every bit of those two hours," he said, drawing back from his earlier bold assessment.

"I can review with you, if that helps?" Bayley offered.

Draven waved him away, showing his annoyance. "No, that would slow me down. You'd be more useful looking out for any disturbances."

Bayley left Draven to his work and camped himself at the entry desk. Two hours passed and Bayley had heard nothing, so he readied to check on him when Dane walked into the Trojan site four hours earlier than usual. This was either enormously bad luck or they'd walked into a trap. The only encouragement Bayley felt was that Dane was alone.

Chapter Twenty-Nine

OUT RANKED

I woke to an unfamiliar alarm that activated my com. Activity in the Trojan site had been detected by a personal drone. Latatious had been true to his word, authorizing a personal drone, his breadth of influence on full display. The drone's report vindicated my decision as Bayley had entered the area with one other. I requested the drone's recordings of events be transmitted to my com and an encrypted copy sent to Latatious.

That done, I headed through the deserted corridors to the Trojan site, all the while viewing the drone transmission locked on Bayley's movements. Curiously, he sat at the front desk not showing any interest in the Trojan machine. Had he detected the drone? That was unlikely, given outlawed drones were quantum small, invisible to the eye. Perfect spies.

I wasted no time sounding Bayley out, hoping to catch him off guard. He was clearly surprised and agitated as I approached. "Why are you here?"

Bayley didn't answer immediately, instead inviting me to sit with him. Was he buying time? I sat down and perused the desk for any sign of weapons before pressuring him for a response.

"The site is under surveillance and all records are transmitted to our head of security. Again, why are you here?"

Bayley looked around the room, looking for the surveillance equipment, still stalling for time.

"I'll call security if you don't answer."

Bayley lifted both arms as if surrendering, before finally replying. "I'm sorry for troubling you at this terrible hour, Dane. I felt the same way, when I was asked to accompany an agent."

"What agent? You don't seriously believe I'd…"

A familiar voice called from behind, interrupting me. "Good morning, Dane. I'm sorry to have alarmed you unnecessarily," said Hali, as she approached and sat down beside me.

The sight of Hali surprised me. She carried equipment in a back pack and appeared eager to leave. "Would you mind telling me what's going on?"

"I can't, Dane. It's part of our investigations, but it will be fully revealed at the right time."

"You can involve an ex-Apollo operative, but you can't reveal it to me?"

"Nothing has been revealed to him. He was just following my orders. I needed access to these premises as part of an investigation, the reasons being of a sensitive nature that I'm not at liberty to reveal to you or your sister."

"I will report this to Zi and my commander," I threatened.

"That's fine. You can also tell your commander that I'm taking Bayley to the UN barracks for questioning. If you have any further questions, direct it to the Earth council," Hali replied tersely, signaling for Bayley to join her as they left.

Hali's aloofness bothered me enough to check the Trojan machine. Everything appeared normal and there was no apparent tampering, so I checked my com. They were both heading north in the direction of the checkpoint. Why would she want to question Bayley at UN quarters? None of it made sense, so I determined to return to brief Latatious on the events. There seemed little else to do but wait for Latatious to return my contact request. At least the personal drone would alert me of any further break-ins on the Trojan site.

An hour passed and Latatious still hadn't responded, so I returned to the site. The Trojan machine opening sequence appeared normal until I began to set up the day's programs. A phantom code had been installed camouflaging a major malfunction. The program files had been tampered with, making it impossible to operate. I slammed the desk in frustration, almost certain the files had been copied, before encrypting a destructive virus. I would have immediately reported the early morning intrusion to security, but for Hali's involvement. If she were working for our enemy, who else was?

There was no other recourse but to brief Zi. Fortuitously, Latatious's com call came through just as I neared her quarters. She sat in her compact eating area which doubled as an office, enjoying coffee and studying reports. Zi's mood even appeared upbeat, but my report would abruptly change that.

"This is a first. You always go to the Trojan site in the morning. For what do I owe the honor?"

I opened my com to receive Latatious's call. "You need to hear this," I replied, so as to brief them simultaneously.

Latatious appeared on the com and dispensed with any pleasantries. "I take it you've been using the personal drone I allocated?"

"Yes. I wasn't aware until the personal drone set an

alarm early this morning, notifying me that Bayley was in the target area."

I waited for Latatious's response, hoping it may satisfy Zi's inevitable response. Her happy demeanour visibly changed, as she folded her arms and focused her gaze at the com, or more precisely anywhere but at me.

"Bayley was recently given clearance to the area. What are your concerns?"

"Initially none. I investigated the area at the time of the incursion. I found Bayley sitting at the entry desk. He was waiting for Hali, who had apparently ordered him to accompany her to the area."

"Does Hali have clearance?" Latatious asked.

I looked Zi's way. She didn't reply immediately, seemingly gaining her composure. "I have received official documents from the Earth council that she be given full cooperation in her investigations. So, I don't see any illegal activities here, and I certainly don't see the need for a personal drone," Zi replied accusingly.

"Dane contacted me with concerns about potential illegal activities. After considered deliberation, I accepted his request to activate a personal drone."

"Preposterous! Personal drones are an illegal activity!" Zi replied.

Latatious deflected to me. "So, what exactly are your

concerns, Dane?"

"At first, I accepted Hali's right to be there, although she appeared in a hurry to leave."

"Did she offer an explanation for rushing away?" Latatious interjected.

"The inspection of the site was to do with the investigation revolving around Zi and me. She had apparently found what she was looking for and wanted to leave for the UN base with Bayley to continue her investigations."

"Did you know of this, Zi?" Latatious asked.

"No, but I don't expect Hali wants to brief us about every facet of her investigation."

"I thought the same, so I didn't give it any more thought, until this morning."

"Go on," Latatious prompted.

"I decided to run the Trojan opening routine earlier than usual, as a precaution. I soon learnt it'd been tampered with and rendered inoperable. Key operational files were copied then destroyed, or in other words, our intelligence was hacked and stolen. The upshot is I recommend we instigate a search for Bayley and Hali."

"Bayley's whereabouts?"

"The last personal drone check verified he was heading for the UN base."

"Zi, you're responsible for giving Bayley a security pass.

Can you contact him and verify Dane's report? If there is any hint of suspicious activity, organize a security group to apprehend him immediately and keep me posted hourly. Is that clear?"

"Perfectly," Zi responded.

"Thank you. You're excused," Latatious ordered.

Zi left, making clear her displeasure, not once acknowledging my presence during the com meeting. I had slighted my sister. Worse, I had not confided in her.

"Has she left?" Latatious asked, his mood also dark.

"Yes, we're alone."

"You have taken steps that could compromise us both. Next time don't involve anyone else until you pass it by me. Clear?"

"Yes. When I saw the Trojan was compromised, I thought I should notify the base commander."

"You only witnessed those events by using the illegal equipment I supplied. So, I'll tell you who you should see. Are you sure there hasn't just been a malfunction?"

I wouldn't win either way. If Hali's story checked out I'd be reprimanded for requesting an illegal drone, and Latatious would be ordered to justify such an approval. If my suspicions were correct, I'd betrayed Zi's trust and destroyed her growing relationship with Bayley.

"I'm certain the Trojan has been compromised. I had to act."

"What's Bayley's current status?"

I checked the drone's positioning again. "He is in the perimeter, but he has veered from his initial course."

"How far?"

"Not enough to predict a change of course. It could be an adjustment to move around an obstacle, although their speed would suggest otherwise. They've accelerated, suggesting a different vehicle to standard ferry services."

"Calculate potential courses."

"If they continue the current corrections, they would be heading for the Olympus Mons base."

"Monitor Bayley until he's returned to the base. Assist your sister with a retrieval mission if it's required and follow through on Hali's involvement. Then keep me regularly posted on events."

Latatious cut the transmission to a difficult meeting. Now I had to face a second with Zi as I entered her office. She paced the office while making a com call.

"Bayley, report to me on an urgent matter," she said, her despondency showing it wasn't her first call.

"No answer?"

"Not yet. But my messages are clear," Zi replied, before sitting at her desk. She looked my way for the first time since being briefed, while I pulled up a chair and sat out the silence, prepared for the inevitable interrogation she'd unleash. But an incoming com call broke the steely quiet.

"Hali returning your call."

"Thanks, Hali. We had an incident at the base last night that I'm hoping you can help us with. Where are you?"

"I'm in my quarters. I can come and meet with you if that helps?"

Zi's cheeks turned pale as she took in the ramifications of Hali's response. "That would help. Could you join Dane and me at my office? It's an urgent matter."

"I'll come now."

The silence continued longer until I had to say something. "Zi, I didn't…"

"Don't. Please don't try and justify your actions. I've always tried to help you and never asked a lot in return. So, I'm just asking you to not go there. Explanations will have to wait."

I nodded and held my tongue. Zi was right. She'd always been the one to help me, with little reciprocation. Mercifully, Hali arrived, drawing Zi away from the internal anger she held in check. She greeted Hali, then looked to me to report the events of last night, which I described in detail.

"So, the question is why were you assisting Bayley and why did you lie about taking him to the UN base?"

"Whoever you saw last night wasn't me. You clearly saw someone who looked like me," Hali responded.

"Can you verify your whereabouts?" Zi asked.

"Yes, you can verify my location during that period with Codi, but we can't reveal the work we were carrying out as it is related to the ongoing investigation."

"Can you remain in your quarters until I notify you otherwise?" Zi pressed.

"You're aware that you have no jurisdiction over me, but I assure you that I will be working with Codi here on the base. I won't be going anywhere."

"That's sufficient assurance for me. Thank you, Hali."

Zi checked her com as she watched Hali leave. Bayley still hadn't responded. "Where is Bayley now?" she asked, a hint of resignation in her voice.

"He's moving rapidly toward the Olympus Mons base."

"ETA?"

"Less than three hours. I'm sorry…"

"Don't! We can talk about this later," Zi snapped, before calling security on her com. "Organize a security operation. I want three vehicles, fully loaded and our best people on board. We need to intercept a vehicle heading for the Olympus Mons base," Zi ordered.

"Do you want me to command the operation?" the security commander replied.

"Yes, you will command the military side of the operation. I and one other will join you, and we need to be ready to leave in five minutes. This operation is a high security threat, so your best crew."

Zi stood and looked at me, determination in her eyes. "Is there enough time?"

I studied the com. "At their current speed, we can still intercept them."

"If they're capable of higher speeds?"

"Improbable. They have a standard vehicle. Slow moving but difficult to detect with normal radar. At top speeds they'll get close to the perimeter and drone support."

I ran alongside my sister as she determined her strategy. On reaching the three military vehicles, Zi barked her orders to the three teams.

"Commander Jarvis, you'll command military operations. I'll remain in the support vehicle to carry out negotiations with our targets, one human, the other a biot. Dane will command the third lead vehicle as they'll take the more challenging westerly route. Assign your very best driver to him."

"Rickard is our best driver. We've lost many men along that dangerous route," Jarvis cautioned.

"Thank you, Jarvis, but Dane has more experience with this terrain than anyone on Mars. We must stop this vehicle before it reaches the Olympus Mons base perimeter. Dane knows the area better than anyone on Mars," Zi replied, looking my way.

The westerly route was extremely challenging. Zi either meant what she said about me, or it was her payback for my treachery. It didn't matter. I had another chance to help Zi, and I wasn't about to waste it. "We'll gain a good twenty minutes along that route, so I suggest we dispense with any more talk and get on with it."

All three vehicles were armed and quickly in pursuit. I followed Zi until we reached a telltale boulder outcrop that signalled our turn-off. We veered left and immediately experienced difficult terrain, while Zi's two vehicles disappeared to the right of the large outcrop. Our trail winded higher across the easterly base of Olympus Mons, before we cut back down to the flat plains.

Rickard was a skilled driver, capably handling my directions. He knew the terrain well, almost taking the accepted safe route across the mountain's base, but I had other plans.

"Go left of that boulder."

Rickard shook his head. "That's a dead end."

"Not where I'm taking you."

Rickard accepted the challenge in military fashion, peeling on his well-worn driving gloves, preparing for the challenge. We approached the safe trail but I directed him left to a higher trail rarely used and for good reason. He turned into a near vertical climb, seemingly aimed straight toward the Olympus peak. The trail was little more than an ancient stream clearing carved when water flowed on Mars. Rickard now drove on instinct, relying solely on my direction, climbing to levels he had never been. The two other crew members held tightly to their seats as Rickard held his nerve, holding sufficient acceleration to ascend higher, before at a thousand meters I released the pressure valve.

"Go right around that large boulder and prepare for a steep decline."

The silence of the team gave way to terror as we drove off what appeared a steep cliff face, our only view the pale pink Martian sky. We were airborne for seconds before the vehicle gained traction, turning our sky view to a panoramic view of the plains and the reassuring feel of tires on land.

"Hold the steep descent to the largest boulder you can see, then make a hard-ninety-degree left turn and accelerate hard."

Rickard made a perfect turn, before accelerating hard

across the mountain toward another steep decline. Dust streamed up high, at times blocking any view. Many had met their deaths on this stretch, either not sufficiently accelerating or misjudging the narrow trail afforded them.

"Good. Hold your speed. You've nearly navigated the ridge. When I say turn, go right twenty degrees in lowest gear. That will be the cross down to the second ridge."

We drove no more than a ledge, any sign of a vehicle trail long gone. I waited, relying on memory alone to identify the final blind turn. "Now!"

Rickard responded, turning his vehicle toward the unknown. Only an experienced biot could meet this challenge, as the vehicle engaged the last steep drop from our lofty perch. Gears screamed as we descended to the relative safety of the second ridge and the final straight descent back to the plains. Only then did I check the com. We were five minutes ahead of Bayley's vehicle.

"Position the vehicle behind this boulder, secure your weapons and wait for Jarvis's orders." I then contacted him. "Your men are ready to encounter the target vehicle. What's your position?"

"We're five minutes behind the target vehicle. Engage them and hold them there. I repeat, you must not let them pass," Jarvis ordered.

"Do we have any drone activity?" Rickard asked.

"None. So, use artillery as a last resort. You're close enough to the perimeter for the sound of any engagement to be picked up," Jarvis replied.

"Will do, commander, but it's unlikely they'll stop without firepower."

"Understood. Keep us updated," Jarvis replied.

In a short time, the telltale dust trailing Bayley's vehicle came into view. We moved from our position of cover into the direct trajectory of the approaching vehicle. If they carried weapons we were about to find out.

"Engaging warning lights. Weapons at ready, men," Rickard ordered.

Instead of decelerating, Bayley's vehicle accelerated and veered away from us. Rickard repositioned the vehicle, while his men prepared to fire warning shots.

Rickard looked my way. "On your orders," he said.

I checked my com. Any firing of weapons would draw drones to us. We had no more than thirty minutes to act before we would be encircled, but we had to stop Bayley before he entered the perimeter. At least outside the perimeter, the drones would be illegally engaging us. I nodded to fire.

Rickard's men fired warning shots a hundred meters short of them to no effect.

"Commander. We have fired two warning shots and

they have not responded."

"They're calling your bluff. They know we don't want to risk destroying the intel they're carrying. Move the vehicle closer and fire at their wheels. They cannot make it to the perimeter," Jarvis ordered.

Rickard maneuvered through the dust and rock storm in front of him as they fired upon us. Rickards men retaliated, unleashing a hail of bullets around the vehicle's wheels, until we drove unsighted into a small crater, flipping the vehicle sideways. Our pursuit was over. We climbed out and waited for Zi's team to reach us, all the while watching Bayley's vehicle limp away in a northerly direction away from the perimeter.

Our two pursuit vehicles arrived, momentarily surveying the carnage, before picking us up. "Close call, brother," Zi said, as I joined her vehicle.

I monitored the com. "They must be heading to a nearby lava tube."

"Have all weapons ready for engagement and ready to fire on my orders," Jarvis ordered, continuing the chase.

"Can we stop them with a long-range missile, Commander?" Zi asked.

"Yes, but we run the risk of destroying the Trojan data."

"Hold fire and pursue."

We reached the entry to the lava tubes, but not before

they'd made their escape. I caught sight of two men enter the lava tube. "I know the other agent. It's Draven."

"Where did you meet him?" Jarvis asked.

"He was one of the agents on the Deliverance."

"Capabilities?"

"Cloaking. Spying. It makes sense, now."

"What do you mean, Dane?" Zi asked.

"He used a replicator. It's obvious now. Draven replicated Hali," I said, annoyed that I hadn't thought of the possibility at the time.

"We'll send a team of three men," Jarvis offered.

Zi turned to me. "Is it enough?"

"If it was just Bayley, I'd say yes, but Draven is another story."

Zi studied her com. "If they know what they're doing, they can reach the perimeter inside an hour."

I knew every inch of this lava tube. "The personal drone still has a fix. Bayley knows what he's doing. I suggest we take two teams. Jarvis, take a team and pursues them. I take another and go around them."

"Agreed. I'll join the commander," Zi replied.

"Ma'am. Fighting a military agent is not a place you should be. Let my men take care of this."

"Absolutely not! I'll be needed to negotiate both the tunnels and Bayley should we capture him. You do your job, Commander, and I'll do mine," Zi ordered.

I feared Zi's heart ruled her decision making, but I could see her mind was made up. "I'll take the second team further north and enter the lava tube there."

"Why not all of us?" Zi questioned.

"There's drone activity near that area. It's risky. Besides, I know that area better than you."

I showed her my com and what I planned. "We should beat them to this point in the cave. Then they will be surrounded by both sides."

Zi labored her decision, so I pushed her. "It's worth the risk."

"Very well. Take the two vehicles to the second lava tube entry. I'll go with Jarvis and his team and guide them through the maze," Zi said, before exchanging knowing gazes. She remained too upset to say anything beyond what was needed, but her face was pained. It was possible this may be the last time we speak. I squeezed her arm before turning to join Rickard and his men, immediately regretting not turning to say something.

Our two vehicles kicked up a dust storm as we plowed toward the second lava tube entry. The thought of Zi disappearing into the lava tube played on my mind. My parents had done the exact same a decade earlier and never returned. As the trailing dust settled, I saw aerial activity build from behind. Drones had picked up the land battle and investigated. Large explosions ignited around the two disbanded vehicles, warning shots and a sign of what would follow. Large plumes of Martian earth exploded high into the air.

Rickard sensed the danger. "How long until we reach the lava tube?"

"Ten minutes. There's some cover along the way, otherwise we're out in the open."

"You head directly for the lava tube. I'll follow a few minutes behind. If they locate us, I'll draw their fire and head to the cover. With luck, that will buy you the time you need."

Rickard had navigated an impossible trail on Olympus Mons. If anyone could evade a fleet of drones, it'd be him. There was no time to argue.

"Good luck," I said, before my driver, Spence, accelerated to the lava tube.

We made it half way before the telltale dark pattern of swarming drones headed directly toward us. I turned to the driver. "If you can make this vehicle go faster, I suggest you do it now,"

Just then, the first explosion sounded a kilometer behind us. Return fire ignited into the sky, momentarily punching holes in the swarm, before the drone collective rejoined, igniting a series of surface explosions, before it turned ominously quiet. If Rickard fell, we would be next. I looked ahead of us and could see the lava tube entry a kilometer away, then looked back expecting the drones to be headed our way, but they continued to circle Rickard's position. He'd made it to cover, drawing the fleet to them. Through their sacrifice, we would make it to safety.

Zi ably guided her team through the lava tube, quickly catching Draven and Bayley, giving Jarvis control. His team of three military biots outnumbered the one human and one biot they pursued, but they had no records on Draven's capabilities, usually an ominous warning of a dangerous adversary not to be underestimated. The other intangible was Zi chased someone she cared for.

"I will need you to fall back to a safe distance, ma'am. I'll leave one man with you. You'll be safe in his hands." Jarvis ordered. Zi nodded, before he and his two other soldiers moved forward to engage their enemy.

"Lock weapons to stun not kill, men," Jarvis ordered, as they moved forward in waves, alternating positions peloton-style.

The tunnel veered right into a narrow-curved column. Jarvis moved to the front and heard the sound of stone falling some twenty meters ahead. He signaled his troops to hold their positions as he investigated, his weapon cocked and loaded. Movement was detected on his visor. Bayley remained out of Jarvis's view as he followed him around the extended curve of the lava tube, cautiously checking for traps. He readied to engage his prey when the sound of weapon's fire raged behind him. Jarvis fell to the ground, fearing he was surrounded. He heard the sound of Bayley running further from him, whereas it had turned silent behind him. "Report your position!"

Neither of his soldiers responded, prompting Jarvis to retrace his steps. Both lay motionless on the ground. Draven had somehow positioned himself between Jarvis and his remaining soldier. Zi was in danger.

"Soldier, we have two men down. Hold your position and defend it. The agent, Draven, is cornered. I am tracking him back toward you, so keep alert and defend your position. Shoot to kill."

"Affirmative. We are secured."

Jarvis checked his men, both were decommissioned, one from a single knife wound from behind, to his core, the other a similar stab wound from the front, also to his core. *How did Draven elude him?* Jarvis continued tracking his ghost-like adversary, but there was no sign of life, except for his remaining soldier and Zi. Draven had vanished.

"Where did the soldiers perish?" Zi asked.

"Where the tunnel veered right."

"Which route did you take?"

Jarvis looked baffled. "What do you mean? There was just one tunnel."

"I have often hiked this area. The lava tube parts just ahead. The left side tube winds around five kilometers to the Cathedral cave, whereas the right side is more direct."

"I think you're mistaken, ma'am."

Zi knew these tunnels as well as anyone and was less than convinced. "Show me."

They returned to where the decommissioned soldiers had fallen, the only change being they lay at the fork of two lava tubes. Zi was right, and Jarvis now realized why. He brushed his hair back, annoyed at his miscalculation before contacting Dane.

"We have two soldiers down. I repeat two soldiers decommissioned. The agent, Draven, is using an AR device. Set your visor to extra sensory, targeting the heat ratio of a biot core and anticipate revised reality."

"Dane, have you made it to the lava tube?" Zi asked.

"Affirmative. Just me and Spence. We lost Rickard and the other men to a drone fleet."

The increasingly perilous hunt prompted Jarvis to address our diminishing fortunes. "Dane, the enemy is moving towards the Cathedral cave along the short route. We will take the long route and not engage them until they move forward beyond the Cathedral cave toward you. Station Spence at the entry into the Gate cave with orders to kill anyone that tries to get through. We will hold the other end of that tunnel. Do nothing else but hold that entry. Is that clear?"

"We are approaching the Gates cave. I remember that connecting tunnel. It's around five hundred meters in length. We will have a clear aim on anything that moves down it toward us."

"Have Spence secure that passage. Create a fortress and shoot to kill anything that moves, including any changes in the composition of that tunnel. The agent has and will use AR to confuse you."

"Spence and I are both listening, Jarvis."

"The final confrontation will be somewhere between the Gates cave and the Cathedral cave. If Draven and Bayley enter that tunnel, we've got them cornered. No amount of AR weaponry can get them out of this. Remember, shoot to kill anything that moves down that tunnel."

Chapter Thirty

SHOWDOWN

We quickly secured our fortress against an elusive enemy. I knew little about Draven, let alone who he reported to. What was certain, Draven and Bayley possessed the Trojan files, managing to achieve what a fleet could not.

"The barrier is finished," Spence informed.

I studied it, less certain than he. I would have destroyed the tunnel if Zi and our men were not at the other end. Perhaps that would be the final solution, if we failed. It seemed fate again drew Zi and I back to the Martian depths to defend our parent's legacy, perhaps paying the ultimate price.

"I've set up the armory. You choose," Spence offered, pointing to a cache of weapons.

He looked secure in his heavily fortified barrier, ready to defend. A pair of explosive devices caught my eye, and I immediately knew what I should do.

"I'd be more of a hindrance to you, but you already know that, don't you?"

"They won't pass me, Dane," he replied, practicing his line of sight with a military grade laser rifle."

I nodded in agreement, then picked up the explosive devices, a sniper rifle and climbed over the barrier into the lava tunnel. "I'll set up some surprises for them along the way, just to make sure they don't pass you."

The soldier remonstrated, but I ignored him and walked twenty meters into the lava tunnel. "If they look like getting through, blow this tunnel to hell," I said, laying them behind two discreet and separate areas.

"Okay, that's fine. Now come back," said Spence, signaling me to return.

"I can't do that, soldier. My sister will need me more than you. Just remember to not let anyone through here. Anyone," I emphasized, turning to walk away.

"Wait!" he said. I turned back. "You may need this," he said, throwing me an extra round of bullets. "Good luck!"

I picked up the bullets, nodded and turned toward the Cathedral cave, knowing I had little time to prepare for Bayley's and Draven's arrival. Jarvis had already lost two of his men, leaving Zi vulnerable. I looked at my rifle and moved forward determined to make a difference. I may not have been a military man, but I was more than handy with a rifle.

I crept cautiously through the final twenty meters to the Cathedral cave. The personal drone calculated Bayley and Draven were ten minutes away, time to set up in the cave and position my rifle. There was a hidden crevice I once used in my youth to hide from Zi that was well protected and offered a wide view. I climbed through the tight passage up to the small enclosure. It hadn't changed a lot over the decade, with good cover, but it only offered a restricted view of the cave below. It was not as I remembered it, but it had to do as Bayley and Draven were quickly closing, leaving me to check and re-check my rifle and wait.

Draven and Bayley emerged from the tunnel, sparing little time to prepare for a confrontation. I dared only an occasional glimpse, a partial view through two large boulders, but mostly I listened. Draven passed the backpack with the Trojan files to Bayley, before barking his orders.

"There's the tunnel to the adjoining cave. Run a reconnaissance on the area. They had troops following us, so it's possible there could be more stationed at the other end."

"Why not engage them now?" Bayley asked.

"We don't know the number or how they've setup. The

whole tunnel could be booby trapped. I'll take care of what is following us, while you seek out what we are walking into. Clear? While you're there, conceal the backpack in the tunnel before you return."

"Done."

"You'll also need this," said Draven, passing him a twentieth century handgun.

"I could do with a little more fire power."

"I'm laying a laser inhibitor in the cave, to eliminate modern tech weapons. They'll have to use hand to hand combat to get past me," Draven replied, setting a scan through the cave that would nullify any modern technology weapons.

"They're trained soldiers, skilled in hand to hand," Bayley said.

Draven smirked with confidence. "They've not fought someone like me," he replied. Then just as Bayley headed for the tunnel, he called to him. "Remember, when you return, come in with your rifle cocked and ready to fire. They should be easy targets when I'm finished with them."

Bayley left the Cathedral cave and silence ensued. My stocks had risen as only Bayley and I possessed the advantage of low technology weapons. I wondered whether to risk a shootout, but then I'd give my position away. Something told me the element of surprise would be required against this agent, whose greatest skill was that very strategy.

The reconnaissance soldier, Harvey, was the first to walk into the cave, his adversary not just Draven, but to his shock, four Dravens. The soldier attempted to fire his pulse gun, but it failed to activate, causing him to back away to com Jarvis, when it too failed.

Draven was unarmed except for a single dagger, which he removed from his sheath and pointed his assailant's way, inviting him to battle. Harvey, like all military biots, were robotized killers, programmed to fight in the fires of hades if their commander required it. He welcomed Draven's challenge, exchanging a steel salute with his blade.

In that moment between standoff and battle, both combatants exchanged an inscrutable glance that signaled the opening gesture, acceptance that what they now started would only end with one standing. War-like adrenaline saturated the cave like the Martian dust as they began a dance, they'd spent their lives honing. Both were masters of the blade.

The soldier relished rather than feared Draven's advantage as he rotated 360 degrees to confront the four assailants that encircled him. It was a Russian roulette encounter, with only one holding the real weapon of death.

But which? The soldier flicked his handle, extending his knife to a sword, showing he too brought tricks to the arena. Masterfully, he swept the sword in a Samurai-like movement of grace and skill glancing all four assailants, clicking real metal on only one, establishing his real target.

He attacked Draven, slicing, carving and driving his sword in every possible direction and angle but each time Draven evaded his assault untouched, toying with him. The soldier grew bolder with every exchange as if the challenge was all that mattered. Ever faster, he launched attacks that ultimately pushed Draven into the rock wall. Cornering Draven, he felt emboldened to make a devastating but risky assault, successfully finding the small opening in his defense allowing Harvey to plunge his sword deep into Draven's core.

The sound of steel driving through Draven's body echoed through the cathedral signaling victory, but to the soldier's shock, Draven stood tall, before the flickering of his holograph gave way to the cold rock where he stood.

"You're fast, soldier. But I'm as quick as light," he said, pulling his knife from the soldier's back, spilling his blood to the Martian dust, decommissioning the young soldier with a single decisive incision.

All went silent as Draven lay in wait for the next adversary, Jarvis. Jarvis and Zi soon entered the cave, the decommissioned body of Harvey their deadly welcoming. Their host, Draven, revealed himself along with the three holographic avatars, blocking the lava tube Jarvis and Zi had entered from, prompting Jarvis to direct Zi across the other side before facing him.

"You'll meet the same fate as your soldier," Draven announced, inviting him to the center of the cauldron.

Jarvis obliged, not being drawn to Draven's avatars, immediately identifying his real adversary in a knife combat, showing his vision extended beyond Draven's holographic tricks. He rammed home the difference, easily defending Draven's lunges. If Harvey was a master of the Samurai, Jarvis was his mentor. Blades flashed to the sound of sweeping arms attacking and defending in equal measure, before Jarvis concluded it with a brutal trip or throw. Ever more confident, Jarvis cornered his prey against the rock wall ready to avenge his fallen comrade.

Draven's left arm had been decommissioned and his single weapon lay in the dust where he fell as Jarvis ominously closed the kill. Like a bloodied boxer cornered in the ring, Draven waited for the decisive blow. Jarvis came at him quickly, driving his knife deep into Draven's core, assuring victory with a vengeful twist of the knife, felling him where he stood, but Draven had one final surprise, a failsafe army of quantum drones that held the commander's grip to his decommissioned body, unleashing a pre-programmed mutually assured destruction that saw both warriors fall to the Martian dust.

Zi rushed to Jarvis's aid, but all too late as both lay in waste. She looked around in the silence of the cave as biot synthetic blood spilled into the fine dust, unsure of what to do next. She briefly looked in my direction, sensing a place she knew well, before the sound of an explosion roared from the tunnel connecting the Cathedral and Gates caves.

Zi reacted. "Dane," she cried, before running toward the tunnel, but it was Bayley who emerged, scanning the cave whilst shaking the dust from his uniform.

"Are you hurt?" Zi asked.

He walked past Zi more intent on inspecting the three fallen biots.

"Bayley! Can you hear me? Are you okay?"

Bayley picked up Draven's knife, and only then turned her way. "I can hear you perfectly."

He approached her with dagger raised, causing Zi to back away. Dust continued to swirl from the tunnel creating an ominous mauve fog. What was once a hallowed place filled with joyous child hood memories was now a Cathedral for the dead. She looked into Bayley's cruel eyes, shocked yet resigned to pay the same price as her father.

Terror turned to sadness then resignation that this bitter day would be where her trust finally died.

"Why? You owe me that."

Bayley turned, reacting to the noise of a small rock that rolled from the entrance of the tunnel, further filling the litter strewn entrance. Then he turned to face her.

"I gave you what you most sought. Love."

"You call it love. You've deceived me more than anyone I have ever known. You're not human."

Bayley moved closer, holding his knife to his heart. "An ironic observation. You were starving for love. Was I wrong to deny you some joy in your loveless life?"

"Better a loveless life than to suffer your dark deceit. Who do you work for? Zhang?"

"You slight me, Zi. I report to a higher order than you'll ever know."

"Don't justify your moral code. Your compass only knows deception, hate and fear. The language of war."

"Whereas your code is awash with greed, self-delusion, and fantasy, unjustly holding onto the most precious deposit in the solar system for a highly disputed aim and supporting lies and half-truths to further that cause. I'm charged with exposing your lies," Bayley said, just a breath from her.

He moved his dagger ever so slightly, before firmly

grasping Zi's neck with his free hand. "Unfortunately, you won't see the day when I fully expose your illegal operations," grasping her neck ever tighter.

In the cold silence, Bayley watched the life begin to drain from Zi, before a single shot rang out and echoed across the chamber. He let go his prey and turned to locate the line of fire. A sniper fired another single bullet that ripped through his shoulder, then another, forcing him to release his grasp and run through a hail of bullets to his escape, the tunnel through to the Gates cave, then on to the perimeter.

Chapter Thirty-One

CAVALRY

Zi lay slumped against the cave wall, gulping in large breaths. She didn't recognise me at first, dazed from the lack of oxygen, shocked by the betrayal. She drew back in fright on my approach. "Zi, it's me, Dane."

Her wide, uncertain gaze surveyed the surrounds of her attack as she took time to formulate my words. "I'm sorry," she repeated, unable to hold back her tears.

"You're safe now," I repeated, holding her close, until painful tears subsided. She stood up and looked around the cave, frightened Bayley may return, but only the fallen warriors remained, making her shudder.

"His hands were like steel. His eyes weren't human. He's a monster."

I stood by her side and gently pressed her arm. "You're

right. He isn't human. I shot him four times, and the bullets didn't slow him. He's a biot."

"An agent," Zi said, lowering her sad eyes to the blood-stained ground.

I didn't want to leave her alone and vulnerable but I voiced my concerns. "He's heading for the perimeter."

She balked at first, knowing what I meant, before standing straight and responding. "Stop him if you can, Dane. Stop him for me."

I brushed Zi's tears clean then made her a promise. "I know these caves better than anyone. I'll make sure he pays for what he did."

I turned and headed toward the Gates cave, not daring to look back. Zi shouldn't have been left alone in her state, but my com showed Bayley was heading for the perimeter. He had a head start, but the multiple bullet wounds would slow him down. Now I knew he was a biot, the next time I fired would be directly at his core.

At the entry into the Gates cave, I passed my fallen comrade, Spence, decommissioned by explosives. Bayley had located one of my booby traps and thrown it into the Gates cave before somehow detonating it. His final barrier passed, Bayley had a clear run to the perimeter and the drone's protection. He had a start but he was injured, and I knew the terrain.

Tracking his telltale scuff marks and biot blood was easy. He was jogging at a pace with the damaged leg dragging the ground ever more perceptibly the further he went. Bayley was slowing. On reaching the surface, the trail was clearer and fresher, meaning I was quickly closing in on him. I took the higher ground knowing there would be a vantage point up ahead offering me a clear shot. I was running on adrenaline and a steely desire to get retribution for Zi as well as my parents. I cared little for the ramifications, willing to pay the consequences for permanently decommissioning this monster.

At the track's high point, I positioned the rifle on a large boulder that provided good cover, a stable position to sight my rifle, and a clear view for the kill shot. He soon limped into my sight, talking into his com, no doubt signaling for support. I could have fired a single shot into his core and end him, but I lowered my aim, held the handle firm to my cheek, and then with the lightest of touches, fired a single bullet into his good leg. It cracked through the knee joint, immediately felling him.

I ran toward him, knowing the single shot would soon draw drones. With rifle ready to fire, I cautiously approached. "If you have a weapon throw it to the ground, or I'll finish you now."

He was studying his shattered leg, then he looked up at

me, casting a wry smile. "I have no weapons. I can't seem to lose you, my friend."

"I'm not your friend. I see how you treat those you claim to be close to."

"She needed affection and love. So, I gave it to her."

"That wasn't love." I cocked my rifle to finish him as time was against me, but he goaded me.

"Your machine can do so much for the future. Why would you waste it on a small terraforming project?"

"Our invention, our choice."

"You condemn the majority of humans, so that a few may prosper. Not content to have nearly destroyed Earth, you want to do the same again on a second planet."

"You're hardly in a position to moralize. You work with a caste organization that deals in deception and murder to further your own cause. How will intergalactic exploration help the billion humans who remain?"

"Perhaps you've had your time?"

"We've just started. Push your back pack toward me, or I'll decommission you here and now."

Bayley didn't release his backpack, instead looking to the horizon behind me. "Go ahead and shoot me, but you won't have time to save yourself."

Swarms of drones headed toward us. Within seconds, fleets of them closed in from every direction, cutting off any chance of escape. Left with one last act of defiance, I cocked my rifle against Bayley and dug it into his backpack. One shot would destroy the Trojan files and Bayley's core.

The machine filled sky turned the clearing into a gladiatorial stadium of drones, bearing witness to my impasse. A small path cleared for a single ship to hover down to the surface. Caesar had arrived with his Praetorian guards to appease the throngs, soon announcing his intent for all to hear.

"Release him and I'll let you live," Hogan offered, through loud speaker.

I surveyed the dark sky, pulsating with drone wings, knowing a single shot would seal my hostage and my own fate. I dug the rifle nozzle hard into the backpack, making sure one shot would destroy what they most wanted. "Do that and destroy any chance of developing the Trojan."

"He won't care. Give him what he wants," Bayley implored.

"Drones. Prepare to fire on the target," Hogan ordered.

Red laser lights poured down, focused on their target, preparing to unleash fury on us.

"This is your final chance. Give him up, or I'll turn your pitiful stand into a memorial crater."

I looked across the plains, now as red as an Earth

sunset. I couldn't save myself, but I may have saved Zi. I held the gun firm on my hostage, waiting for our end, when out to my right, a small opening appeared, a pulsing light on the horizon. A second star ship hovered into the cauldron, separating the drone army like a giant theatre curtain.

"Identify yourself," Hogan ordered.

"This is a UN starship. You are ordered to stand down."

Hali's voice boomed from the ship's speakers as her ship hovered just above Hogan's, sparking a standoff.

"You have no jurisdiction in this area. We are seeking to nullify a hostage situation. Leave this area, or I'll turn my drone fleet on you," Hogan threatened.

"That would be considered an act of war against the council of Earth. Desist or suffer the consequences."

Hogan would be in violation of UN regulations, if there were witnesses. Hali hovered inside the cauldron, vulnerable to his drones, and I didn't see any cavalry on the horizon.

"Retreat, or I'll order these drones to fire on you," Hogan responded, calling Hali's bluff. Half of Hogan's fleets turned their deadly arsenal on Hali, making her ship shine like a red star. "You have ten seconds to leave, or I will fire."

Hali's ship powered its engines but did not retreat.

"She's as mad as you are," Bayley said, as Hali's ship engaged its defense force field.

Hali had seemingly made a courageous but futile gesture, given a fleet of drones would easily penetrate her shield. But then the force field expanded across the drone army, casting a fog-like clamp that disabled them.

"Surrender or be destroyed," Hali warned.

Hogan responded with force, turning his ship's weapons on her, but within microseconds, she took control of his drones, turning their weapons on Hogan's ship and destroyed it.

Hali then turned her attention to me. "Dane. Stand back from your hostage, drop your weapon, and raise your hands above your head."

This would be my last chance to avenge Zi, and Hali sensed my hesitation. "There is nothing to gain from decommissioning the biot, Dane. Zi is safe. We located her at the southern end of the lava tunnel."

Her reassurance convinced me to stand down. Within minutes, UN guards had secured the site. What I hoped was a rescue turned against me as the guard recited a scripted montage to Bayley, then me.

"You are under arrest for crimes against the Earth council. You do not have to say anything, but it may harm your defense if you do not. Anything you do say may be given in evidence."

My ordeal was over, for now. We were taken to the ship and held in separate confinement. I looked to Hali as I was taken away, hoping for support but none was offered as she ordered the guards to take us away.

Epilogue

UN guards accompanied me to the visitor's room, sitting me at its single table, opposite an unoccupied chair. A large mirror window dominated one wall, in all likelihood, screening a monitoring room. My confinement to UN barracks had extended beyond a week and little interaction bar my caste legal aid advisor named Bryant. We'd discussed potential charges, with attempted murder, smuggling, and conspiracy to murder being just some of my potential indictable offences.

Bryant had shared no information about my family, so when Zi walked into the room instead of him, my spirits lifted. She still had the bruising from Bayley's assault, and she'd visibly aged from the ordeal. Sitting opposite me, I was struck by the sadness in her expression, but it didn't stop her from extending her hand across the table to show her concern.

"How are they treating you?"

"As well as can be expected. The worst of it is they

don't tell me anything, and I've had no contact with Lia or Chryse."

Zi passed a com file across the table, making me look nervously at the security window. "It's alright, Dane. They cleared it. It's from Lia."

"Thank you, Zi," I replied, pressing the com file close to my chest.

"I just spoke to Lia. They're both well and hope to join you as soon as they can."

"Will there be a trial soon?"

"There may not be a trial, if I have my way."

"My legal advisor doesn't share your optimism, Zi."

Zi shook her head and sat forward in her chair. "I'm working with the authorities now. I'm making it clear to them that you were an unwitting accomplice in the delivery of the Trojan machine."

"But…"

Zi spoke over me. "You carried out your official duties to deliver terraforming equipment to my base. I told the investigation team headed by Hali that the Trojan machine was instigated by me in liaison with Latatious. You knew nothing of it."

"That's not…" I looked to the security window, emphasizing either of us should not say anything incriminating.

"This meeting is not being monitored. Hali gave me assurances, so speak your mind," Zi replied.

"Zi. I knew all along about the illegal cargo," I whispered, not convinced we weren't being monitored.

"That isn't the story we want from you. We want you to tell them you knew nothing of the contraband, and you were unwittingly drawn in to a plan orchestrated by Latatious and overseen by me."

I stood up and turned to the security window, hoping someone was listening. "You know that's not true. I'm not going to let you be a scapegoat for me again."

"Sit down, Dane! Hear me out." Zi implored.

I waited momentarily for a response from outside the security room, without success, so I reluctantly returned to the table. Knowing my sister, it was likely she'd already falsely admitted her guilt. "You have sacrificed so much for me. I can't let you do it all again."

"You saved my life, Dane! Isn't that enough repayment?"

"I could never repay what you've done for me. I won't allow anyone to lie on my behalf. Least of all you. The thought that you'd accept incarceration to save me is too much."

"Hear me out, brother. At least do that."

I couldn't bring myself to talk anymore, instead nodding.

"I have been negotiating with Hali who's heading up the

investigations. I know I can broker a plea bargain with her if you'll let me."

"Illegal smuggling, lying to the world council, and that's just the start. Your career and life would be ruined."

"Incarceration would be involved, but it's what I want," said Zi.

"A Martian sent to an Earth prison. You'd never survive."

"Incarcerated yes, but I'd stay on Mars, in a place of my choosing."

Zi's hopeful expression made me believe she truly wanted to be incarcerated. There could only be one reason for that. "Helena. Hali's offered you a chance to work with her."

Zi nodded. "It's what I want."

"And what of your life's work? The Elithium mines and terraforming Mars?"

"I've played my part. Codi is ready to take over the facility with your help and…" Zi smiled, waiting for me to finish her words."

"And Lia?"

She nodded. "Yes. Lia and Chryse."

"Are you sure this is what you want?"

"I know this is what I should do. I want to spend time with the mother we thought we'd lost. I'd gladly work under incarceration to get to know her. To be honest, I wouldn't miss my home. I've given ten years of my life to the terraforming project. It's time others stepped up. You and Lia would be the best ones to see the next phase through. Codi would oversee operations, you'd manage the Trojan project, and Lia would develop the immigration program."

"Are you sure this can really happen? Does Hali truly have the political connections?"

"I believe she has. She just needs you to cooperate. Can I assure her that she has your loyalty and support?"

I had worked alongside Hali for a decade and had received nothing but loyal support from her. It was time I reciprocated. "Yes, you can tell Hali I'll do all I can to help you and her."

Zi sat back in her chair, a wry smile formed on her lips. "If she weren't a biot, that news would gladden her heart."

"It will. I've learnt over our years of friendship that Hali does have some emotions buried deep in her core. So, go ahead and tell her. But what happens next?"

"Hali has organized a meeting to confirm all the new postings. Then contracts will be drawn up."

My ears pricked up. "All the postings?"

Zi smiled knowingly. "Yes, all the postings. Once I confirm your support with Hali, Lia and Chryse will be given clearance to immigrate to Mars."

The meeting with Zi felt surreal. We seemed to have had an overwhelming victory over Apollo. "There must be a cost?"

"I'm giving my full support to Apollo. We will also share the Elithium resource equally between us, until an amalgamation is negotiated."

"Negotiated with who? Apollo and Gaea have never agreed on any terms. Why the change?"

"For one, Helena's memory implants have been fully exposed. Apollo had to agree or lose everything. But more importantly, the Earth council has agreed that Mars have a ruling council similar to that of Earth. Both organizations will be equally represented on the Mars council but the ultimate power will rest in the hands of biots representing the AI body."

My head was spinning from Zi's revelations. "This has happened so quickly. It sounds more like a long-planned coup?"

Zi was about to reveal more, but her allocated time was up. "The monitors are back on, so we'll talk more next week," she said, before leaving me to be escorted back to my quarters.

Alone, I wondered about Zi's revelations. Did she really wish to work with Apollo? Our mother was reasonable enough motivation, but her time as hostage at the Apollo base may have impacted her. Hali's sudden rise in standing also seemed too good to be true. At that moment I wished Lia was with me. She always levelled me and helped me see through the fog of situations. I took the com file from my pocket and studied it, wishing I could view it, but my com had been taken from me, meaning I could only view it on a public com. I remained powerless, knowing it would come down to Hali and hoping she indeed had the influence Zi claimed she possessed.

Another week passed. I'd heard precious little. Even Bryant had clammed up, so I put little confidence in our morning meeting. His pensive mood further discouraged me, until he put his com on the table, stirring me to make a request.

"Can I use your com to play a file I've been given?"

He cast a suspicious glance at the file I produced, "Where did you get that?"

I immediately regretted showing him. "My sister was given permission to bring it to me."

That seemed enough to satisfy his suspicions. "You can use my com later, if the guards will allow it, but we have a meeting to attend first."

The com came to life, screening the holographic image of Hali who sat at the end of a conference table.

"Welcome, Dane. You're the first to join me for a team meeting. Bear with me as the others come online."

I nodded and waited with apprehension. Was this part of an investigation, or worse the beginning of my trial? I cast a suspicious glance Bryant's way, while the holographic image broadened to include the other participants, but he offered no clues or feedback, instead focusing on Hali's image. Hali addressed each as they appeared. Codi and Zi were the first, surprising me, before the remaining three attendees shocked me, they were so unexpected. Ander and my mother flashed on the screen, before my wife appeared to round off our group. All in attendance, Hali proceeded with the formalities.

"Welcome everyone to the first committee meeting of my newly formed Mars government. Some of you are aware of the positions I have created, some are not, so I want to start by personally congratulating you on your new roles. Firstly: Codi as Governor of the Gaea Base; Dane as Manager of the Gaea Trojan & Terraforming Project; Lia as Manager of the Gaea Human Immigration Project; Zi as Governor of the Apollo Base; Helena as Manager of the Apollo Neutrino Communication Project and finally a special welcome to Ander, who we were fortunately able to reprogram. He will be appointed as General of the UN Defences."

I looked to Bryant, not convinced this was really happening. Was this how a digital implant felt? Disoriented and placed in an alternate world of twisted facts. But he repeatedly nodded reassuringly that this was real, indicating I concentrate on Hali, but the formal meeting was over in a blur of what felt to be distorted realities.

I turned to Bryant. "Is this a set up?"

"It's very real, Dane. I've had to wait on this formal declaration, before being able to release you."

"I'm free to go?"

"Yes. You won't be charged and there's a UN official waiting to escort you to the Gaea base."

The doors to the meeting room opened and the UN guard entered the room, ready to escort me home, but I still remained uncertain. "So, who exactly has been charged?"

Bryant smiled. "I can't tell you that, but I'm sure you'll be properly briefed by our new Governor at the appropriate time. I do know that both Apollo and Gaea senior operatives, both here and on Earth have been restructured. I dare say you and your newly appointed fellow committee members will have a large say about exactly who is responsible."

Bryant stood up and offered his hand. "Good luck," he said, before leaving.

I sat a while longer, testing the patience of my security guard. It seemed all Zi had revealed to me was true and I was really released into a new world, a Mars I and those I loved, could truly shape.

Michael Leon

Michael Leon the author of *Cubeball, Emissary* and *Phantoms. Sentient* is his fourth novel. His work ranges from speculative fiction to fantasy romance.

You can find out more about his work at:

michaelleon.com.au